UNSPOKEN

This book is a work of fiction. Names, characters, places and incidents either are the product of the author's imagination or are used fictitiously. Any resemblance to actual persons living or dead, events or locations, is entirely coincidental.

© David H Walker, 2024
All Rights Reserved

David H Walker

UNSPOKEN

> To my mind, you're like Saul, the son of Kish,
> who went out to seek his father's asses,
> and found a kingdom.
>
> Johann Wolfgang von Gœthe,
> *Wilhelm Meister's Apprenticeship*

1

It's no use telling my story. What would be the point? The reason I remember things is because they happened to me. No one else can relive them like I did, so why make the effort?

Take Mrs Horton. She would launch into full flow if ever you let her catch your eye. She'd go jabbering on and on, and you couldn't make out a thing she was saying. She'd shrug her shoulders and even grin a bit, you know, sorry I'm not making sense, and she'd look at you while she flapped her hands to show how hard she was trying. Other times her eyes would have a beseeching look, pleading with you to give a sign that you at least understood how much she meant it as she forced the sounds out. I made an effort to be polite if I was in the mood, but in the end I knew my eyes would glaze over in spite of myself. She noticed it too, and sometimes her eyes would fill up with tears. Desperate, defeated tears, and her hands would drop into her lap and she would twist her fingers together, making the knuckles turn white.

It didn't help that she'd had a stroke that had paralysed her tongue and larynx and left one side of her face sagging. All that came out of her mouth was a breathy, hoarse gurgle from the back of her throat. She would move her lips to try and shape the flow into words, but it still came out as an incomprehensible gabble. 'Ouagh-ouagh-ouagh,' with an occasional gulping sound as she paused for breath.

When she eventually realised she wasn't getting through she would fall silent and give a lop-sided smile. As if she felt sorry for me, not being able to share in her thoughts. But she was by nature a diffident person, so she didn't insist.

It was especially awkward when she wanted you to do something for her, like open a window or close the curtain, or switch the light on, or find her glasses. I had to raise my eyebrows and point or make gestures until she nodded. Or I'd check what page her newspaper was open at, and then I'd know to give her a pencil so she could do the crossword. I used to examine the crossword afterwards, when I was taking the paper away with the rest of the litter. It was always the cryptic crossword she did. I would check the answers she had filled in. As often as not she had done them all. Her writing was clear and firm and easy to read, but when I looked back at the clues, I couldn't see any connection. I fancied she had just made up words that would fit the spaces.

Everyone felt sorry for her, hunched in her wheelchair, lifting her palsied face each time the door opened to admit a newcomer to the sitting-room. Her speech impediment, as the district nurse called it, sent everyone into contortions. The staff and other residents knew that the chances of managing a proper conversation with her were slim. Some had contrived mannerisms for avoiding her eye, like waiters in a restaurant, so they could pass by without attending to her. Others would lean in and smile, or shake their heads apologetically. Or they would speak to her without actually making sounds, miming their words as if trying to make themselves heard over the din of machinery. Mrs Horton could have heard them perfectly well, but for some reason they felt they should show sympathy by enunciating laboriously in silence, mirroring the way she struggled to get her words out. However when it was their turn to listen to her, they would say something like 'Yes, it is isn't it?' and move on. As for Mr Pickvance, he had a way of gesturing at his watch as if he was pressed for time.

The one person who didn't do any of this was Doctor Storth.

On the day he arrived and entered the sitting-room, Mrs Dugdale the landlady introduced him with a flourish.

'This is Doctor Storth,' she announced, tucking in her double chin and thrusting out her ample bosom.

'Call me Hughie,' he said.

From the way he pronounced his name it was obvious he was Scottish.

Despite that, Mrs Smith sat up at once, put on her horn-rimmed glasses, tipped her head back, and looked him up and down. You could tell by the expression on her face that she was thinking, 'At last, one of us.'

'He'll be staying with us a while,' went on the landlady. One or two people nodded, to show they were prepared to put up with his company for the duration. Mrs Smith's smile grew broader. She sat forward, anticipating a proper introduction. However Mrs Horton's chair stood between them, and Doctor Storth came to her first.

'This is Mrs Horton. She has a sp–...' began Mrs Dugdale. But before she could finish, Dr Storth reached across in front of her and offered his hand, which Mrs Horton took in her crooked fingers.

'Hughie Storth,' he said, leaning towards her. She gurgled a greeting of her own, and he placed his other hand on hers and smiled. 'I'm very happy to make your acquaintance, Mrs Horton.' The Scottish accent made his words fall like balm. Mrs Horton gurgled again, softly, and her skewed cheeks wrinkled in the ghost of a grin.

He turned to look around the room, directing a faint smile to no one in particular, to signify that he was pleased to be there.

Everyone was content with that, and got on with what they were doing before his arrival. All but Mrs Smith, who held herself erect in her chair and beamed up at him.

'Geraldine Smith,' she said as she proffered her hand.

There was a hint of reserve in his reaction, as if her greeting was unctuous enough for the two of them. He complimented her on the view she had through the window from her comfortable chintz-covered armchair (woe betide anyone who tried to get to it before her). His speech was precise, his sentences short and to the point, a bit like a businessman with no time to waste ; though the brief conversation he had with her was perfectly cordial.

'My late husband used to play golf with a hospital consultant,' she simpered in her best cut-glass accent, her voice husky from too many cigarettes.

'Aye, well, many's the time I've watched them teeing off on the Old Course at St Andrews,' he said, 'but I've never tried my hand at it myself.'

'You come from there?' she asked.

'That I do. Born and bred in the Kingdom of Fife.'

'And is that where –' she breathed the 'h' in the word – *'hwhere* you… practise?'

'Practise?' He paused. 'Oh, you mean –? Och, no, I'm not a medical doctor.' An Englishman would have ended the sentence with 'I'm afraid'. Hughie had nothing to apologize for. Nor did he owe anyone an explanation, and he ignored Mrs Smith's questioning look. He tipped his head towards her and turned to move off. 'Well, I must get on…'

As he strode across the room heading for the door, it was noticeable that he walked with a limp. And when he paused alongside Mrs Horton on his way out, to smile and say goodbye to her, Mrs Smith's eyes fell to the raised boot that he wore on his left foot.

During the days that followed, people wondered what Dr Storth was doing among us. He seemed to spend most of his time upstairs in his room. Ruth the cleaner let slip that his table was covered in papers and books, most of them in a foreign language she thought might be Spanish 'or something'. When she came in to tidy and dust, she said, he sat hunched over his documents – 'can't be very good for his eyes'. Mrs Smith said nothing, but everyone knew that she was jealous of the room he was renting – a first-floor front room with a bay window overlooking the sea. Where he got the money from was anyone's guess. Even with a widow's pension left by her bank-manager husband, Mrs Smith's finances couldn't stretch that far.

Though he spent each morning and most evenings shut away with his books and papers, no one would have called Dr Storth anti-social. He greeted the other residents cheerfully at breakfast, for example. He didn't often invite contact, preferring to eat on his own, but he was always ready to exchange comments with those at the next table, about the state of the sky or the sea beyond the window, and about the prospects for a walk later in the day. He was open and pleasant enough, though he didn't waste words ; he simply said what the situation called for, with a lilt in his voice that softened his most terse remarks. He could even be curt without causing offence.

Mrs Smith always had breakfast on a tray in her room – there was no way she could arrange her hair and make-up to be presentable that early – so in the mornings Dr Storth didn't have to deal with her attempts to draw him into conversation. Not that he would have found it difficult: he had a natural gift for diplomacy and could turn aside leading questions so tactfully that no one realised when they were being rebuffed.

People did notice that he tended to spend time with Mrs Horton. At first he would pause on his way out of the breakfast-room to say a few words, then he offered to refill her teapot. Mrs Horton took all her meals alone at a table set back from the rest, because eating was a struggle for her. She found swallowing difficult, and made a noise when drinking tea, since her lips couldn't close properly on the edge of the cup. Most people pretended not to notice, and thought it best to avoid looking at her as she fumbled her food and chewed messily. But Dr Storth was ready to help. Forthright when he spoke to others, he didn't stand on ceremony when dealing with her. Far from embarrassing her by trying to be tactful, he simply asked if he could share her table at lunch. While eating his own meal, he helped her with the business of getting morsels into her mouth, murmuring encouragement and softly laughing with her when she spilt food or drink – which she was the first to find amusing. He would tell her when she had food on her chin, and occasionally reach over to dab at spills with a napkin.

Mrs Smith was disappointed by this growing intimacy. It was unseemly – unprofessional, even – for a Doctor to be on such familiar terms with an old lady suffering an affliction. She considered it more proper to keep her distance and observe decorum in her dealings with others, particularly when they were challenged like Mrs Horton. Millicent, who dropped by each day to share mid-morning coffee, duly pursed her lips and nodded in agreement as Mrs Smith gave her the benefit of her insights into the appropriate etiquette.

'You can see he has a good bedside manner,' she observed, reluctant to abandon the notion that Dr Storth was a clinician of some kind. 'Perhaps,' she purred, leaning in to Millicent, 'he has had a change of career...' Then with a meaning look, she added, 'I wonder what might have brought that about?'

Millicent began to imagine that Dr Storth had been demoted – or even 'struck off', as they said on the television news when reporting medical scandals.

Mrs Smith pondered, then pursued her line of thought.

'He's too young to be retired... So how can he take so much time away from work? I understand he's studying something in his room. But what kind of work is that? Does he have a proper job? Is he in work, do you think?' she added darkly.

Perhaps he had lost his job, they both agreed tacitly. And they speculated, each in her own way, about what could have caused him to be dismissed.

Meanwhile, Dr Storth and Mrs Horton got on famously. They discovered common ground when it transpired that they shared a love of crosswords. In the early evening, they would get together in the sitting room to pore over the cryptic clues. This shared activity didn't call for speech, so Mrs Horton was not disadvantaged. The two of them would read the clue, then ruminate in silence until one of them thought they had the answer. If Mrs Horton got it first, she would fill in the squares and sit back in her chair to let Dr Storth see what she had written. She would watch contentedly as he mulled it over. He would murmur so she could follow the paths his thoughts were taking, and she made encouraging sounds when he was on the right track. Finally, as he saw – or agreed – that the various enigmas contained in the clue cohered in the answer she had written, the two of them would nod together knowingly. When *he* got the answer first, he would take the pencil, write it in, then hand her back the pencil so she could plot the way to it, jotting down as she went, in the margin of the paper, notes which meant nothing to all but her and him. When, together, they confirmed the solution to a particularly tricky or abstruse clue, they would congratulate each other with a softly audible cheer of satisfaction, which Mrs Horton could manage quite well despite her speech impediment. And on completion of the puzzle, which between them they achieved quite regularly, they would celebrate with a handshake. When the others in the room turned to look at their antics, Dr Storth would invite them to applaud his 'partner in cruciverbalism', as he called her. Mrs Horton, they agreed, had rediscovered a sense of fun.

The affinity between the two of them, sustained by this all but mute pastime, sometimes gave rise to a form of conversation which, to onlookers who couldn't help but hear, was as enigmatic as any cryptic crossword. They spoke in low voices, so as not to disturb those around them. Mrs Horton would mumble amorphous syllables whose pace was the only pointer to their meaning – ranging between excitement and deliberation, perhaps. Dr Storth kept up the dialogue with lilting responses or brief questions, their cadence coloured by his Scottish intonation. Occasionally he would murmur something that provoked a flow of guttural sounds only he, it seemed, could make sense of. Those around mainly pretended not to be listening, but the silence that fell over the rest of the room at certain moments gave them away : people were hanging on every word – or sound – of the strange tête-à-tête.

Their chats never went on for long – Mrs Horton quickly grew tired, and Dr Storth had work to get back to. But they made people realize that Mrs Horton could be a lively interlocutor, engaged and responsive. There was a side to her character that had been overlooked till then as the old lady sat apart, having abandoned hope of making herself understood. The others in the room were left agog at the transformation.

One day Mr Pickvance, finding himself in the hall at the same time as Dr Storth, grasped the chance to satisfy his curiosity.

'Well I take my hat off to you. I've tried listening to her, on and off, for months on end but I can't make out a word. Do you actually understand what she says?'

Dr Storth stopped and eyed him dubiously.

'Who, Mrs Horton?'

Mr Pickvance nodded, a bit shamefaced at not naming the lady.

'Well,' said the Scotsman, 'some of it escapes me – she has a strong Yorkshire accent, you see.'

He stared unblinkingly into Mr Pickvance's eyes.

'Do you… mean... you can tell that?'

Dr Storth relaxed his gaze and grinned. 'Only joking,' he said.

Mr Pickvance allowed himself a strained smile.

'So – ?'

'Actually I can more or less fill in the spaces. I used to teach Phonetics once upon a time, and I have an interest in language. If you understand how the sounds are formed you can tell how they are being deformed in Mrs Horton's mouth. She can manage some fricatives and velar consonants – voiced and unvoiced of course –, but she has problems with palatals, labials and dentals, consonants normally involving the tongue…' He could tell he was losing Mr Pickvance's attention. 'With the right kind of listening, you can guess at the sounds she's trying to pronounce. They form their own sort of pattern, d'ye see.' He paused, having decided it was best to drop the technicalities. 'I think she's taken to me because she can speak my name – it has no consonants in it, just the aspirate "H" that she can manage perrrfectly well, simply by breathing out.'

Mr Pickvance was following a different train of thought as they stepped out into the front porch. Dr Storth was about to head off towards the pier when Mr Pickvance latched onto him again.

'So you taught then, did you?'

'Yes. I gave a course in Phonetics as a temporary sideline.'

'So what do you... are you a teacher now?' He warmed to his theme. 'My sister used to teach – for 40 years…'

Dr Storth stiffened slightly.

'Actually I'm a Reader.'

Mr Pickvance fought to keep the puzzlement out of his voice.

'Reader? What – you mean you read for a living? What sort of things do you read?

Dr Storth laughed.

'Well no, that's not literally what the word means where I work. I'm called a Reader.' He paused, and looked at Mr Pickvance. 'It's a title... it denotes a certain position in the university hierarchy.' For once he looked a bit awkward, not accustomed to explaining himself, and offered a kind of apology : 'Which means... yes, I do read, so it's no' entirely a misnomer.'

2

'Hmm, a Reader, you say? To judge by the way he looks at that poor woman, I'd say he's reading her thoughts,' tutted Mrs Smith when she learned about Dr Storth's title. 'You can tell by the way he lavishes attention on her. There's more to his kindness than a concern for her well-being.'

It was true that Dr Storth and Mrs Horton had grown remarkably close. They had developed a regular routine. When he came down for a break from his work, her eyes would brighten and he would smile to find her in her usual place in the sitting-room, waiting to meet him. They shared a table at lunch and dinner. Their conversations were easy and relaxed, as if they were old friends. They were clearly not mother and son, for their rapport had none of the latent tension that inhabits a parent-child relationship. Neither could anyone mistake them for a married couple, for the age difference was very marked between them. She was an elderly widow, somewhat frail, whose pastel twin-sets, grey skirts and thick stockings hung loose and crumpled on her shrunken body and limbs. She wore her white hair in a fluffy permed cloud that seemed to lift her features and lighten her wrinkles. He was a man of forty or so, stocky and well-groomed, with dark black wavy hair, a neatly-trimmed bristling moustache, and skin that reddened in the sun. His jaw was square, which gave a determined look to his expression ; though when he looked into Mrs Horton's eyes his long dark lashes seemed to charm her.

Often they sat in silence but were perfectly comfortable when they had nothing to say to each other. Occasionally Mrs Horton would reach across the table, touch Dr Storth's hand and give it a gentle pat. When they did talk, no one heard what transpired between them, for their conversations now were conducted *sotto voce.* Their comfortable companionship came as a surprise to the other guests. Even those with their own concerns, who normally paid no attention to the pair of them, were made aware of the change because the tranquillity of the room was no longer disturbed by the hoarse barks that used to mark Mrs Horton's efforts to speak out. Now she made no attempt to address anyone else, apart from a sociable twitch of the cheek by way of greeting ; she would respond with a nod or shake of the head to everyday questions or comments about the weather.

Then she took to communicating via written messages. It became clear that when the need to convey something specific arose Dr Storth was not to be her go-between. Even when they were together at table, it was not for him to say on her behalf that she required more milk on her cornflakes or hot water for the teapot. Instead, she reached for the tear-off note-pad that she now kept close by, and wrote her request in pencil, in her firm, clear hand. She would wave the pad at the waitress or myself to catch our eye. 'Cup of tea please', we would read ; 'please turn the lamp on', 'rather cold – could you hand me that blanket please?' It was striking that she took pains to be polite even when scribbling rather banal or trivial requests for practical assistance. She did compile a series of pre-written answers to routine questions such as which fruit-juice she wanted, or whether she preferred kippers to kedgeree. To be honest we found it a relief to be able to understand her immediately ; it spared us a discussion featuring mumbles and croaks that invariably created confusion and awkwardness all round. In fact I suspect Mrs Horton adopted this approach to avoid inflicting on her fellow-guests a cacophony which they found disagreeable. She was a considerate person.

However, some found the change unsettling, illogical though that may seem. They had previously gone to some lengths to avoid provoking fits of embarrassing gurgles by attempting to converse with Mrs Horton. Now they were pained to think that Mrs Horton was snubbing the company in some way, and had become stand-offish.

A consensus formed that Dr Storth was behind the old lady's new-found reserve.

This state of affairs exasperated Mrs Smith. The Scotsman had designs on Mrs Horton, she was convinced. She was firmly of the opinion that he wanted her to himself for some nefarious reason. She would fume each time the two of them quietly shared a private joke together.

By rights, she should have been relieved to be free of Mrs Horton's incomprehensible gargling. But really – sent to Coventry by a woman who couldn't even string two words together! She who had always been the soul of courtesy and had suffered hours of tedium for her pains!

Millicent nodded dutifully, a mirror of her indignation.

Things came to a head one bright morning when Mrs Horton leaned across and placed on the arm of Mrs Smith's chair a leaf from her note-pad on which she had pencilled a message.

Mrs Smith gave a cursory glance at the piece of paper, shot a look at Mrs Horton, and went through the ritual of removing her heavy round, horn-rimmed spectacles to replace them with half-moon reading glasses which hung on a chain round her neck. She picked up the message between two fingers as if it were something distasteful, and perused it. Her face was expressionless as she read it a second time. Ignoring Mrs Horton, she addressed Millicent who was sitting on the other side of her.

'My dear, would you be so kind as to pull the curtain this way a little?'

Millicent duly rose, crossed to the window and opened up the curtain so that sunshine spilled into the room. Mrs Smith replaced her horn-rimmed spectacles and crumpling the paper, dropped it into the bin. Mrs Horton blinked and squinted in the glare as the light from outside struck her full in the face.

I found the note later, as I tidied the room and took away the litter. It said : 'I wonder if you could draw the curtain slightly? The sun is getting in my eyes.'

It was not long after this incident that Dr Storth began taking Mrs Horton for walks. The late Spring weather had turned fine and he would push the old lady along the promenade in her wheel-chair. They would pause to admire the view across the sea and sometimes sat together on a bench, their heads bobbing as they chatted in their special way. He would lean close and listen intently, nodding encouragement as she babbled. And he would talk to her, though what he found to say was anybody's guess. Occasionally they would skip afternoon tea in the guest house and on these days they could be seen together in the café that overlooked the fishing port.

In their absence, tongues were free to wag. Some speculated that Dr Storth might be a long-lost son Mrs Horton had had to abandon at birth. Others suggested the affinity between them was due to their both being disabled : he had evidently suffered from polio in his childhood, which had left him with one leg deformed and shorter than the other, hence his limp.

Mr Pickvance, the man who had learned that Dr Storth was a phonetics expert, had his own hypothesis : he was investigating speech impediments, and had hit on Mrs Horton as a subject for his work.

'He must have heard she was living here, and moved in to study her,' he said. 'He told me he "knew how to listen" to her. Struck me as a funny thing to say.'

'I don't know about that,' said Ruth the cleaner. 'Since he set up his typewriter on his table he's for ever rattling away on it. You say he's a reader? He's more of a writer, if you ask me.'

'There you are, said Mr Trethewey. 'After each session with Mrs Horton, he goes back to his room and writes up his observations.' He pronounced this last word with particular emphasis.

All of this was nothing but naïve fiction, according to Mrs Smith. She took out her cigarette-holder with its black jade mouthpiece, and fitted a 'Craven A' cigarette into its onyx end. It had been a gift from her late husband, she liked to say. She brandished it especially when she wanted to catch people's attention. She lit her cigarette, inhaled and blew out a plume of smoke. She coughed, clamped the cigarette-holder between her teeth in one corner of her mouth, and spoke from the other corner in a manner she had perfected over the years.

'He's after her money,' she rasped.

She took out her cigarette holder and ostentatiously tapped it over an ashtray beside her chair, confident that all eyes were on her. Then she held it in the air, letting the smoke spiral up alongside her rouged cheek, and spoke again.

'One has seen this sort of thing before. A plausible young rogue befriends a lonely older lady and worms his way into her affections.'

She puffed again at her cigarette-holder and held it in her teeth while she brushed ash from her skirt. She still had all her own teeth and was quite proud of being able to do this.

'It ends with her altering her will in his favour. Your Doctor Storth is a confidence trickster.'

Now Mrs Smith was not without her detractors. It was well known that rather than join them for breakfast she came downstairs at the break of dawn in her green satin pyjamas and silk dressing gown, cigarette-holder between her teeth, carrying a rosewood tray inlaid with mother of pearl – a souvenir from Singapore, she said. In the kitchen she would set her own breakfast things on it, then slip out to collect the milk from the front doorstep and pour the cream from the top of the bottle into her china jug. Then she would retire to her room, leaving Mrs Dugdale to fume and apologize to the other guests who might notice the milk on their cereal was thin and watery.

'She's been at it again, you know. I've tried to reason with her, but she must have her little luxuries.'

So Mrs Smith's pronouncement might just be for show. All the same, her words left the other guests in a quandary. If Mrs Smith was right, shouldn't they look out for Mrs Horton – shouldn't someone warn her? Who would be the one to do it? Would anyone dare take the initiative and denounce Hughie Storth – if that was his real name? They looked at each other, sharing their unspoken thoughts.

During the next few days most of them avoided Mrs Horton's eye, though some would consider her with renewed sympathy, seeing her as the defenceless victim of an unscrupulous Scottish marauder. And when Dr Storth made an appearance, greeting them in his usual affable way, the responses were subdued. To reciprocate cordially, despite their suspicions, was to risk becoming an accomplice in his scheming.

For his part the bluff Doctor, briskly going about his business, seemed impervious to the slight chill that descended when he entered the room.

Time went by, nothing untoward occurred, and the little community went back to its routine. But every time Dr Storth helped Mrs Horton on with her coat and into her wheelchair for another stroll, a collective tremor went through the residents as they imagined him carrying her off in pursuit of whatever plan each had conjectured.

Sometimes however Dr Storth failed to make an appearance at all after breakfast. On those mornings the guests, who without realising it had become accustomed to the distant chatter of typing from upstairs, remarked on an unusual silence. Instead of retiring to his room to work, Dr Storth would pull on an anorak and head off along the coastal path. On certain days he was seen to put on a collar and tie and go out alone, carrying a briefcase, like a man with a business appointment. He rarely came back from these outings before evening, and sometimes no one saw him return – though he never missed breakfast, which he continued to share with Mrs Horton, the two of them resuming their curiously silent but warm rapport.

In the Doctor's absence, Mrs Horton might have been expected to occupy herself with her crosswords. But no : nowadays she saved these to share with her Scotsman.

Instead, she turned her attention to a notebook with stiff covers, in size and shape resembling a school exercise-book or a jotter. And she also revealed that she owned an elegant fountain-pen, with which she began to write in this hard-back volume. Head bent over, she would scribble away, paragraph after paragraph in a firm, ink version of that handwriting we had become familiar with from her pencilled notes. Naturally no-one got to actually read what she wrote, though anyone passing by and glancing down could immediately see that the pages were filling up in even lines, the writing marshalled into tidy blocks, page following page with barely a crossing-out. It came as a surprise that this elderly woman, facial features askew and unsteady on her feet, who could barely speak and had difficulty coordinating her movements at mealtimes, was able to set down words in neat, precise and orderly sequences.

But what was she writing? The proof of her thought-processes was a shock, it had to be admitted. When all she could manage was mumble, and later when she formed the habit of sitting silently, it was natural to ignore her – as if her mute presence signified inertness, as if she was merely filling a space in the air. But when people realised that she was *thinking*, that there were cogent activities going on in her head, they were – putting it bluntly – disturbed. She was reflecting on… what? They had been troubled by her giving up the effort to speak, but now that they had an inkling of what they were being deprived of by way of reflections, remarks – conversation, in short – they were really quite alarmed. Was she writing about her memories of childhood, perhaps? Was she away in another place and time? Or was she actually describing what she saw and thought about now, this room, them sitting in it…? From time to time she would pause, holding her pen off the page, and raise her eyes to stare into the distance, waiting for the next words to come. Could she be observing them? Would the next words she wrote be judgements on their appearance, on the things they murmured to each other in the hush of the sitting-room? Her presence was no longer passive, something they could disregard : it inhibited them, even affecting the way they behaved. They dropped their voices when talking ; they became awkward, self-conscious, and began to watch their every gesture, for fear of being caught out in an ill-considered movement or a facial expression that could be minuted, consigned to paper by the meticulous record-keeper who had emerged in their midst.

In between times, Mrs Horton read, in a way she had not done before. Discarding the Mills and Boon romances, donated by the staff, that were the staple fare of the sitting room, she acquired substantial volumes which she plunged into with evident relish. Inquisitive residents noted books with titles such as *Jane Eyre*, *Cousin Bette*, *Middlemarch*, *The Devils* – this latter causing something of a frisson when it appeared in the wizened hands of the mild-mannered old lady.

Mrs Smith, contemptuous of the changes in Mrs Horton's habits, took to hiding behind her broadsheet newspapers – *The Daily Telegraph* and *The Financial Times*, which the newsagent delivered specially at her request. As Mrs Horton opened her novel or resumed her writing, she would clear her smoker's throat and put on her half-moon reading glasses. Then she would rustle out her newspaper ostentatiously, hold it up to screen herself from her surroundings, and peruse the Stock Market listings – to check the value of her shares and dividends, she said.

On the days following Doctor Storth's solo outings, Mrs Horton would greet him by flourishing the novel she was currently reading. Their conversation would turn on the characters and stories she was immersed in. He would nod and listen attentively as she struggled to form her thoughts into speech – from time to time she would give up in exasperation, frustrated by the flow of ideas she could only express in pitiful croaks ; she would reach for her notebook to scribble down feverishly what she wanted to say. In response, he would occasionally talk at length, Mrs Horton hanging on his words eagerly. From time to time, she would open the volume and leaf through it to find a passage that had struck her. He would be ready to oblige by reading it to her when she asked : softly, so as not to disturb their fellow guests – who all the while would be straining to follow the meaning in his lilting, mellifluous tones.

However, she never showed him her own writings.

3

It was in the kitchen that word first went round : Doctor Storth would not be in for breakfast that morning. Mrs Dugdale had had a phone call from someone speaking on his behalf, explaining that he had been 'unavoidably detained' and would be unable to return to the guest house.

The waitress passed on the news to Mrs Horton, who was visibly bewildered at his absence from the table they shared. Few of the others remarked on Dr Storth's failure to appear. Since Mrs Smith took breakfast upstairs in her room they were spared her reaction and there seemed no cause for concern.

However that day was long for Mrs Horton. She had last seen Dr Storth when he left the house dressed in his collar and tie and carrying his briefcase. Normally when he went out like that she would not see him again until the following morning. So she had already missed their lunch and afternoon walk together ; and now the phone message Mrs Dugdale had received contained no indication of when he would be back. We could only speculate that if it was business that had held him up it could be late at night ; it might be another day before he reappeared among us.

The staff could tell that Mrs Dugdale had concerns of her own. If Doctor Storth could spend one night away, who was to say he hadn't found another place to stay? That room he rented was her best and the rate she was able to charge for it made a difference to her income. He had paid a month in advance, but it was already approaching the end of his fourth week and he had given her to understand he would be staying on.

The next day dawned and still there was no sign of Dr Storth. Not even a phone message this time. The residents exchanged puzzled looks and tentative explanations ; but after all, short-term guests came and went fairly regularly, so this case was not that unusual from their point of view. Someone thought they remembered a previous instance when a visitor had left suddenly without paying the bill, but such matters were none of their business, and they saw nothing to trouble their routine.

However when by the third day Doctor Storth had still not put in an appearance, it began to look as though he would not be back at all. Mrs Dugdale took it upon herself to go into his room to see if there were any clues as to what might have happened to him. She emerged frowning and tight-lipped, and asked Ruth to clear the room of a few oddments left behind, and prepare it for the next guest.

So he had upped and gone without giving notice. Ruth later let slip that he had left his typewriter behind, but apart from that and a few personal items she found inside a cheap cardboard suitcase he had arrived with, there was nothing of value.

'He only took what he could cram into his briefcase,' she concluded.

Mrs Dugdale instructed Ruth to take the few oddments down into the cellar, where they could stay 'until he comes back to claim them,' she said.

One guest murmured that there might be a case for reporting his disappearance to the police – especially if he had absconded without paying an outstanding bill. But Mrs Dugdale said 'there was no need for that,' in a tone intended to shut down such suggestions. She had no wish to have the police involved in her affairs, many of which hinged on cash-in-hand arrangements to avoid tax. If Doctor Storth didn't come back to reclaim his few possessions she could sell them off – the typewriter would cover the unpaid rent, and he had forfeited his deposit, she added as an afterthought.

Mrs Smith saw no reason to hide her satisfaction. 'I dare say that's the last we've seen of him,' she purred. 'I knew from the start he was up to no good – he had a distinctly louche air about him.'

She smiled down at Millicent, her faithful confidante. She deliberately spoke in a hushed tone that had everyone in the room discreetly striving to hear. Although the details were common knowledge, she contrived to make it plain that she knew more than she was prepared to say. Having achieved her aim and sensing all eyes were on her in the hope she would divulge more, she fell silent, drew out her cigarette holder, and fitted another Craven 'A' into it as if unaware that she had become the focus of attention.

'Imagine,' she said to no one in particular as she lit her cigarette, 'if the truth were to come out and we all found ourselves under investigation because of the time he spent here.'

As Mrs Smith came to reoccupy centre stage in the group, Mrs Horton shrank into her chair, bereft at the loss of her erstwhile companion. No one could tell whether she shared Mrs Smith's suspicions, but explicable or not, Dr Storth's disappearance left her distraught.

Mealtimes once more became a trial as she resumed her solitary task of attempting to feed herself without mishap.

The hours in between saw her slumped, staring at the floor or directing an unfocussed gaze at the sky beyond the windows. She seemed to have given up on her crossword puzzles and her reading, as if henceforth they carried painful memories of a lost camaraderie. After a day or two she roused herself, brought in a pack of playing cards, and took up patience instead. But she did continue her habit of communicating via written messages, which enabled her to make requests unobtrusively while avoiding the pathetic gurgles that would draw attention to her sorry plight.

The guests had mixed feelings about this state of affairs. On the one hand it came as something of a relief. They had endured almost two weeks of feeling on edge while she sat hunched over her notebook, her pen running back and forth, filling the pages with notes that for all they knew might concern them. (Mrs Smith had let it be known that she considered it a gross impertinence to make such a show of writing when in company.) At least they could relax now, as Mrs Horton subsided into a forlorn torpor. On the other hand, as the days passed and Doctor Storth's disappearance ceased to be a subject of conversation and a source of distraction, they could not ignore her dejected silence. It radiated a pall of melancholy across the sitting-room and seemed to hang over them all. Occasionally one of them would try to lift her spirits with a jaunty comment she could respond to non-verbally : she would raise her eyes and sketch a wan smile but clearly her heart was not in it.

Suddenly however she began reading again. She brought in her notebook and sat running her eyes over the pages she had written. Occasionally she would unscrew the cap of her fountain-pen and modify a word or sentence, or else she would add a note. But mainly she read intensely, thoughtfully, her brow furrowed, with pauses for reflection when she would stare at the sky through the window, oblivious to her surroundings and her neighbours.

This went on for a week or so. Then one morning, after we had finished clearing away the breakfast things and I put my head round the door for one last look in case we had forgotten a plate or a teapot, Mrs Horton unexpectedly glanced up and caught my eye. Then she crooked a finger to call me over.

As I stood before her, she looked past me to left and right, evidently checking that no one else was paying attention. Then she slid towards me a page torn from her note-pad. It was folded double, and with a small gesture of a back-turned hand she signalled I should take it away with me rather than open it there and then.

Naturally I assumed at first that it contained a small tip by way of a 'thank you' for something I had done for her – as part of my normal job, I should add. But I couldn't feel a coin as a I pushed it into my pocket, so I was left a bit mystified.

When I came off my shift, I went up to my room and it was there that I opened the small crumpled square of paper. It didn't contain money. It contained writing.

'Would you take me for a walk in my wheelchair, please? I'll buy you a cup of tea for your pains.'

My heart sank. Don't say she had picked me out to be her new companion. I didn't mind her, and was happy enough to lend a hand now and again – but for all I could tell this might be an invitation to a long-term arrangement. I valued my independence and I foresaw a commitment I could do without.

Then I saw her in my mind's eye : a good-natured old lady who was evidently in some distress on finding herself without company. Mrs Smith's snide remarks came back to me as well : and I have to admit it was partly to put her smug Roman nose out of joint that I decided to go along with Mrs Horton's request.

I had time off between lunch and tea-time, so the following afternoon I manoeuvred her wheelchair down the front steps, helped her into it, and set off along the promenade.

It was a blustery day, the wind coming in gusts off the sea and snatching away attempts at conversation. In any case the best Mrs Horton could do was cry out from time to time and gesticulate at the flock of birds advancing with the tide, swooping down to the water's edge and taking off again as the waves rippled in over their feet.

I answered with 'Uh-huh', though I tried to make it sound like an expression of interest. This seemed to work, since Mrs Horton would launch into a sequence of snuffles and barks that the wind gave me an excuse for not understanding. All the same, I did occasionally offer snippets of proper speech, hoping that what I said would serve as replies to her impenetrable utterances. By the time we reached the café at the end of the bay, to a casual onlooker we were conversing like old acquaintances.

I had to prop open the door of the café so I could manoeuvre the wheelchair through the gap. The air inside was heavy with steam and I felt the warmth return to my cheeks as we headed for places by the window. A plump woman behind the counter called out a cheery greeting and the waitress crossed in front of us to move a chair aside so we could wheel Mrs Horton up to the table. She grinned at Mrs Horton, glanced at me and then looked back at the old lady, a twinkle in her eye.

'I see you've got a new beau looking after you today.'

Mrs Horton managed to purse her lips lopsidedly, and blew out through them. I can look after myself, was what that said. And as I got the message (which had escaped the waitress), it was the start of a peculiar understanding between the two of us.

We didn't communicate much while we waited for our tea and Chorley cakes to arrive.

It was unusual for me to be sitting face to face with Mrs Horton. Mostly I'd just give her sidelong glances, and try not to stare at her – it was my way of sparing her embarrassment. It seemed impertinent to look directly at her wonky face, her crumpled cheeks and drooping lips. But I could hardly avoid it here, without actually turning away from her – which would have been rude. I did try staring out of the window as if admiring the view, and made some remarks about the sky and the seagulls ; but I couldn't keep that up for long, so I was glad when our food arrived. Finally I looked into her eyes, determined not to let my own stray to her disfigured features.

I needn't have worried. The eyes that had been looking me over while I avoided them were waiting to fix me at last. An ice-blue, penetrating gaze sparkled across from beneath the sagging eyelids.

She nodded from the teapot to her cup, and I poured her a drink. I said 'Say when!' as I added milk, and blushed as she chuckled and raised a finger. It struck me that she had a laugh just like anyone else, even though drinking was an awkward manoeuvre for her.

She broke off a piece of Chorley cake and covered her mouth with her hands, catching crumbs that fell back from her lips as she chewed and swallowed.

I thought there must be more for me to do than witness the spectacle. But biting into my own cake felt like I was deliberately showing off superior skills. I ate as tactfully as I could, envying that straightforward approach to her eating difficulties that Dr Storth had shown.

Those bright eyes fixed me once more. This time she arched an eyebrow – I'd never noticed that she could do that – and I realised she was giving me a quizzical look.

There was no room for misunderstanding here: Well, what do you have to say for yourself? I read in her expression.

I would have to find something to say. I cleared my throat.

'So… how long have you lived in Cottsea?' I finally managed to utter.

'Or ngy hife,' she replied, matter-of-factly.

Leaving it to me to make sense of these sounds.

I looked at her. She repeated her words, such as they were. They came from somewhere right at the back of her throat, apart from when she brought her teeth down onto her bottom lip to make an 'f'.

'Or ngy *hife*,' she repeated, emphasising the last word.

'Life?' I said – and she nodded. Then the penny dropped.

'All your life?'

She nodded again, and gave a skewed smile of satisfaction. Contact had been confirmed.

'So I dare say you could tell us a lot about the place.'

She nodded a third time, closing her eyes as if to show how much patience it took to deal with obtuse people and patronising questions – unless she was contemplating the memories she could not voice. But when she opened her eyes again they had an urgent look. She drew a determined breath, and began painstakingly to articulate more sounds.

'Ah wonk koo kork awauk hooey.'

It was my turn to nod, as I gave a vague smile, to signify I was bewildered though willing to try and understand.

'Ah wonk –' She broke off. 'Hooey,' she said. And repeated : 'Hooey'.

I shook my head apologetically. 'I'm sorry, I can't – '

'*Hooey*,' she said again, followed by a stream of sounds I couldn't make out. At the same time her hands were flailing between us, as if they might help carry her meaning across.

I felt cornered. She wasn't going to stop until I understood. I struggled to grasp the words behind her incomprehensible utterances.

'Hooey, hooey,' she kept saying. Then more gargled noises.

I turned this over in my mind, then tried mouthing it myself.

'Hooey… hooey,' I said.

She nodded vigorously, as if I had grasped her point.

Then at last I did.

'Hooey… – Hughie,' I said smiling with relief despite myself. 'Oh, you mean Dr Storth.'

She heaved a sigh and gurgled something that – however it sounded – plainly meant 'That's right'.

At last we had a subject of conversation.

'I didn't have much to do with him, but I thought he was a nice man,' I said.

She murmured in agreement.

'I don't know why he's called Doctor though, if he isn't actually a… doctor.'

Mrs Horton looked into my face, trying to work out why this should puzzle me. She said one syllable that might have been 'Oh…': you know, it's not a great mystery.

It's a funny thing trying to keep up a conversation with someone who's hanging on your every word, showing every sign that she's eager to hear you speak, but who can't say anything to keep the discussion going from her side.

'The two of you seemed to get on well,' I tried. 'You must miss him, now he's left.'

33

This time she launched into speech again, but quickly gave up as she saw my brows furrow, reflecting a futile attempt to follow her.

Then she began to scrabble in her bag. I watched her pull out her notepad and a pencil. She folded back a sheet of paper and started to write. When she had finished, she turned the pad around and slid it across the table so that I could read it.

'He has been abducted,' she had written.

Up until then the conversation had been innocuous, banal, if a little stilted. I had struggled for things to say that might engage her interest. After all, what could I know about the mind of a seventy-year-old?

Now, as I read what was in her thoughts, it occurred to me that she was in the grip of a senile delusion, the kind of obsession that an ageing mind can be prey to. Until then I had been chatting with her as best I could, assuming she was a normal person. Suddenly a gulf had opened up between us, and I must admit my instinct was to recoil. How should I respond? Should I just dismiss the idea like those who never took the trouble to listen to her anyway, and who didn't want to get involved with her fading world?

And if I were to take her seriously, what kind of eccentric notions might I be drawn into?

Meanwhile her eyes looked at me steadily. They had none of the vagueness or abstraction of one who had left reality behind. She wasn't inviting me to step beyond that table where we sat, into a realm of speculation and fantasy.

She reached out and tapped the piece of paper with her finger.

She meant what she had written.

4

And she had written other words to back up her conviction.

It turned out she had learned a lot about Dr Storth during their walks up and down the promenade and sometimes further afield. Mrs Horton was not just a subject for his alleged scientific work, as some supposed ; a sort of fellow-feeling had grown up between them. Perhaps this was because Dr Storth was disabled himself, having suffered in his childhood from polio, which had left him with one leg deformed and shorter than the other, giving him a curious rolling gait as he pushed his protégée along. The sight of this limping man wheeling the lopsided old lady had become a regular feature of village life – so much so that Dr Storth's absence was quickly noticed among the community beyond our guest-house. No one said anything, but whenever I took her out – or was she taking me out? – I could feel people thinking how bizarre it was to see an able-bodied chap behind the wheelchair.

It also turned out that in the course of their odd conversations he had got into the habit of expressing himself quite freely. He probably talked on impulse, to fill the silence caused by her inability to speak in a normal manner. Often, it seemed, he would take advantage of having a more or less mute interlocutor, to simply think out loud. And perhaps he fell into the mistaken belief that his secrets would be safe with this literally tongue-tied old lady.

It happened to be the case, however, that Mrs Horton took in everything he said to her and proved perfectly capable of writing most of it down afterwards. This possibility didn't occur to anyone, least of all to Dr Storth, until much later.

So it was that some days after I walked Mrs Horton back from our first outing together, she insisted that I should get into the lift with her and accompany her to her room. There she handed me her notebook and wrote instructions at the top of a slip of paper which she inserted into it like a bookmark : 'Read up to this page and NO FURTHER'. She gave me one of her penetrating looks as I read these words, then touched the side of her nose with one finger and pointed it at me. The inference was clear : this is strictly between ourselves.

I've never been a great reader, and I found the prospect of her handwriting especially off-putting. But at my next break I dutifully sat down, opened up the first page, and read :

Because they pay no attention to me, they think I'm not paying attention to them.

Because they can't make out what I'm saying, they think I can't understand them.

Because I can't say what I'm thinking, they think I have no thoughts.

This young Scotsman. He insists on calling himself Hughie, which strikes me as an infantile diminutive. But there is presumably a part of him that hasn't outgrown his childhood, when his parents gave him that name out of affection for him. In any event I'm excused from using it as such since I can't speak it anyway.

Mrs Smith persists in addressing him as 'Hugh', as if calling him to order, but it does no good. And I'm not surprised she doesn't impress him, with her patronising manner. Or perhaps it's her grotesque appearance that puts him off. Someone should have told her years ago about keeping her hair dyed red when the roots show vast expanses of white. Keeping it so long, brushing it out morning and night, heaving it tight as a drum into a bun at the back of her head. She spends hours on it, but I suppose it keeps her occupied. She doesn't seem to have much else to fill her days. Apart from defending her armchair and surveying the room as if it belonged to her.

That armchair. Mr Trethewey took a fancy to it before he knew any better. And she found him sitting in it one morning when she deigned to join us after breakfast. She sailed in like a galleon, great bosooms billowing under a tight green jumper and cardigan, cigarette holder clamped between her teeth like a bowsprit. Seeing he had usurped her chair, she took up a position standing alongside, breathing through her teeth with that raucous smoker's gasp she uses to announce her presence, and clenching her jaw so that her cigarette holder twitched, threatening to flick ash onto Mr Trethewey's trousers. He looked up and got the message right away, rising and murmuring excuses, and retreated sheepishly to a modest wing chair by the window.

Someone should draw a map of this room, marking out the hazards and pitfalls an unsuspecting newcomer has to negotiate. There are more shoals and quicksands in here than out on the beach.

Young 'Hughie', as I must resign myself to calling him, seemed untroubled by the atmosphere that greets each new arrival. I was impressed – not least by the discreet brush-off he served up for Mrs S. He is a young man with aplomb, is my first impression. But for the time being I shall reserve my final opinion.

He has taken to sharing my table at mealtimes. I think it suits him to be a bit removed from the rest of the guests, and I can't blame him for wanting to avoid their dreary conversations. But it does seem a bit extreme to seek out a companion who doesn't speak at all.

The thing is though, he knows how to listen. Oh, I don't fall for that smattering of phonetics he claims makes him capable of understanding my gargling. There may be something in it I suppose, but when I tested him by saying 'haggis' he hadn't a clue. At least he laughed when I wrote down the answer, and he had to admit he wasn't infallible. Then, just to make the point, I said he was a 'presumptuous jumped-up squirt' and he didn't demur. I meant it in a friendly way so when he claimed to hear 'promising young scholar' I let it go. At least the twinkle in his eye when he said it shows he's self-deprecating. And I think he understood I have one advantage over him : I can be rude to people to their face and get away with it.

But a listener : he acknowledges I might have thoughts and things to say, and they might be worth hearing. He gives me some of his time and takes pains to understand me, which I appreciate.

And in return I think I've sharpened his technique for solving cryptic crosswords.

I don't know what made him offer to wheel me out for walks. Perhaps he gets tired of being cooped up with his paperwork and writings. He does go out on his own quite a bit, but on those days I think he sets off with a purpose : he looks preoccupied. So perhaps he likes to relax by rambling along with no particular destination in view, and pushing my wheelchair is a task that takes his mind off other things. For my part I'm not demanding company. As a matter of fact, I think he finds that I'm a good listener too. I've begun to understand that when he has a number of things going round his head, he uses me as a foil, to talk through what's preoccupying him. I sometimes see myself as a sort of ventriloquist's dummy, sitting wordlessly beside him on the promenade bench as he projects his thoughts. He laughed when I told him that. He said my deadpan expression was right for the part. I gave him a tap on the wrist for being cheeky, and shot him a look that said 'Don't mock the afflicted.' But he could tell I was only joking.

He's a scholar. A Reader in Comparative Literature, whatever that is. He tells me he found a manuscript in a library in France and is trying to make sense of it. It appears that the Carnegie Trust for the Universities of Scotland, no less, has provided him with money to come and live at the seaside while he carries out this valuable work.

I said, 'If you like going to libraries, could you get some books for me from the local library?'

He stared at me. Of course he couldn't tell what I was saying at first, but I think he was surprised that anyone might find something to say in response to his tale of rooting about among dusty manuscripts. I dare say he's accustomed to stunned silence and glazed eyes. I repeated myself and he listened carefully. In the end I wrote down what I had said. I saw a look of disappointment flit across his face when he got the message – he'd been hoping I would show some enthusiasm for his investigations and here I was asking him to run an errand for me. But he agreed readily enough. And when I told him what books I wanted to read he perked up.

'It looks like we have similar tastes in literature,' he said. And then he went on to explain that he'd been working on the manuscript of a fairly obscure French novel.

He noticed me raise my eyebrows.

'Oh yes, I should have said, French is the language I mainly work in.' He gave me a twinkling look. 'Though I'm also proficient at Double-Dutch, as you'll have noticed in my conversations with you.'

I replied with something rude, which fortunately he didn't understand, though he got the gist of it and gave me a cheeky grin. Dear boy, he really does have a nice face to go with his sense of humour.

He said he had planned to produce a new edition of the novel, that put right some of the printing errors in the published version and restored some passages that the author had cut for one reason or another.

'And then,' he said, 'among all the manuscript folios, I came across this bundle of papers that were handwritten like the rest, but in a different hand.'

At this point he became excited. He put his hand on mine. Nice warm fingers on my arthritic knuckles.

'This second manuscript was in English,' he said. 'I read through it and it was obviously a translation from the French. An English version of a chapter intended for the original novel.'

He squeezed my hand.

'But there was nothing like it in the published novel. Or in the French manuscript.'

He could tell it belonged to the novel, he said, because several of the characters were the same. And there were some 'themes', as he put it, that it had in common with the published book.

'So I deduced,' he said with an air at once self-mocking and self-satisfied, 'that I had come across a translation of a chapter that had been cut from the novel. But what I couldn't find was that part of the original French manuscript which the translation had been made from. It has disappeared.'

He was about to go on, but I interrupted him because what he said struck me as very odd. I'm no critic but there was an obvious question to ask. Rather than try his patience – and mine – by attempting to speak it, I asked him to wait a moment while I scribbled out what I wanted to know.

'Did no one ever notice there was a piece missing from the published novel? Doesn't the story have a hole in it?'

He read my words and I saw he was eager to give me an answer.

'Well no, you see, because when I looked through the original manuscript again, I noticed that at one particular place there was a flurry of variant texts.'

He could tell this was beginning to sound like Greek to me, and stifling his excitement he forced himself to speak more slowly and in terms I could understand.

'What I mean is, you can tell where this chapter had originally been by the fact that at a certain point the author has rewritten the end of one chapter and inserted extra passages at the start of the next, to provide a transition and cover over the gap. In other words he didn't want anyone to suspect this chapter had ever existed. As if it was something he wanted to... hide perhaps.'

So you're trying to find this bit of the original French manuscript, I said as best I could. It was the obvious thing to say and I think he got it, because he nodded.

'You've come to a funny place to find it,' I continued.

He didn't understand me but he noted the ironic tone of my voice and said, 'What?'

I repeated myself, and when he still didn't grasp my words, I wrote them down.

'You're wondering why...'

I grunted. It's all I can do at moments like that.

'It's a bit complicated,' he said. 'But strange as it seems, and unlike the rest of the novel, the action of this chapter takes place in a seaside village in England.'

I raised my eyebrows : how do you know?

'It mentions English place-names. Not real ones – as I discovered when I tried looking them up in an atlas – but authentic fakes.'

'...?'

'Well, for instance he calls the place Bournsea.'

Not a million miles from ...

'I checked through the author's published journalism and a series of letters which have found their way into print. I discovered that he had visited

the Lake District in the autumn of 1917. That was when he was working on the novel.'

By now he was really warming to his subject. Whether I was interested or not – though in fact I was – I was going to get the full story.

'So I got hold of an Ordnance Survey map and studied the towns and villages on this part of the coast. That's when the name Cottsea caught my eye.'

While he was speaking a small fleck of foam had appeared at the corner of his mouth. He licked his lips and continued, excitement mounting.

'It wasn't much to go on. But then I noticed one or two nearby place names and geographical features that called to mind locations in the story. For example he writes about Fluke Sands – and just along the coast here you have Flounder Beach. That's what decided me to come and carry out a closer inspection.'

'So that's why you've been going out for walks?' It was a rhetorical question. I don't know if he made out what I was saying. I needn't have tried, really. I only wanted to keep the conversation going – to show I was interested.

'And that's why I've been going out for walks,' he went on. 'I've been surveying the lie of the land. And I'm pretty certain that he based his village on Cottsea. You have Overstrand where he has "Upland Way"; he writes "Nethermere" for the spot called Underness. He talks about a railway line with a level crossing. Well the railway doesn't run any more as I'm sure you know, but you can see where it used to be – and I found that remains of the level crossing are still there. He even mentions "Cottam Hill", which he refers to as an isolated hill in a wide flat land, which can be seen for miles

around. I climbed up Barham Knowle, and I'm sure that's it. Even after forty years or so, the view from the top corresponds to what he describes.'

I nodded. All this seemed fairly plausible. And it's interesting to think that the out-of-the-way place you've spent most of your life in should have found its way into a literary classic. Perhaps there was scope for a boost to the local tourist trade.

But what was this book? Is it any good? Do people still read it? Questions jostled in my mind and they would only jumble in my mouth if I tried to spit them out. So I jotted them down.

'It's called "Away from the Storm" – À l'Abri de la Tempête – the storm being the Great War, of course. The author's name is Paul Daubignac. He appears to have died during World War Two. And no, unfortunately neither he nor his book are very well known... But they have their place in literary history.'

He looked at me, half-intent, half-amused.

'And if I have anything to do with it, that place is about to get bigger.'

Oh yes? I raised my eyebrows again.

'If Daubignac based the fictional location on a real place, then the chances are that the events in the story are based on actual events. And the nature of those events may explain why he decided not to include this chapter in the novel. That's the next avenue I propose to investigate.'

I had reached the place where Mrs Horton told me to stop. Some of this went over my head – talk of manuscripts and French novels and the like... What would a foreign writer want with Cottsea, a humdrum place looking out over dull mudflats? The whole set-up struck me as bizarre. Dr Storth had been investigating a translation of a manuscript which had never been published and which had disappeared. He had found this trace of it buried in an archive somewhere, but to all intents and purposes, the original had ceased to exist. But had it ever existed? He was apparently the only one who knew about it. He had spent time in Cottsea digging up the so-called reality behind this non-existent fiction… My head began to spin.

And now he was gone without any explanation. But if Mrs Horton's theory was to be believed, his absence was part of a pattern. He had gone missing in mysterious circumstances – while investigating a disappearance.

5

The next time I saw Mrs Horton was in the breakfast-room the following morning.

'I read –' I began as I leaned in and served her.

She started, stiffened, and gave me an urgent look. She raised her finger to her lips and I fell silent.

For the rest of the meal she virtually ignored me and I went about my business in the usual way. But when I came to clear away her table, on her empty plate was a piece of paper folded over a scribbled message.

'Take me for a walk, please?'

It was a fine day so instead of heading directly for the café, we sat side by side on a bench overlooking the shore. The tide was a long way out. The beach and the sky were both empty.

I handed over Mrs Horton's journal. She glanced down at it in her hands, turned her head, raised her eyebrows and gave me a questing look that said, plain as day : 'Well?'

I'd been dreading this moment. Suddenly I was back at school, and the teacher was asking me to give an account of my homework.

'I don't know French,' I said. 'And I've never had much time for reading.'

She let out a heavy sigh that made her slack lips flap somewhat.

She said something. I couldn't grasp the words but the intonation was eloquent.

What difference does that make?

'Well,' I said reluctantly. 'If we were in a detective film, I'd be saying something like "How can you know he's been abducted?"'

She nodded, and remained silent. Eventually I said,

'And who would have a motive for abducting him anyway? There's nothing in that account you gave me to show someone might have it in for him.'

True, her response said.

I had to go on. And to my surprise I found I had things to say.

'This manuscript – this translation. How does he know it's a translation, if the original French version has disappeared? Who's to say it isn't something someone wrote on their own... – maybe after they'd read the novel?'

She said what I took to be 'Hmm', then opened her journal and flicked through it to the page where Dr Storth referred to the manuscript alterations aimed at masking over the missing chapter.

'OK, so it's probably a genuine translation,' I conceded. Then an idea occurred to me. 'Was the whole novel translated? Was it ever published in English?'

That was a question Mrs Horton liked. The answer, as she shook her head, was a definite 'No'.

But I was warming to my investigation, so I stuck to my guns.

'Are you sure?' I asked.

She shook her head emphatically. But there was something in her attitude that didn't put me off musing some more. It wasn't often I had found myself being listened to in that way. The novelty of the experience encouraged me to continue talking ; and I discovered that the more I talked, the more I became interested in finding something useful to say.

'Look,' I went on. 'Suppose the writer wanted his novel translating. He would hand over the entire manuscript wouldn't he?'

Mrs Horton was nodding, which was her way of egging me on, I supposed.

Another thought came to me.

'Perhaps he might begin with a sample to see what sort of a job the translator would make of it. But you'd expect him to do a try-out with the first chapter, wouldn't you?'

By now I felt I was swimming on my own, some way out from the shore. I began to flounder.

'But what if –' I stammered. 'Anyway I've no idea how these things are done. Perhaps it's a translator who enjoyed reading the book who makes the first move?'

Mrs Horton rocked her head : she was non-committal. I felt a little stab of indignation : look, I didn't ask to get involved in all this riddling. Can't you help me out a bit?

She was gazing across the bay, oblivious to my quandary. Now she'd drifted off into a world of her own. Was it my job to keep her interested? What the hell was I doing here? I was a bit tetchy as I spoke again.

'Why else would someone take the trouble to translate only one part of the novel?'

Mrs Horton pursed her lips : Who knows?

'You'd think that if they liked the novel enough they'd aim to translate the whole thing,' I said. 'And in that case you'd expect them to start at the beginning, wouldn't you?' Then something else struck me. 'But suppose they did do the whole thing – and couldn't find anyone who would publish it. You said even in France the book didn't have much of an impact. Okay, so they might chuck the translation away in a fit of pique…'

Mrs Horton shrugged, but not in a dismissive way : she couldn't say.

'Perhaps they couldn't bring themselves to do that, after putting in a lot of work. But then you'd think they'd keep the whole thing. So who would hang on to only one random chapter, from the middle of the book? And what would make them do that? What's so special about that chapter?'

Mrs Horton crinkled the corner of her eye and put her hand on my arm: I was getting warmer.

'Something in that chapter was worth keeping,' I said in spite of myself – but all of a sudden, I was delighted at having been led by her curious method to reach a conclusion that felt like progress.

Next thing I knew we were shaking hands – like she and Dr Storth used to do on solving one of their crossword puzzles.

But I hadn't finished yet.

'Dr Storth mentioned events in it… Did he tell you what they were?'

She shook her head. She suddenly seemed downhearted, distracted even. Not because he hadn't told her the story, more likely because she was missing him.

On impulse I tried to get her attention again.

'Maybe something in that chapter could be connected with Dr Storth being abducted…' I murmured – then bit my tongue. My thoughts were running away with me. I glanced at Mrs Horton, ready to apologize. From the look on her face it was obvious she had intended this to happen. And at that point I knew I was hooked.

All the same, I felt I had to add, 'If he has been abducted.'

49

Mrs Horton crossed her hands in her lap and stared out across the shore again. A breeze had got up and was tugging at her fluffy hair. She let out a sigh and I wondered what she was thinking. I could hardly ask her – I didn't know her well enough, and in any case a chap my age had no business intruding on an old lady's thoughts.

To fill the silence, I said, 'I wonder who the translator was? Did... does ' – I corrected myself – 'does Dr Storth know?'

Mrs Horton shook her head. Then she said something like,

'Hangah-hing.'

Here we were again, me trying to make out what she meant while she repeated 'Hangah-hing, hangah-hing,' and once more, with emphasis, 'Hangah-*hing*'.

I mouthed my own version of the sounds.

'Something ending in "ing"?' I asked.

She nodded.

'Hang,' she said.

'Hand?' I suggested.

She nodded.

'Hand... ing,' I repeated.

A dog appeared out of nowhere, accompanied by its owner, a man who was gazing at us nonplussed as we gurned at each other.

Mrs Horton glanced at him, then came down with a fit of giggles. The man moved away.

She stopped giggling and then raised her hand as if holding a pen, and scribbled in the air.

'Oh, handwriting,' I said.

She placed one hand on her heart and gave a mock sigh of relief.

'So,' I said, 'the handwriting is a clue.'

She nodded, gave me a thumbs-up, but then held out her open palms and shrugged her shoulders as if to say that in fact it wasn't much help...

Suddenly I had a vision of us playing charades, where someone thinks of a book or film title and can only gesture mutely as the other players try to guess it. I couldn't help smiling, and Mrs Horton tried to grin too, bless her. Evidently she was thinking along the same lines.

Funnily enough, this was a big step forward in our efforts to communicate. I relaxed as we both started behaving like we were acting out a parlour-game.

I said, 'Did Dr Storth say what kind of handwriting it is?'

She pursed her lips, and leaned her head to one side : Well, sort of.

'Big? Small?'

Middling.

That didn't get us far. Then I had an idea. I'd read somewhere that schoolchildren in France are taught how to write on squared paper, which makes French handwriting somewhat standardized – different from English, which tends to be much more varied.

'Is it French handwriting?'

She shook her head. Definitely not. We were getting somewhere.

'So, English then.'

Presumably.

One more question occurred to me.

'A man's or a woman's?'

Mrs Horton cocked her head and moved it left and right, pensively.

Anybody's guess.

I wondered if I would have been able to identify Mrs Horton's writing as that of a woman. I glanced down at the register in her lap, and felt her eyes follow mine.

So, I thought. We have two possible kinds of translator. What would make a man want to translate a French novel – or a part of it? Why would a woman want to?

'What's that chapter about?' I blurted out. 'Is there a story in it? Come to think of it, what's the novel about?'

Mrs Horton shrugged : search me.

'So Dr Storth didn't tell you?'

No.

Events, I thought.

But then Mrs Horton's face went into a sort of convulsion. Her shoulders began to shake, and a bleating sound came out of her mouth. It took me a moment to realise that she was crying.

'Hoo-ey,' she sobbed. 'Oh, Hoo-ey.' She reached into her handbag for a handkerchief.

She had been almost smiling a few moments ago, and we had been chatting – after a fashion – more or less light-heartedly, playfully even. But now here she was in the grip of what I could only call grief. She really was missing Dr Storth, and she was genuinely worried about him. It struck home to me that *this* was a mystery of substance. In comparison, the other questions were beside the point.

I couldn't just sit and watch, so on an impulse I moved to put my arm around her shoulders. I wanted to comfort her, though I had no way of knowing exactly what was making her so upset.

She sat up rigidly, as if she didn't welcome my arm around her. She remained self-contained in her sadness, and her body language made it clear she wasn't going to lean into me for comfort. I patted her shoulder and withdrew my hand.

I couldn't help wondering if she would have reacted in the same way to Dr Storth. And then I wondered what it was about Dr Storth that had made her so attached to him.

It didn't take her long to regain her composure. We sat side by side in silence for a moment, each of us embarrassed in our own way about what had just happened.

She put her handkerchief back into her handbag and closed the clasp. I thought she might be shaping up to go back to the guest-house, but she didn't move, just gave a sigh.

'Can I ask a question?' I said. 'What was – is – Dr Storth like?'

I couldn't put my finger on what I had felt just a few moments earlier, but it was something like jealousy. And it prompted me to recall the rumours and speculation that had been going round about him. Did he really deserve her concern? Could she be certain he was what he claimed to be?

Mrs Horton must have read my mind, because she turned to me sharply, with an amused look in her eyes.

'A cong hang?' she suggested.

A con man.

I nodded. She snorted. She had evidently got wind of Mrs Smith's insinuations, and didn't think much of them.

Rather than try to explain herself in speech, she reached into her bag and drew out her notebook once more. She lifted the cover and leafed through it, turning the pages back and forth until she had found the place she was looking for.

He's good company and we get on very well. I've no idea what he sees in me except that I'm a docile listener. The other day he compared me to his students.

'When they don't speak up in class it's a sign that I've failed to get through. Their silence can be quite dispiriting. Yours is a refreshing change!'

Today he announced he was going to the library. I wrote down the title of a book I wanted him to bring back: Crime and Punishment, by Dostoievsky. He looked at it, then at me, and frowned. And then the penny dropped. His eyes twinkled and his face creased into a grin.

'Now look here,' he said. 'I hope you don't think I'm some sort of Raskolnikov, plotting to bump off a rich old lady and run away with her money. I'll have you know I already have a well-paid position. I've got better things to do with my time than conduct an experiment in remorse!' He paused, laughed, and then said very firmly : 'My research may be taking me up all kinds of byways, but I'm not about to embark on another career!'

I couldn't be sure what that novel by Dostoievsky was about. But when I finished reading and lifted my eyes, she was looking back at me with her misshapen face – and her eyes were brimming with what seemed like tears. It may just have been the breeze, or they may have been watering as old people's eyes do. But I gathered that she had been happy to take Dr Storth at his word when he claimed he was no threat to her.

I smiled to let her know I understood that much, even though I hadn't read the novel. One more novel I'd like to get my hands on.

I felt another pang of that odd feeling, tinged with resentment. My company was no substitute for Dr Storth, and it bothered me.

I was beginning to appreciate what he saw in her – and it wasn't just that she was a docile listener.

In fact she had been reading my thoughts again, during the silence that had settled on us. She reached across me and took the journal from my hands. She retrieved the book-mark she had used before and tore a piece off to make a second one. She turned several pages and inserted this, pointing at it to mark where I should resume reading. And a few pages further on she placed the stub of the first one. It still said on it: 'Read up to this page and NO FURTHER'.

She held the volume out to me. I hesitated, then tucked it inside my jacket.

She gathered up her handbag, pulled her coat around her, and indicated it was time to go back for tea.

I let the brake off her wheelchair and manoeuvred it to face the way we had come. I was glad to have something to do – something to ease the tongue-tied state I now found myself in.

'All set?' I asked, and as she grunted her reply she reached back over her shoulder and touched my fingers where they curled around the handle.

I may not be in Dr Storth's league, I reflected. But maybe I could help her search for him.

6

Today he took me for a walk on the seafront in a new direction, past where the esplanade veers away inland, along the path that follows the sea wall. It isn't meant for wheelchairs, so my ride was a bit bumpy. The wheels would get stuck in ruts and Hughie kept having to wrench them free. We hadn't gone very far before he was panting heavily. It would have been hard work for an able-bodied man, let alone one with a bad leg like Hughie. I felt rather sorry for him, and tried to protest that he needn't put himself through all that for my sake.

'Ach no, you're all right,' he said, stopping to catch his breath. 'I can manage fine.'

We set off again, and I was jolted from side to side as he continued on the route he seemed determined to stick to. I recalled playing on this bit of the foreshore when I was little, but hadn't been near it for years. I clutched the arm-rests to steady myself. It occurred to me there may come a point where I'd have to say that I'd had enough.

After a while we reached a spot Hughie had evidently been aiming at. To my great relief the surface of the path became smoother as we came to where it meets the narrow lane that emerges from a grove of trees and slopes down to the beach. Alongside the junction there is a bench, and Hughie manoeuvred me into place so he could sit down beside me.

'This tarmac was put down after the war,' he explained. 'Before then the lane was a track that was mainly used for carting mussels from the mud-flats.'

He looked at me and I nodded – as well I might, since I can recall sitting at this very spot and watching the men bring the mussels ashore when I was a girl.

'Sorry! Of course you know that,' he said.

I decided it would be too much of an effort to try to spell out all the things I remembered. I did notice, though, that the solid timber bench I had been familiar with had gone, no doubt battered to pieces by storm waves and gales lashing in from the bay. Its replacement was a concrete and wooden plank affair, serviceable enough but with none of the associations that came back to me from forty-odd years ago as we sat in silence and gazed out over the bay. No point trying to speak about those things now, I thought. Given my 'speech impediment', it would be like putting rose petals through a grinder.

Next to me Hughie seemed to be growing fidgety. I turned to look at him, and realised he could hardly contain himself. I raised my eyebrows and leaned a bit to one side, which is my way of asking:

Well?

He didn't need further prompting.

'You may think you know about this place,' he said with one of his eager boyish grins. 'But I bet I know something you don't.'

I have a restricted repertoire of facial mannerisms at my disposal, but I opened my good eye wide and this must have conveyed surprise coupled with scepticism, because he raised his eyebrows and puckered his mouth to make an 'Oh yes I do' face.

So I sat still, and waited for it to spill out.

He turned and placed a hand on my arm.

'This is the setting where an important event happens.'

I looked around, wondering if I had missed something, or whether an incident was imminent.

'No,' he said. 'In the story – the manuscript.'

I made an 'Oh' sound.

'Yes,' he went on. 'Two characters meet and talk on a bench here. Not this very one, I imagine.' He gestured at the concrete seat.

No, I thought, it was probably the one I remember.

But Hughie was talking about a fictional bench, obviously. I drew breath to try and say something of the sort, but he anticipated the words I would have had to struggle with.

'Of course it's in the author's mind that events happen. But it's very striking that he describes a location just like this.' He leaned closer. 'As a matter of fact – as opposed to a manuscript of fiction – what I think is that he was familiar with this spot and recreated it as the setting for part of his narrative.'

I looked around again. Beneath our feet the path was a pavement, the bench was concrete ; weeds and lichen covered the top of the sea wall, while sea lavender and marram grass had taken over the foreshore. None of this would have been the case in 1914 or so. In fact, none of it was the case, I recalled. How could Hughie be sure that this was the place the writer had in mind?

I had a sudden urge to put the question into words. I gurgled a bit and raised my palms, gesturing around us, pointing to the concrete parts of the bench, and I must have managed to get my puzzlement across, because Hughie spoke again.

'Naturally, it's not as it was then. The bottom of the slope down there has silted up and become overgrown with the passage of time, and in fact the entire coastline has changed. But' – he held up a finger and wagged it at me – 'I've succeeded in retracing the path the protagonist followed to arrive here.'

He went on to explain that during his walks he had managed to map the fictional world onto large chunks of the coastline and countryside in and around Cottsea. He repeated the names of various features he had told me about – the ones he had deciphered behind their fictional counterparts : Overstrand, Barham Knowle, Underness.

'Daubignac describes quite a few other landmarks – the level-crossing, for instance. He gets a wee bit poetical when he evokes the view across the bay...' He pulled a wry face. 'Anyway, I collected up all the bits of description in the manuscript, and the surveys I carried out on foot enabled me to do some triangulation. Bit by bit I believe I've grasped the essential topography of the fictional landscape – and I can now say it has its sources in the actual terrain around us.'

He was evidently very pleased with his achievement – I could tell from the way he brandished the words like 'triangulation' and 'topography'.

I felt this called for a written comment – so I pulled out my notebook and wrote,

'Well done!'

He responded with a satisfied smile. But I wasn't finished, though it took me a few moments to sort out my thoughts and write them down.

'And have you traced all the particular places where the events happen?'

He eyed me with a quizzical expression on his face. I think he might have forgotten having mentioned 'events' to me.

'Ah, yes... well,' he began uncertainly. 'There's one location I'm still unsure of. I suspect that that one,' he said, underlining the words by his tone of voice, 'will turn out to be pure invention – a fiction. In which case it would follow that the events which are said to occur there were made up. Possibly.'

I thought, yes, but that doesn't mean the happenings depicted as taking place on a particular bench by the actual sea were not imaginary.

And I wondered to myself about the memories that had come back to me as we sat there. Could they have less substance than the goings-on narrated in a Frenchman's novel?

He walked me back by a different route. Here the path was properly surfaced and my wheelchair rolled along easily. Hughie had run out of things to say. He was off in a world of his own, part fiction, part speculation, I supposed. The sound of his irregular footfalls lulled me as my mind drifted among my own musings.

*

When I was young I used to have trouble keeping my thoughts to myself. I was notorious for letting slip whatever crossed my mind, and it got me into quite a lot of hot water with people I happened to offend. Not any more. I can blurt out anything that occurs to me and no one will understand it. They don't even pay much attention. It just contributes to the impression that I'm rambling. And to be honest, that suits me.

For example I can let that dreadful Mrs Smith know what I think about her and get away with it. Even when she really irritates me my anger doesn't show on my face, since all it does is sag. The best I can manage is a doleful rictus which only makes me look gormless.

She has this way of contriving to reclaim attention when the conversation in the room has wandered away from topics she can pontificate about. She'll suddenly stand up and declare to no one in particular that she needs to go and powder her nose, for example. And she'll disappear for a few minutes, then come back and sure enough, her proboscis will be caked in the stuff, some of it flaking away. She reminds me of that line in the 'School for Scandal' : 'widow Ochre caulks her wrinkles'. She insists on slathering her mouth in scarlet lipstick too. And when she has done all this and returned to her throne, she will take out her compact case and examine her makeup in the mirror as if her artistry merited scrutiny from everyone in the room.

I usually murmur 'What do you think you look like!' and if she acknowledges me at all she will affect to appreciate my gargles as if I'm paying her a compliment. But last week I made sure I had my old compact in my handbag. I never use it of course : there's nothing worth looking at in my crumpled countenance nowadays – certainly nothing that can be rectified. But when she started doing her little cameo, I made a show of examining my face in the mirror, prodding at my fallen folds of skin and pretending to touch up imaginary eye-liner on my drooping eyelids. While I was doing this I heard her close her compact case with a sharp snap. She had got the message.

People observe my misshapen features and take pity on me. They are often mistaken to do so.

*

Yesterday, when Hughie and I had finished doing our crossword, I thought I'd take the opportunity to ask him a question about something that had been on my mind since our conversation. So with the pencil I still had in my hand I wrote in the empty space at the bottom of the newspaper:

'Do you think you know this area now?'

He thought for a moment.

'Och wee-ell,' he said, drawing out the word. 'While I've been out and about I've got to know bits of it. But I've been mainly concentrating on finding the spots that interest me.'

Then something else occurred to me, so I scribbled again.

'And did those spots turn out the way you imagined from reading about them?'

'That's an interesting question,' he began.

Mrs Smith shifted in her chair. I knew what was coming next.

'Time to go and powder my nose.'

She couldn't have known what I had asked, and Hughie was speaking sotto voce, so I suppose she hadn't any idea what we were talking about. She was jealous, that's all. And had decided to be rude in that special way she has.

Hughie gave her one of his disarming smiles as she crossed the room. After she had gone, he carried on talking.

'When you read a story, you imagine the settings by drawing on what you already know. I do, at any rate. I mean, it may seem odd, but I had Glenrothes in my head while I was reading certain parts of the novel. You flesh out the descriptions with mental pictures from places you've actually been in.'

This was obviously a topic close to his heart, because he didn't wait for me to nod before continuing.

'And yes, I must admit that when I started to discover the places that feature in the manuscript, they didn't turn out as I had imagined. But funnily enough that didn't stop me recognizing them for what they were.'

He put on a rueful grin.

'Strange, isn't it, to use the word "recognize", but that's definitely the sensation I had. I suppose it's because I "knew" them beforehand, from having read about them in the story. Especially those where turning-points in the plot occur.'

I was writing back before he finished what he had to say.

'Such as the bench...?'

He peered at my scribble and I was able to watch his reaction form.

'Hah! Well, of course it wasn't the actual one ... but I could visualize the original on the basis of benches I've seen in public parks and the like.'

I managed to get my reply across with a raised eyebrow and a warbling sound.

'The original? Really?'

He shot me a quizzical look in his turn, unsure whether I was just making fun of him. Then he snorted.

'Oh I see. You've brought that crossword-busting intellect to bear,' he said with a grin. 'So you want a philosophical analysis...'

I nodded. If I could I would have given him a faux-naïve stare.

'O.K. Without going back so far as Plato... The original bench is past and gone, and all I have to work on – though obviously not to sit on – is the description in the manuscript, which I deduce is derived from a bench that used to be located atop the sea wall where we were yesterday. But in my imagination I summon up the fictional bench, built only of words on a page, as a composite of images prompted by real benches I recall from my own experience.'

He fell silent then. I looked down and folded my hands in my lap.

'So,' he resumed, 'I have to confess I have no experience of the original bench, as we might call it.'

He spoke his conclusion in such a droll, mock-serious tone that I had to laugh. He laughed along with me.

Had I been younger, I would have blurted out some words as I used to do. Instead I took the time to write them out.

In the past I often found myself wanting to take back the spoken words I had let slip.

This time I held them out for him to read.

'I had direct experience of that bench. And what happened there was not all fiction.'

He read thoughtfully. Then he looked up and flashed me an amused, teasing grin.

'Should I ask what transpired there?'

I looked back at him, knowing my expression was inscrutable.

At that moment Mrs Smith sashayed back into the room, sporting a freshly-dusted set of features.

Hughie and I eyed each other without a word. Then he muttered:

'You and your poker face.'

We broke into giggles and Mrs Smith cleared her throat before taking out her cigarette-holder.

Hughie duly watched her attention-seeking performance for a moment, but his thoughts were elsewhere. Eventually he murmured:

'I wish I could get a fix on that other place I mentioned,' he said. 'I think he must have planted a bit of pure fiction on the map. He gives it a name but I cannae find anything that might correspond to it.'

I lifted my brows by way of a question, and he went on, 'He calls it Oddfellow House. Have you ever heard of it? Does the name ring a bell?'

I thought a bit, then shook my head.

7

I'd read further than Mrs Horton intended. I'd told her I wasn't much of a reader, and I'm sure I would never have bothered with the novel she and Hughie talked so much about. But I was caught up by these pages she had written in longhand. She had a life she could put into words – and that kept taking me by surprise, I admit. There was much more to her than the decrepit remnant who appeared to pass her days staring vacantly into the middle distance, her features resembling the aftermath of a landslip.

There was no love lost between her and Mrs Smith, that much was clear. I didn't have a lot to do with Mrs Smith, but I saw enough to know that she was a snob. She felt she deserved more consideration than she was shown in our establishment. I'd got used to her funny ways, though. She wanted people to believe that she didn't really belong in Cottsea and would be more at home in Chelsea. Sometimes she was cranky to the point of unpleasantness, and the way she treated Mrs Horton seemed downright malicious. But in those bits of the notebook I wasn't supposed to read I learned that Mrs Horton could give as good as she got. I put it down to exasperation. I mean, when you're stuck in a wheelchair and dependent on the goodwill of others, you might feel entitled to get irritated by people who are so wrapped up in themselves that they have no time for you. And I would try to imagine what might be behind Mrs Smith's funny mannerisms. After all, she must have some kind of inner life too. I found myself wondering what kind of revelations there would be in her diary, if she kept one.

I decided I would propose wheeling Mrs Horton along to the bench above the sea-wall, in the hope that she might explain exactly what that bench meant to her. I knew the place myself, of course, and had often sat on that same bench smoking cigarettes and drinking beer under-age. It was notorious as a spot where couples came to snog after dark. And I suppose I was vaguely intrigued, though not as much as Mrs Horton, to discover that it might have been of interest to a visiting French author.

But behind all that was the question that still obsessed Mrs Horton : what had happened to Hughie? She couldn't accept that he might simply have left of his own accord. She read and re-read her diary, evidently searching among her entries for possible clues that would help her find him. She would read with a pen in her hand, adding notes in the margin, and from time to time she would gaze out of the window as if pursuing a thought that had occurred to her. The passages she was studying came after the pages she had given me to read. I had no idea what could be in them to prove that he had been abducted, or point to his whereabouts.

All that changed one morning when Mrs Dugdale came into the sitting-room and announced that a letter had arrived from Dr Storth. It contained money, she said, to cover his unpaid bill, and he was very apologetic about his sudden departure. Brandishing the letter, she explained that he had been called away suddenly on urgent business and had to change his plans for the future. He made no mention of the typewriter and other items he had left behind – and gave no forwarding address. The postmark on the envelope was illegible, Mrs Dugdale said, but the stamp had a thistle beside the head of the Queen, so it must have come from Scotland.

'Here's a funny thing,' she commented. 'It's definitely addressed to me : "Mrs Martha Dugdale", it says on the envelope. But he got the address wrong – he must be one of those absent-minded Professors people talk about – and it was delivered by mistake to Mrs Wormold's boarding-house at the other end of the Esplanade. Good job she knows me. She popped in with it this morning.'

She announced all this to a room where very few now remembered or cared about Dr Storth. Most had only an intermittent grip on events anyway. The daily routine had erased Hughie from their lives. But at the mention of his name Mrs Horton had pulled herself up in her chair. Was she relieved to learn that he was safe and well? Or put out that her kidnap theory had proved wrong? I watched her expression. Her face might have fallen, but it was hard to tell.

When Mrs Dugdale finished speaking, Mrs Horton held out her hand as if asking to see the letter. The landlady hesitated for a moment, then waved it in front of her face briefly, long enough for Mrs Horton to read the signature. Then she leaned down towards the old lady.

'There was a page addressed to you,' she said, and handed Mrs Horton a sheet which had been carefully folded from the top and bottom, and on which Mrs Horton's name had been written across the line where the flaps had been tucked one under the other.

Mrs Horton's fingers fumbled with the paper.

A stage whisper arose from the corner where Mrs Smith held court. 'It looks like something he pushed into the envelope as an afterthought,' the painted widow murmured, waving her cigarette-holder and wafting smoke across the room. 'Saving money on a second stamp... exactly what you would expect from a Scotsman.'

Millicent duly simpered.

Meanwhile Mrs Horton had unfolded the sheet and was running her eyes over the writing on it. Her collapsed face gave nothing away. She read to the bottom of the letter, read it a second time, and stared out of the window for a few moments. Then she folded the paper and slipped it into her handbag.

After breakfast my time was taken up with housekeeping and I saw nothing more of Mrs Horton. But in the late afternoon she asked the landlady if she could have tea in her room as she was feeling under the weather. Since I was her favourite, I had the job of taking it up.

I put the tray down on her table and Mrs Horton gave me a grunt – her way of saying thank you. Then I made to leave : but she caught my arm, and when I turned she ushered me to a chair alongside hers. I sat down, and from a chest of drawers at her bedside she took out the letter that Dr Storth had written to her. Without a sound she handed it to me to read.

'Dear Mrs Horton,

I am afraid my sudden absence will have given rise to Angry Remarks, a habitual entertainment among the chairbound.

Meanwhile my work is at an impasse and my prospects unclear, to the point of being cryptic.

This being so, I may have to change direction. I told myself initially Public Relations is one route to follow, but that road went no further than the first letter I wrote.

Then my thoughts turned to that American uncle you'll recall. To pursue a cricketing analogy, after absorbing the end of the batsman's innings, he plumps for a place I'd never heard of.

In short, my predicament is a conundrum.

I can say no more for the time being.

Yours,

Hughie.'

I was mystified. 'What a peculiar letter,' I said. 'Do you think he always writes like this?'

Mrs Horton sniffed and her chin lifted.

'Does it mean he's given up what he was doing? Gone away and started looking for a new job?'

I stared down at the paper. I was tempted to suggest it was some kind of prank.

'Is it really from him?' I asked.

Mrs Horton reached out and I gave her back the paper. She took up a pencil and circled the signature. She wrote alongside, 'Mrs Dugdale's letter was signed "Hugh"'.

I thought for a moment.

'Maybe that's how he signs a formal letter.'

Mrs Horton shook her head, pointed at the signature on her letter, let out a grunt, and gave a thumbs-up sign. I understood : this is his real signature. So there was something about the other letter that was bogus, since he had signed it in a way that wasn't authentic for him. However odd Mrs Horton's letter might seem, it was to be taken seriously. But everything about it was bizarre. The way he expressed himself struck me as contrived, the sentences weren't properly linked up – and there was stuff in there that I found downright impenetrable.

I said all this to Mrs Horton. She nodded her head, but seemed lost in thought. She tapped her pencil on her teeth.

Then she drew another circle, around the words 'Angry Remarks'. I had noticed the capital letters, which looked old fashioned – or maybe it was the way things were taught in Scottish schools, I didn't know.

But Mrs Horton hadn't finished. Above 'Angry' she wrote 'Cross'. Then she paused and looked at me, and I noticed there was a glint in her eye. I was mystified.

Next, she wrote 'Words' above 'Remarks'.

'Cross Words,' I read out.

She nodded eagerly this time, and fixed me with a stare that made me read them out again. As I did so she reached across and pointed with her pencil at the word 'cryptic'.

At this point I thought she was having me on – or else in some strange way Dr Storth was.

'Cryptic crosswords?' I said.

Her eyes gleamed and the skin around them bunched up slightly : the surviving traces of her smile. She took back the letter, spread it out on the table and invited me to watch her as she took her pencil to its contents again.

She circled the word 'initially', and then underlined the first letters – the initials, I twigged as she did so – of 'Public Relations'.

I'd seen her play around with words in this way when doing the crosswords with Hughie…

Then she put a circle round 'first letter', and drew a wavy line from that circle back to 'road', then to 'route'.

Then, having already underlined 'P' and 'R', she bent over the paper and carefully traced lines under the words that followed, up to the first letter of 'road'.

P…r…is one r

Prisoner.

I stared down at the separate pieces again, and saw them cohere into that single word again.

I swallowed. Was this still a game? For a grotesque moment I felt as though I was back in a children's adventure yarn.

Mrs Horton was waiting for me to look up, and when I did she stared into my eyes.

This was more than just a puzzle. It seemed as though her hunch may be right. Dr Storth had been abducted and was being held against his will.

Mrs Horton stared at me in silence.

'But where could he be... imprisoned?' I finally managed to say. But even as I spoke the words they seemed ridiculous, overblown. I still couldn't take them seriously.

In an effort to shake myself out of the stupor I felt, I turned over some details in my mind.

'The letter came from Scotland,' I said.

Mrs Horton shifted in her chair.

'euh hank gig.'

The stamp did. And of course it was the kind of thing a Scotsman would have in his wallet, wherever he happened to be.

Just one, as it happened. So he could mail only one envelope – with two letters in it.

I ruminated out loud. Perhaps he persuaded his kidnappers that it would dispel suspicion if he wrote an innocuous letter of explanation to Mrs Dugdale and enclosed money to pay his outstanding bill. That way, no one would come demanding payment from him. And a Scottish stamp would throw any possible pursuer off the scent.

And having convinced his captors of this, he wrote the letter to Mrs Dugdale as a smokescreen and slipped in a brief note like an afterthought, to his old friend Mrs Horton.

But this apparently casual scribble was the key to what had actually happened.

Mrs Horton nodded along as I speculated, though I was only half convinced I was talking sense.

'But suppose all this is true,' I said. 'What can we do about it?'

She wasn't listening. She was looking back at the letter, and I followed her eyes.

She was staring at the next paragraphs. I stared at them alongside her.

What about this 'American uncle', followed by a reference to 'a conundrum'?

She aimed a wordless query at me. American uncle?

'Did Hughie say he had relatives in the USA?' I asked.

Mrs Horton shook her head emphatically. So if she could 'recall' this person it would not be from anything he had said to her.

I suddenly got the feeling that she was holding out on me. That however high the stakes were, the thrill of this little game had momentarily overcome the anxiety she might feel for Hughie.

I raised my eyebrows and gave her an expectant look, and she relented.

'(Uncle) Sam,' she scribbled on the bottom of the sheet.

I considered what she had written.

'I'm no further forward,' I said.

'Absorbing,' she pointed her pencil at.

Well, yes, it was absorbing ; but if Dr Storth really was a prisoner, we should be feeling something stronger than that.

No, no, her impatient dumb-show said. I was missing the point.

She ran the tip of her pencil under 'the end of the batman's innings'.

I stared at her blankly. She raised her brows and jutted out her chin, prompting me to try harder.

'He's out.' I said. Then : 'Oh, he's escaped! Maybe he's got back to Scotland after all!'

I didn't realise she could do a 'Tut!' But she managed it somehow, to show her disappointment with my pathetic effort. She pointed at the phrase again.

'OK,' I said. 'So how does a batsman's innings come to an end?'

She liked this. Her mouth made an eager shape.

'Clean bowled. Run out,' I tried.

She wrote 'Sam' again on the paper, and tipped her head to one side, urging me to bear that in mind as I went through the possibilities.

Absorbing. Sam, after absorbing... 'bowled'.

Seam? Seal? Slob? Sambo? Could I get any more letters 'absorbed'? Blade mows. Bowls dame. Demob laws. I began to wish I'd played Scrabble more often.

How about LBW, then. Slawbm. Nope. I drew a blank.

I looked up at Mrs Horton. Her lips hung limply, her eyes were vacant.

Catch. I borrowed her pencil, wrote the word down, examined it, set 'sam' alongside it, and ran through more combinations, each more nonsensical than the one before. I sighed, and stared at the letters that danced before my eyes.

Then I felt Mrs Horton's hand on my arm. I turned to her. She was tapping her pencil on her teeth again. She started to write.

'S... catch... am.' And again: 'Scatcham'.

I stared at her blankly, half expecting another 'Tut' from her. She pointed at a phrase in Hughie's letter : 'plumps for a place I'd never heard of'.

I thought for a moment.

'Well, if it *is* a place, it's certainly one I've never heard of,' I said.

Mrs Horton nodded her head pensively.

The following afternoon I was planning to walk her to the bench and find what she knew about it. But as we left the house, she pointed in a different direction. She seemed impatient and made gestures with her hands, urging me to hurry along. She obviously had a particular destination in mind ; at each street junction she would wave us on or indicate to turn this way or that.

Eventually we were in front of the entrance to the Library.

All of a sudden I felt out of my depth, never having had much to do with the place. But seeing me hesitate Mrs Horton actually wrote out some instructions for me before we went in, and once I was at the reception desk I knew what to do. Mrs Horton sat quietly in her wheelchair and the lady behind the counter, seeing I was acting on behalf of this poor woman, was very sympathetic. She treated my words with the respect due to an elderly lady.

'Mrs Horton would like to consult some Ordnance Survey maps of the area,' I said.

'Yes, of course,' the librarian said, and while I wheeled Mrs Horton along behind her, she led the way to the appropriate shelves.

Soon we had maps spread out on a large table and were scanning them for a place-name that recalled the one we had deduced from Dr Storth's letter. I had the northern section of our area and found myself poring over the coastline and seaside villages. Mrs Horton was tracing the course of the River Lyre, which rises in the fells to the southeast and flows up through the inland region to the estuary at Cottsea. I found it interesting to recognize the fine detail and symbols representing spots I was familiar with. Places I had heard of but never visited surprised me by the way their names arranged themselves around the picture I thought I knew. However among the names I didn't recognize, none stood out. I looked across at Mrs Horton, who was leaning over her map, palms splayed out on the paper, intently tracing lines with her fingers. I could see nothing of note in mine, and as time went by I began to get bored, and wondered how long this search would go on. I considered how we had come to be here, and on balance our quest seemed preposterous.

Suddenly Mrs Horton gave a sharp intake of breath and let out a sort of gasp. I glanced up and she caught my eye, tipping her head to signify she had something to show me. I went round to her side of the table and looked over her shoulder at where her gnarled index finger was pointing. I had grasped the scale of these maps, and about a mile or so from the river, alongside a green patch signifying woodland, there was the name : Scatcham. It was just a small group of buildings, isolated in a landscape of fields. A line indicating a track led to it from a lane that ran by at some distance.

Mrs Horton looked up at me and as her head twisted back, her lips fell into the closest approximation of a delighted grin that I ever saw her manage.

8

But she wasn't satisfied with her discovery. She scribbled on a page of her notebook that lay open beside her.

'Need a cadastral map,' I read. I hadn't a clue what that meant. But with Mrs Horton's conviction to back me up, I addressed myself once more to the Librarian.

'Oh, we don't have cadastral maps in England,' she said. 'They only have them in Scotland.' She paused. 'And in some other countries – France, I think.'

Behind me, Mrs Horton was stirring and trying to say something. Rather than give way, I thought I could take it upon myself to pursue the enquiry on my own terms.

'Erm… what *is* a cadastral map?' I asked.

'It's a map of an area that shows who owns the land and property. It's a larger scale than the OS maps,' the lady obligingly explained.

I looked back at Mrs Horton – who, as far as I could gather, knew this already.

The Librarian followed my gaze and addressed her next comment directly to Mrs Horton.

'In England,' she said, 'it's the Land Registry that records ownership and boundaries.'

'And are there such things as Land Registry maps?' I asked. 'Do you have them?'

She shook her head.

'We don't have any here,' she said.

I saw Mrs Horton's face sink to her chest.

But the Librarian brightened.

'There are several volumes of local history among our holdings. Some of them contain reproductions taken from Land Registry maps. You might find what you're looking for there.'

She led the way once more to another set of shelves. Soon Mrs Horton and I were seated side by side at the big table, each with a heap of books to left and right. I examined a few from my collection, opening them one at a time and flicking half-heartedly through a few pages. The smell of musty paper filled my nostrils. I really couldn't see me reading this lot. I glanced down one table of contents and my heart sank at the prospect of working through chapters with headings like 'Neolithic' and 'Anglo-Saxon'. I wiped dust off my fingers, and looked towards Mrs Horton. She had picked out a heavy, thick tome and needed both hands to hold it open on the table before her.

What struck me was that she wasn't reading the first pages. She was running her finger down what appeared to be columns of print at the back of the book. I leaned towards her so I could make out what she was examining. She noticed my movement and looking up, realised I was at a loss : where to begin? She heaved the book up so I could read what she was poring over. I saw it was the Index : a list of all the names and places mentioned in the book. She turned over a few pages and there was another list, headed 'Table of illustrations'.

The penny dropped. Now I knew what I was looking for and how to get at it. I went back to my volumes.

Actually some of them were little more than brochures : publications put out by amateur historians, produced on a shoe-string budget, typed pages mimeographed and stapled together. None of these had an index, though some had occasional hand-drawn illustrations, so I couldn't ignore them completely. I scanned them for a mention of the name 'Scatcham', then set them aside. With each reject I felt a mixture of disappointment at finding nothing and relief at getting closer to the end of what seemed like a fruitless exercise.

Mrs Horton was concentrating on the bigger bound volumes. They were obviously older ; the pages were yellowed and the print was austere, paragraphs set in forbidding blocks.

I thought I should tackle a proper hardback, and pulled towards me one that was entitled *Parishes in Poverty : the Flight from the Land in Nineteenth-Century Rural Dioceses*. I ran my eye down the contents, then the first paragraph of the introduction, and gathered that it was focussed on our area, using it as an example of what happened to the outlying villages during the industrial revolution. I turned to the index, flicking through the alphabetical headings – and suddenly there it was : '*Scatcham*', with a page reference.

From listless and uninterested, I felt a rushing sensation through my veins. Mrs Horton must surely have noticed, I thought as I tried to find the place, my fingers making the pages tremble. No, she was engrossed in another book. I'd wait till I had checked my reference, then show her.

Here was page 73. Three paragraphs. Should I read from the top line to the bottom? No, I'd skim it line by line and trust that my eye would catch what I was hoping for.

Sure enough : two-thirds of the way down, the word leapt off the page. I stopped, ran back to the start of the sentence and read : 'In the Domesday Book the hamlet of Scatcham features as *Escache*. The manor and ten acres of land were granted to Roland de Bignac in 1122. The line died out in the fifteenth century and the land reverted to the Crown. Thereafter it remained broadly in the hands of yeoman farmers. The industrial revolution was to have little impact on this stable and self-reliant agricultural community.'

It wasn't much, but I was quite proud at having found it. I shuffled in my chair, then coughed to catch Mrs Horton's attention.

I pushed the book towards her, open at page 73, and she took in the lines I pointed to. She nodded. I was disappointed that she didn't seem more impressed. Then she tipped her head towards the bulky volume that lay open in front of her. She invited me to hold down the page nearest to me so we could both focus our attention on a sketch map which filled most of the facing page. She was running her finger along the stretch of river that ran across it, and quickly found Scatcham.

We both contemplated what lay before us. Considerably larger and in much greater detail than the Ordnance Survey map, this depiction showed the lane leading from the main road up to a cluster of buildings surrounded by fields. Some looked like houses while others must be barns and other farm outbuildings. The name of the hamlet was marked in block capitals, but alongside one of the houses, in a smaller, italicized script, were the words 'Quainton Grange'.

Mrs Horton's finger stabbed at that name, and she tapped the page excitedly. Then she tried to speak. Sounds came tumbling from her mouth, but I couldn't make sense of them. She grew impatient at the puzzled expression on my face, and repeated the sounds. I could distinguish something like:

'Oggherro houh.'

And again:

'Oggherro houh.'

Finally, with a sigh she reached for her handbag and heaved out her notebook, which she set on the table between the map and me. She flicked through the pages, forward and back, until she found what she wanted. She pointed to some words in a passage I remembered having read :

'He calls it Oddfellow House. Have you ever heard of it? Does the name ring a bell?'

When I lifted my eyes from her handwritten lines, she was pointing back at the map. I read again : 'Quainton Grange'.

I pursed my lips, not wanting to admit that I was still flummoxed.

She moved both of her hands, one over her notebook, the other over the sketch map, and placed a finger over part of the names.

I read on her notebook : 'Oddfellow'.

And on the map : 'Quainton'.

I mouthed each of the two words in turn.

Mrs Horton stared at me expectantly, waiting for the connection to dawn on me.

And then it did. Odd fellow. Quaint 'un.

I gasped, and grinned.

'Oh I can see it now. Quaint – odd,' I said.

Mrs Horton presented her cockeyed face to me and nodded silently.

I fancied I knew the satisfaction she and Hughie must have shared when they hit on a crossword solution together. But the feeling was short-lived, for Mrs Horton placed her hand on mine, gave it a slight squeeze, and mumbled something that sounded like, 'Now then.' It was her way of reminding me that this was not a game. And I understood that she wasn't about to stop at this discovery.

'What do we do now?' I asked.

The answer was simple : we would find a way of getting to Scatcham, and we would take a look at Quainton Grange. I wasn't accustomed to facing this kind of challenge. As a boy I used to ride my bike around the countryside, but that was years before. I had passed my driving test, though I'd never had a car of my own to drive. If a place wasn't near a bus route I didn't go there.

None of that was a problem for Mrs Horton. She had learned to cope with her disability and she wasn't short of ideas as to how we would get where she wanted to go.

We wouldn't hire a taxi because that would entail taking a third person into our confidence. No, we would borrow a car. To be precise : a van, with space to put her wheelchair in the back.

Borrow a van? Who did I know who had a van and would be prepared to lend it to me? Did Mrs Horton have any acquaintances with the right kind of vehicle? She shook her head.

Even if there was someone I could call on, they'd want to know where I was going in it – and we couldn't tell anyone what we were really up to, could we?

I wondered if we should go to the police and persuade them to start a missing person enquiry, but I knew before I raised the question that it was a non-starter. The only solid evidence we had to explain Dr Storth's disappearance was the letter he had written to Mrs Dugdale – that suggested there was no mystery at all. And I couldn't see PC Postlethwaite the local bobby calling up the CID on the strength of the clues in Mrs Horton's letter.

Then I had an idea. The people in the village had become used to seeing me wheel Mrs Horton around the streets and along the promenade. Why not let it be known that I'd decided to take her a bit further afield, so she could revisit some of the places she'd frequented as a young woman? We could say we were going out for a picnic. I'd discovered that playing on Mrs Horton's disability made it possible for me to accomplish things I'd never contemplate on my own account. Who could refuse a favour for an old lady who couldn't get about as she would like? And who could harbour misgivings about the nice young man who was volunteering to take her out sight-seeing?

There was an odd-job man called Witscombe who occasionally did work around the house for Mrs Dugdale. He had a little van that would accommodate a wheelchair in the back. I wheeled Mrs Horton round to his premises. He took one look at the poor old lady slumped in her seat and he didn't need any persuading. He didn't work on Sunday, he said, and we were welcome to borrow the van then. Mrs Horton had suggested I ask about insurance and offer to pay (she would provide the money) : when I raised the issue the man rubbed his chin and said, 'Oh go on, it'll be fine.' I thanked him effusively, directing my gaze at Mrs Horton, and he was pleased to be doing a good deed for a helpless old lady.

The following Sunday we folded up Mrs Horton's wheelchair and stashed it in the back of the little van, and then we set out. Mrs Dugdale had been only too happy to make sandwiches for our picnic – it suited her to have one less to cater for in the dining room – so we were well provided for as we rolled through the countryside. The first part of the route followed roads I was familiar with. Mrs Horton had a map spread across her knees for when we struck out into the remoter regions where the clusters of bungalows gave way to isolated cottages and open farmland. The high, wide sky was overcast but the air was clear ; hedgerows, low trees and the occasional church spire stood out against the flat fields between us and the misty ridge of hills that rose up on the horizon.

Mrs Horton asked me to stop the van when at one point we found ourselves on a raised lane, built up as a crossing over a former peat bog that had long ago been drained to become agricultural land. It was a good vantage point and she wanted to take in the view. She stared out over the ploughed fields, invited me to share a glimpse of the river Lyre in the distance, and nodded quietly, as if in conversation with what she saw. Then without a sound she touched my arm and we set off again.

As for our ultimate destination, we had a plan of sorts, having discussed at some length how to approach the place. We couldn't know exactly what we would find when we reached Quainton Grange, but in any case there was no point trying to sneak up furtively. Even assuming the terrain was level, the wheelchair didn't lend itself to surreptitious manoeuvres. So we agreed we would first drive by and take a look, and then consider our options.

The name of Scatcham began to appear on the white signposts at each road junction, and eventually I pulled over to consult the map and check where the turning was that led up to Quainton Grange. That was when Mrs Horton began to show signs of nervousness. Her lips started to writhe and tremors ran through her sagging left cheek. She would knit her fingers together, then pull her hands apart and rest them in her lap, then clasp one in the other to stop them from twitching. The sight of her in such a pitiful state made me feel unusually sorry for her.

In an effort to reassure her I said, 'Look, we can just drive past and then go home if you prefer.'

She gave a start, pulled out her notepad and began to scribble, while we remained stationary with the engine running. I could see her handwriting was more shaky than usual.

She held up the page.

'Just driving past would do no good. Have to DO something.'

I breathed out.

'Okay. As we agreed, we knock on the door and say we're trying to find a Miss Keighley. That should give us time to see if we're in the right place and what kind of people Hughie is being held by.'

As I spoke the words I was convinced that this whole business was nothing but a wild-goose chase. We had embarked on what anyone could tell was a daft escapade, on the strength of a stupid note that was probably nothing more than a whimsical joke at Mrs Horton's expense. Dr Storth was almost certainly back in Scotland where he belonged, and the sooner we got this over with and got back to Cottsea, the better we would be.

But I told myself the worst that could happen was a few minutes' embarrassment. And after all it was a small price to pay if that was all it took to show Mrs Horton there was nothing to her fears. True, it wouldn't reunite her with Hughie but she would have to get used to him having gone.

Meanwhile Mrs Horton seemed to have calmed down, so I put the van in gear and we moved off. I steered us into the second turning on the right and we entered a narrow lane. It had a tarmac surface, which I found reassuring, but there was a ditch on one side and by the time we had driven some way I was wondering what would happen if we met something coming in the other direction. The lane went up and over a hump-backed bridge, then veered left, plunged into woodland, and became little more than a cart-track. I began to fear for the van as we bumped and swayed over the uneven ground. I had visions of a stone shooting up and scratching the paint or cracking a window – and I worried about the bodywork if I had to scrape along the hedgerow to let someone else by.

We emerged unscathed from the wood and up ahead I could see that the lane led towards a huddle of buildings. The van was already in low gear so we advanced slowly, giving us time to take in what we saw. I was concentrating on keeping to the track, so I could only glance at what was probably a barn, some low buildings that might be pigsties, hen houses and the like.

Then I realised that rather than passing through this farmstead, the lane came to a dead end in a yard. We were going to have to draw to a halt in full view of anyone around, then do a three-point turn while farmhands got a good look at us, and head off back the way we had come. So much for our plan to drive by more or less unnoticed.

9

There was nothing for it but to drive into the yard, pull up alongside the gaping entrance to the barn, and manoeuvre the van back and forth till we were facing out again.

Farmyards have a funny way of appearing deserted even though the air is filled with the sounds of activity going on somewhere : machines rumbling, buckets clanking, animals shifting and snorting, cocks crowing. I expected to see heads pop out and a barking dog, or maybe a man in overalls and muddy boots, come running after us. But there was no response to our arrival ; the noise of our engine must have been drowned out by the rest.

All the same there was no point in assuming we hadn't been noticed. It would arouse suspicion if we tried to behave furtively in full daylight. Better make it clear we had nothing to hide. I turned to Mrs Horton and said as much. She nodded.

'I think I'll get out, see if anyone comes, and ask for directions as if we've lost our way,' I said.

I had cobbles underfoot as I took a few steps and scanned the surroundings. Through the gaps between the buildings I caught sight of fields where cattle were browsing. Back down the lane there was a stone building with a slate-covered roof and mullioned windows. I caught Mrs Horton's eye through the van's passenger window, and pointed to it. She nodded.

When I raised my head again a man in dungarees was staring at me across the roof of the van.

'Oh, hello,' I said as casually as I could manage. 'I think we might be lost.'

'Where d'you think you might be?' he said.

'We were looking for Quainton Grange,' I said.

He tipped back his cap.

'There's nobbut farm now,' he said. 'Thon building dahn theer's Lodge, all as is left.' He pulled a packet from the front of his dungarees, extracted a cigarette, and lit it.

'Oh,' I said.

He inhaled and blew the smoke out. 'You lookin' for someone in partikler?'

'Not really,' I replied. 'My... aunt here used to know someone who had connections there.'

The man stared through the glass at Mrs Horton, and raised his eyebrows at her as she fixed him with her most doleful gaze.

'Aye, well,' he said. 'I doubt she'll find anyone she knows theer now.'

I wasn't sure how to continue the conversation.

'No, I suppose not,' I tried. Then : 'Do you think they'd mind if we knocked at the door?'

'Can't do any 'arm,' he replied.

I thanked him, got back into the van alongside Mrs Horton, started up the engine, and we moved off.

'This double-act gets better the more we perform it,' I said.

She poked her fingers into the corners of her mouth, and pushed them up into a smile.

I approached the house cautiously. I needed to find a spot where we could park without blocking the narrow lane. Moving slowly towards it we could see the building was old : solid and squat, constructed in stone, roofed with heavy slate and topped with hefty chimney stacks. The leaded window-panes threw off scattered reflections of the sky.

Then came our dilemma. On the one hand it would seem most natural if Mrs Horton waited in the van while I went to knock on the door, as though checking that we were in the right place before we took the trouble to get her out. If I were to roll up with her in her wheelchair it would look like we were inviting ourselves in. On the other hand, Mrs Horton in her wheelchair was our surest gambit for getting in ; and since that was our aim, she should come with me.

So I unpacked the wheelchair from the back of the van and helped her into it. We presented quite a spectacle for anyone who might happen to see us from inside the house. But when I glanced up from getting Mrs Horton properly installed, half expecting to catch the eye of someone watching, I realised the front windows were shuttered and the glass was covered in a film of dust, as if the rooms behind them were not being lived in.

Mrs Horton noticed this too, and she twisted round in her chair to give me a puzzled look, her brows furrowed. The impression created by the blank windows made us both aware that we had no idea what to expect. And while up to now I had been telling myself that this whole carry-on was probably futile, suddenly it seemed quite possible after all that something sinister lay behind those shutters.

I wheeled Mrs Horton up the path to the front of the building. There was an entrance flanked by stone pillars supporting a pediment. This house had definitely seen better days. The paint was flaking on the heavy timber door and the brass knob at its centre was covered in verdigris. Evidently no one had entered that way for quite some time.

'Do you think it's worth knocking?' I asked Mrs Horton. I had visions of someone inside having to clamber over stacks of abandoned furniture and debris to answer the door – which was probably jammed anyway, either deliberately or from lack of use. I noticed that there was no letter-box – another bad sign.

Mrs Horton was staring at the forbidding frontage. She looked at the windows to right and left, and shook her head. She gestured with her thumb and forefinger to suggest we should try going round the house.

The path skirted the façade and led us up the side of the building. There were no windows here but when we reached the far corner we found ourselves facing a small, neat garden with a lawn bordered by flower beds. Wisteria and honeysuckle intertwined as they climbed up the south-facing stonework. In the middle of this side of the house was a porch which evidently served as the usual way in now. I wheeled Mrs Horton up to it and we looked in vain for a door bell or knocker. I was about to rap on the outer door frame when a woman emerged inside the porch. For a while she remained where she stood, and stared at us. She took barely a moment to size me up, but her eyes rested on Mrs Horton, on her wheelchair, on her misshapen face – and finally she stepped forward and opened the outer door.

'Hello,' she said, standing in the doorway. She was elderly but sprightly and her voice was strong. I bet she sings in a choir, I thought for an instant. And I could imagine hours of gardening had kept her fit and had contributed to the tan on her skin, which though lined with age, was taut across her cheeks and chin, and gleamed in the daylight. Her nose was slightly turned-up and she had clearly been pretty when young. The years had accentuated her angular features and strong jaw. She smiled down at Mrs Horton. I watched her from behind the wheelchair and decided I had better break the silence.

'My aunt and I…' I began. The woman looked up at me, and her gaze was unnerving. I dried up. 'Er, sorry to bother you…' I said.

Mrs Horton shuffled. I sensed her frustration at not being able to speak for herself. Her mouth began to move, and her lips struggled to shape guttural sounds into words.

'My aunt has a… speech impediment,' I said, shamefaced, unable to think of a better way to explain things. Mrs Horton made a choking noise.

The woman frowned sympathetically.

'She's trying to find a friend,' I said. The woman stiffened slightly, puzzled. 'An old friend,' I went on quickly. 'Someone she knew years ago.'

'Oh,' said the woman. 'I see. And does – did – this old friend live here?'

'That's what we're trying to find out,' I stammered. 'Her name was Keighley. Ellen Keighley.'

She pursed her lips and thought for a moment, looking down benevolently at the old lady in the wheelchair. It struck me that they were probably the same age despite being so different in appearance.

I had rehearsed my speech with Mrs Horton. Now she nodded, egging me on, and on the strength of the woman's evident feeling for her, I felt more confident as I continued.

'They were school friends. A long time ago.'

The woman thought about this.

'Perhaps you'd better come in,' she said, suddenly.

I had an instant of panic. Had we by chance hit on the name of a real person, someone she actually knew?

She gestured to us, and turned to lead the way.

On the inside the house was faded, a touch dilapidated even, but it had been made cosy. We followed the woman past a staircase, along a narrow, stone-flagged hallway that called for careful steering with the wheelchair. Three doors clustered at the end, one facing back down the hall and two leading off to either side. She stopped in front of the middle door and turned to us.

'This is where I live,' she said. 'Shall we go in here? My name's Hilda, by the way.'

She opened one of the side doors as I mumbled, 'This is Mrs Horton, and I'm Graham' to her receding back. We followed her into the room.

I didn't take much in, I was so nervous. A patterned carpet, armchairs in chintz covers. A low ceiling, a simple fireplace with a bookcase beside it, and a table in a bay window.

Hilda indicated a space between two armchairs where I could park Mrs Horton. Then she said,

'While you settle in, could I... Would you mind if I pop out for a moment?'

She had gone before we could react. In the silence she left behind, we heard the ticking of a grandfather clock in the corner. It sounded a bit menacing. I looked at Mrs Horton, and as I caught her eye we both had the same thought. What if we've been lured into a snare – the same one that caught Dr Storth, perhaps? Are we to be taken prisoner too? Has 'Hilda' gone to spring the trap shut and stop us escaping?

The door opened again and Hilda re-appeared.

'Sorry about that,' she said. 'I felt sure you'd appreciate a little refreshment, so I went to arrange tea for us.'

She smiled at Mrs Horton, who found it too much of an effort to try smiling back, so I smiled for both of us, and murmured 'Thank you.'

'The front of the house makes the place appear rather inhospitable,' said Hilda. 'So we try our best to be welcoming when we have guests.'

Now she was sitting opposite us in an overstuffed armchair she seemed far too kindly to be any threat to us. Keeping her eyes on Mrs Horton, she tilted her face towards me as the old lady's spokesperson.

'So your aunt and Ellen Keighley were at school together?' She turned to Mrs Horton with a smile. 'A long time ago, I imagine.' Mrs Horton nodded, and Hilda aimed another question at me. 'Was it a local school?'

I was stumped. And embarrassed. We hadn't taken the story that far – it was just meant to be an opening gambit, to get us into the house and take a look around.

I glanced at Mrs Horton, who came to the rescue unexpectedly.

'Geengh hach gerh,' she said.

Hilda stared at her. Her expression was attentive, but puzzled.

Mrs Horton spoke again. 'Geengh hach gerh.'

Hilda turned to me for help. I grasped at the first thing that came into my head.

'I think it's Green something.'

Hilda's eyes lit up.

'Ah, I know! Greenhalgh Girls.' And as Mrs Horton nodded, she went on, excitement creeping into her voice, 'But that's where I went to school!'

Mrs Horton stirred. She too seemed struck by this coincidence.

But was it a coincidence? I felt left behind as the conversation went on.

Hilda leaned towards Mrs Horton.

'So *you* went there too? Well I never. I wonder if our paths crossed?'

Mrs Horton shook her head and one corner of her mouth turned down.

Then a thought struck me. Hilda would never recognize Mrs Horton even if they had been at the same school – even in the same year. The old lady's face had aged, but it had also been disfigured beyond recognition. On the other hand Hilda's cheekbones had weathered well despite the years that had passed. Her face was striking and I was sure that anyone who had known her in her school days would know her now.

Mrs Horton's features gave nothing away, of course. Whether she already knew Hilda or not, her expression was inscrutable. Her disability gave her an advantage in this exchange. She had the perfect poker face.

Hilda insisted on pursuing her line of enquiry.

'My maiden name was Woodrough,' she said. 'What was yours?'

Mrs Horton let out a sigh.

'Oh, I'm so sorry,' said Hilda. 'Here I am asking you questions, and speaking is a struggle for you…'

She glanced across at me, eyebrows raised. The old lady was supposed to be my aunt : I should be able to provide an answer. The best I could manage was my own name – she could have been my father's sister, after all…

'Erm, Rawcliffe,' I offered. 'Marion Rawcliffe.' I had seen Mrs Horton's first name on the occasional item of mail that came to the house for her ; but I had never used it before now.

Mrs Horton looked down at her hands. At least she wasn't showing signs of indignation.

Before Hilda could respond to me, there was a knock at the door and she called out, 'Come in!'

A man appeared, carrying a tray. He was tall and gangling, with stooped shoulders and a lined face. The eyes were pouched with age, but his hair, steel grey in colour, stood up in a stiff brush-cut.

'Thank you Thomas,' said Hilda as she rose to take the tray from him. 'That's very kind of you. Do come and join us.' She put the tray down on a low table beside her chair. 'This is Mrs Horton and her nephew Graham. They're trying to track down an old school-friend of Mrs Horton's. And it turns out we all went to the same school!' Then turning from Mrs Horton to me, she said 'This is Thomas.'

The armchair alongside me was vacant. But before he came to sit in it, Thomas crossed the room, said 'How do you do?' and offered his hand to Mrs Horton, who took it in hers after a slight hesitation. Then he came back towards me and did the same. I wasn't used to shaking hands with people. His hand was bony and dry. His manner struck me as odd, though I couldn't say why.

His wife poured and served us tea and biscuits. Mrs Horton took a cup but declined the biscuits. The tea alone would be sufficient challenge for her lips.

'So,' Hilda resumed when everyone had been served, 'when did you last see Ellen Keighley? I have to admit I have no memory of anyone by that name.'

Just as well, I thought to myself. It would have been difficult to improvise details around someone she had actually known.

But I did have a rehearsed story to tell. I glanced across at Mrs Horton and took my cue from the slight nod of her head.

'They lost contact with each other during the war,' I said. 'The First World War. They were both eighteen, and Ellen volunteered to be a nurse.'

I noticed a flicker of interest in Hilda ; and alongside me her husband drew himself up slightly. Of course – they were of the same generation.

Hilda was the first to speak. 'Yes, I remember, a few Greenhalgh girls did that. It was a terrible time for those with men – brothers, fiancés – serving in the forces. And "They also serve who only stand and wait" was really no comfort.'

'They were our angels,' Thomas murmured.

The weight of the conversation was on my shoulders, and I was finding it a burden. I was only supposed to be an interpreter, after all. But though Mrs Horton's lips contracted slightly as she listened to Thomas's words, she showed no sign of having anything to contribute in reply. I was out of my depth when it came to reminiscences from a time long before I was born ; but a silence had fallen and I felt obliged to fill it.

'Were you in the war?' I asked, turning to 'Thomas'. I didn't feel able to address him out loud by his first name. 'Mr …' came more naturally to me with people of his generation – but I hadn't been given the couple's surname.

'A little,' he replied, sounding the t's.

10

Well I knew who she was as soon as I set eyes on her. I remembered her right away, though she couldn't tell me from Adam. She wasn't to know I was once as pretty as her. And a school friend, of sorts.

Naturally I was surprised. I had barely given her a thought in decades. But my lifeless old face hid what I was feeling as well as who I was.

She smiled a lot : a contented smile. At times it could have been ironic. But in that situation I thought I had the best of the irony.

Then again, perhaps she did have the key to the mystery that had brought us here.

Her husband struck me as a peculiar chap. The exaggerated courtesy, the stiff gestures, the crew-cut. And he hardly uttered a word. Young Graham was at a loss to keep up the conversation single-handedly. He tried to get Thomas to talk about his involvement in the war.

'Oh, you know...' the old man said hesitantly. 'I was wounded, so...'

I couldn't make out the end of his sentence, since Hilda Woodrough – as I remember her – leaned across to me and said :

'By the way, I was about to tell you – my married name is Beaumont.' She caught the eye of the man she called Thomas.

I managed to look up at her and pull my lips together. Fortunately the rest of my face was as impassive as ever, and helped me keep my reaction to myself.

Meanwhile Graham decided to try engaging the other man in conversation once more.

'Did the farm – the Grange – belong to your family, Mr Beaumont?'

A silence followed his question. Then the old man stirred and was about to speak when Hilda intervened.

'Ah, it's quite complicated you see,' she said with that smile of hers. 'It was my family that owned the original Quainton Grange. But the upkeep of the old building swallowed a large part of my father's inheritance, and when he and my mother passed away, estate duty meant we had to sell it off. The farmer who took it over with the land had no use for a crumbling shell, as he put it... The last remnants of the original building now form the walls of the barn up there.'

I nodded along as she spoke ; and when she stopped I gestured at the walls around us and raised my eyebrows by way of a question. Hilda took a moment to register what I was trying to say.

'Ah yes, where we are now is the Lodge – the old gatehouse. We've lived here since...' her words tailed off. 'You've noticed that it's also in a poor state. When my husband retired we couldn't maintain the fabric and heat the whole place, so as

you see we've... retreated to the back of the building.'

My being unable to speak was making her more talkative than she might otherwise have been, I suspect. She felt compelled to forestall any silence, knowing that I wouldn't be able to fill it.

In the meantime Graham's attention had wandered to the rest of the room. I glanced at him as I listened to Hilda, and I saw he had noticed the bookcase. I wondered what the books were on its shelves. Many were bound volumes, interspersed with a few paperbacks, but I was too far away to read the titles on their spines.

When Hilda stopped speaking I had to respond in some way, so I scribbled on my pad and showed it to Graham. He read out what I'd written.

'She says it's very cosy here, and it's kind of you to let us come in.'

Hilda gave me that smile again.

'You're very welcome. We don't have many visitors, do we Thomas?' He murmured in agreement. 'You know, being off the beaten track and all that. We've rather lost the habit of conversation, haven't we Thomas?'

It was funny how she kept bringing him into the conversation despite his apparent reluctance – or inability – to contribute. Perhaps he was simply a man of few words – or maybe it was true that he had lost the capacity for small talk.

'But we enjoy our own company,' he responded, carefully articulating each syllable. I wondered if he might once have had a stammer. Maybe I wasn't the only one with a 'speech impediment.'

I was beginning to wish Graham had been schooled in the art of conversation. We hadn't made much headway in our efforts to penetrate whatever secret was contained in these four walls. I wondered if there was a cellar – or an attic – where Hughie might be held prisoner. And I listened out for noises from other parts of the house. I could see that Graham's nerves were on edge. Were we conducting an investigation or just chatting to fill the time, in the hope that by chance these people would let slip something to give themselves away?

I had to admit that they seemed unlikely kidnappers.

Then, bless him, Graham found his tongue again, and came up with another harmless question.

'I read that Quainton was a historic house,' he said. 'Did you manage to hang on to any family heirlooms when you moved out?'

Hilda shook her head. 'My father had already sold off most of the valuables and museum pieces in the hope of keeping the place afloat,' she said. 'And in the end, when all his efforts came to nothing, the rest had to be auctioned off to pay our debts.'

'Every last thing,' murmured Thomas. I wondered if this man had resented having his prospects dashed when his in-laws went bankrupt.

We all fell silent. Then Hilda asked where I was living now, where we had come from. We had decided not to be too precise about our address, since they may have seen the letter Hughie had sent to Mrs Wormold along the road from us. Graham managed an evasive answer, referring vaguely to Cottsea. At which Hilda changed the subject.

'But tell me – what was the connection between Quainton Grange and Ellen Keighley? What was it that brought you here?'

Her eyes flicked from Graham – who froze in a panic – to me. I made a few incoherent noises to buy time and to show I'd registered her questions, then turned to my scribbling pad again and jotted down an idea that had come to me.

'She used to talk about working with the horses here,' Graham read out.

Hilda gave a little gasp, as if a long-lost memory had suddenly come back to her.

'Ah yes, we did have stables back in those days... Of course that was before the Great War, when we were all in our teens.' She pursed her lips. 'Long gone now. And even at the time I must admit I couldn't keep up with all the girls who came to help groom the horses. There were so many of them you know – all so keen...'

I nodded, glad to acknowledge that avenue of enquiry had come to a dead end. No need to pursue the decoy any longer.

'Whereabouts were the stables?' Graham enquired naively.

I had a moment's irritation. It was time to drop the subject before we got in over our heads and here he was, about to cause more embarrassment.

Thomas shuffled in his seat. Evidently he felt called upon to speak, but might not be up to it. He looked across at Hilda, who said airily,

'Oh, as I remember they were just a set of outbuildings off the lane somewhere. I doubt I'd even be able to find the place now, it's so long ago...'

Graham was showing signs of wanting to press her further, which struck me as unwise. Something imperceptible in her tone had rearranged the air, the space between us, and I decided it was time to leave. We could find the site of the stables for ourselves.

I gave the signal by coughing and started to fidget in the wheelchair. Graham took the hint and said,

'Well, we must be going. You've been very hospitable and it was kind of you to talk to us. We're sorry to have taken up your time to no purpose....'

Hilda protested and addressed me. 'Must you go so soon? I was looking forward to the prospect of reminiscing some more with you – it seems we have a past in common.'

Graham told them about the van and explained that we needed to return it to its owner before dark. He turned to Thomas and added, 'Thank you for the tea and biscuits.'

Thomas seemed to come to life at last, as we were about to leave. Casting reticence aside, he stood up and said, 'Oh think nothing of it.' I noticed he had a sort of inverse lisp : he pronounced 'sink' and 'nossing'.

He opened the door and Hilda escorted us back along the hallway. Graham manoeuvred me down the steps and Thomas took his leave of us there before disappearing indoors, where he evidently had something to see to. Hilda followed us along the path round to the front of the house and watched, still smiling, as Graham loaded the wheelchair and me into the van. I wound down the window and she leaned in to speak to me.

'I do hope you'll come again,' she said. 'We must catch up on our school days – perhaps when the men aren't around,' she added with a giggle. 'I enjoyed the chance to speak of old times – such opportunities are rare at our age.'

I nodded, meaning to seem non-committal. As I did so my eyes wandered past her to the shuttered front of the house. She followed my gaze, and turned back to me as if she felt the need to explain some more.

'Yes, it does look blank and unfriendly, doesn't it? But I hope you won't judge us by first appearances... The shuttered windows don't tell the whole story...'

Graham had gone round to the door on his side, and as he got in she began to speak with a note of urgency.

'You know, we do drive out from time to time, to visit a cousin of mine in a nursing home near here. We could come and pick you up in Cottsea on our way back. We could bring you here and give you tea, and take the time to get to know each other better – again?' The last word sounded like a plea. Perhaps after all she led a lonely existence here and she would appreciate some female company. And I had to admit that getting away from Mrs Smith and the others had been a pleasant change for me.

'... And then we'll take you back home,' she ended.

So I nodded in agreement to her suggestion.

'Said the spider to the fly,' murmured Graham as we set off.

I couldn't help a little snort in response.

'I'm glad you find it amusing,' he said, changing gear. *'I thought they were a bit creepy.'*

I shrugged.

'Do you really think they have something to hide? But even if they do, are we any closer to finding Hughie? Assuming he needs finding.'

When we reached the edge of the woodland, out of sight of the house, I signalled to Graham to stop the van. He parked up close to the hedge, but I had no intention of leaving my seat. Instead, I gave him a push and gestured to him to get out and peer over the hedge, into the trees. He was a bit reluctant, but *did as I indicated . Standing with the van door open, he put his head back inside and asked,*

'What exactly am I after?'

I waved him off to see what was there. I had a pretty fair idea of what he would find.

While he was away I pulled out my pad and scribbled on it.

He came back a few minutes later.

I held up my pad and showed him what I had written.

*

… So there I was peering over the hedgerow, trying to make sense of some tumbledown brickwork and scattered rubble, overgrown with grass and weeds, half-hidden in the wood. At first I thought it was a derelict site that had been abandoned. Then I looked more carefully, and saw beyond the ruins there were some ageing walls still standing, and a roof still intact. And a split door that indicated a stable. There was at least one building here that had been preserved. The broken masonry lying around, and the general air of neglect beneath the trees, served to camouflage it.

That was why Mrs Horton had prompted me to take a look. She suspected the stables were here. Heading back to the van I knew she wouldn't be surprised by what I had to tell her. I was also in full conspiracy mode. Mrs Beaumont could well have been misleading us when she claimed to have only a vague sense of where the stables were. When I opened the van door I was bursting to tell Mrs Horton that I had seen an ideal place to keep someone locked up.

Before I could get a word out she cut me short by waving her scribbling-pad at me. Her writing was more shaky than usual, but I could make it out well enough.

'I knew Thomas Beaumont. That wasn't him.'

I stared at the scrawled words, then at Mrs Horton. Her crumpled face was as inscrutable as ever, and I needed a moment to take in what she had written. But as I wrestled with the implications, her clear blue eyes blazed out with an intensity that took me by surprise.

Eventually I gathered my wits.

'So who was that man?'

She tipped her head, shot me a sidelong glance, and raised an eyebrow: how should she know?

Then she busied herself again with her pencil and pad.

'Go back via Neatby. Where the nursing home is.'

This came out of the blue and caught me off balance again. She seemed to enjoy doing that. I thought for a moment and pointed at the sky.

'The sun will be going down soon. We have to get the van back before dark, remember.'

Mrs Horton blew out her cheeks : Pooh, who cares about that?

'Look,' I said, 'If we want to be able to borrow the van again we need to do things properly by Mr Witscombe.'

She reached out, took my hand and squeezed it – and as she did so she gave a vocal sigh that had a note of entreaty in it : Please?

Reluctantly I gave in and put the van in gear. After all, passing through Neatby added only ten minutes or so to our return journey.

11

We drove along in silence. Conversation was out of the question, obviously ; and we couldn't resort to our usual means of communication since I could hardly read anything she might write while I was trying to keep my eyes on the narrow meandering country lanes. So instead I ruminated over her reasons for taking this route back. Had she decided she knew the nursing home where Mrs Beaumont's cousin apparently lived? It occurred to me that as an invalid herself she may have had some experience of living in nursing homes – or perhaps had considered moving into one before deciding on the guest house at Cottsea.

I put this last thought to her as a question : from the corner of my eye I saw her nod.

Then I was thinking out loud.

'I don't suppose there are many homes in this area – it's a bit off the beaten track for families to visit. So it's fairly likely that's the one where this cousin of Mrs Beaumont is being cared for.'

No response from Mrs Horton. I took that to mean she agreed. But then I had to ask a leading question.

'Is this going to help us find Dr Storth?'

No response.

We drove on in silence, winding round the lanes for a couple more miles, gaps in the hedgerows affording occasional glimpses of the river, until the spire of Neatby church appeared above the tree tops on the horizon. Mrs Horton sat up and leaned forward as she saw it, pressing her hands against the lid of the glove compartment.

Something told me this was not a good sign.

'You're not expecting to call in, are you?'

I waited a few seconds in the silence that followed. I repeated : 'Actually call in?'

Keeping one eye on the road ahead, I shot a glance across at her.

She was gesticulating : both of us.

I'd had some experience of dealing with elderly and sometimes infirm people at the guest house, but gate-crashing a nursing home was a different kettle of fish. I spotted a layby, steered the van into it, and yanked up the handbrake. It made an angry scrunch that sounded the way I felt.

'Look, I wish you'd tell me what we're getting into. Why would you want to visit an out-of-the-way place where neither of us has any call to go nosing around?'

Mrs Horton slumped back into her seat. Whatever had galvanised her a moment before fell away as abruptly as it had come, leaving her deflated – and fragile, suddenly. I tried not to dwell on her shrunken frame and her woebegone features, and asked again:

'Do you think Dr Storth might be here?'

I looked into her eyes. What I saw there, to my surprise, was embarrassment. My irritation faded.

While the van was standing still she could write again.

'You never know.'

It took me another couple of seconds to absorb this.

'What are the chances?' I said. And because Mrs Horton seemed so downcast, I bit my tongue.

I released the handbrake and drove off again. Minutes later we were passing through Neatby, where we slowed down. The village was little more than a smallholding or two, plus a Wesleyan chapel and a cluster of modest cottages with well-tended gardens lining the road on either side. Mrs Horton paid no attention to them. But as we left them behind and entered a bend in the road, she placed her hand on my arm and pointed to two stone gateposts and a sign that announced 'Faircroft House', marking the entrance to the care home.

My heart sank, but I dutifully turned into the narrow driveway. It led up a slight rise to three empty parking spaces beneath large bay windows on the ground floor of a double-fronted, two-storey red-brick building which had presumably once been a substantial residence. It commanded a view across open farmland. Dormer windows had been built from the roof to provide extra accommodation. The entrance door still had the original leaded panes of dimpled glass, arranged in a coloured pattern.

As we drew up I eyed Mrs Horton.

'So – do you recognize this place?' I asked.

She shook her head, but was already reaching for the door-handle, clearly determined to climb out of the van and get inside the house. I had to think quickly.

I felt fairly confident that we could concoct a bona fide visit on the basis of our well-rehearsed double act. Wheeling an elderly disabled lady who couldn't speak for herself gave me free rein to improvise, whatever situations we might encounter on the inside. If I should prove less than convincing I could blame my confusion on the old lady.

A ramp for wheelchairs led up to the front door. I pressed the bell and a shape floated into view behind the parti-coloured glass panes. The door opened to reveal a member of staff wearing a blue uniform, a mob cap, plastic apron and rubber gloves. We had evidently caught her in the middle – or at the start – of a potentially messy operation ; but whatever irritation she might feel, when she caught sight of Mrs Horton her face lit up at the prospect of a new resident.

'Hello!' she gushed. 'Can I help you?'

Given her outfit I was tempted to try a joke but thought better of it.

'We were hoping we might pay a visit,' I said. 'My... aunt wants to find out about life in your care home.'

By now the woman was pulling off her gloves, and she offered her hand to Mrs Horton, who just stared vacantly at the badge on the woman's bosom and let her head nod distractedly as if registering the name: 'Sheila'.

'Would you like to follow me?' Sheila said, and led the way down a corridor at the end of which was the door to the manageress's office. She turned out to be a dumpy bespectacled woman who wore her hair in a bob and dressed in a brown twin-set and tweed skirt. She sized us up, introduced herself as 'Doreen' and listened to my invented explanation for our being there. She explained that visitors like us were normally expected to give prior notice. We acted out an exchange of confused glances. She let us stew for a moment, then relented graciously and offered to give us a guided tour of the facilities. It was obvious that she prided herself on being businesslike, and though eager to show prospective clients around would not take long over it.

We were given a peek into an individual room, spick and span and empty, with a window ajar so that fresh air from outside dispelled the ambient smell of soaped bodies and vaguely sour emanations that hung in the corridor behind us.

'And along here,' said Doreen as she headed off and turned into another corridor, 'is the day-room.'

As we drew closer a set of double doors swung apart and a member of staff backed through them, pulling a trolley with left-over biscuits and cups of tea on it. We stood aside to let her pass, then Doreen ushered us into the lounge.

She addressed the room in general : 'We have some visitors today : Mrs Horton and her nephew Graham. They want to see how people get on in Faircroft House.'

A chorus of low murmurs greeted her announcement. The atmosphere was warm and stuffy, and evidently had a soporific effect on the residents who sat or dozed in a collection of high chairs, armchairs and reclining seats, facing in a variety of different directions.

Doreen turned to us. 'One or two of our residents tend to keep themselves to themselves, as you will see. But most of them like having someone to talk to... so do feel free to say Hello and you'll find them quite welcoming.'

She checked her watch, needing to be somewhere else.

'Sheila will be along in a moment. She'll be able to answer any questions you might have. Now, if you'll excuse me...'

She smiled a tight smile, directed it round the room, and then left us alone with those residents who had ventured from their individual rooms for such companionship and desultory conversation as were available here.

I looked about me. Most of the people here were women, and some of them smiled eagerly when I caught their eye. I nodded, mouthed 'Hello', and smiled back. I asked one old lady how she was. 'I've just had some tea,' she replied, 'but I left the biscuit. The crumbs get under my dentures.' I frowned sympathetically, and turned away. I saw another lady listlessly turning the pages of a magazine, while a third was knitting with her eyes closed. I counted three men : none of them seemed disposed to communicate. None of them bore any resemblance to Dr Hugh Storth.

I was obviously out of place, by far the youngest there. But what made me especially self-conscious was being the only person standing, even though the room's occupants were mostly too distracted to take any notice. To start a conversation I would have to lean down and break into someone's private thoughts – assuming they had any. I shifted from one foot to the other, uncertain whether to try singling out a resident by catching their eye across the room and threading my way towards them between the chairs – which were laid out so randomly as to discourage such manoeuvres.

Mrs Horton had no reservations about moving through the little gathering. She blended in with the surroundings – she was just another old lady in a wheelchair. She had left me and rolled herself alongside a pair of residents who at least seemed aware of each other's presence. They acknowledged her as she drew up between them : arriving at eye-level, she was one of their own. I couldn't make out what they were saying to her and each other, but the fact that she couldn't reply properly didn't seem to bother them. They appeared to be introducing themselves to her and they nodded at the sounds she made in response.

I decided to join them as Mrs Horton's nephew. The lady with her back to me turned slightly as I approached, and the light gleamed on her spectacles so that at first I couldn't make out her eyes. But I quickly realised that she was partially sighted : her lenses were of darkened glass, and her gaze was casting about in my general direction rather than aiming straight at me. Her companion continued to look down ; she was registering the sound of my footsteps. She was blind.

'Hello,' I said. 'I'm pleased to meet you. Mrs Horton is my aunt and we've come to get a taste of life at Faircroft.'

The woman in dark glasses said, 'You'll have to stay around till teatime for that,' and they giggled ; Mrs Horton joined in.

The blind woman, staring forward into the middle distance, said, 'Me and Margaret are enjoying getting acquainted with your aunt.'

Mrs Horton looked up at me and managed a murmur of agreement. I noticed that behind their lenses Margaret's eyes tended to roll in search of an object to focus on. She must see only shapes without detail. And it occurred to me that neither she nor her companion could make out Mrs Horton's crooked face. Their perception of her was not coloured by the wretched expression her features fell into in spite of herself. They weren't prompted to pity by her appearance – they took her *at face value*, assuming she looked normal.

On the other hand they were entirely reliant on her grunts and sighs to understand what she was trying to get across. They were denied the clues that Mrs Horton's eyes could sometimes supply as she forced rasping noises from her throat. No wonder they listened so attentively while other people would soon have given up. Could they really make sense of Mrs Horton's utterances?

'I'm Janet, by the way,' the blind woman said to the space in front of her.

'I'm Graham,' I replied. 'And my Aunt's name is Marion.'

'She's quite a chatterbox,' said Margaret, her smile causing her glasses to twinkle.

Mrs Horton made a soft, hoarse laughing sound in Margaret's direction, and at the same time reached out to squeeze Janet's hand. The three of them presented a picture of a curious intimacy.

'Have you lived here long?' I asked, to join in the odd conversation.

Janet stirred.

'Too long. What caused your aunt Marion's speech impediment?'

I glanced towards Mrs Horton and explained she had had a stroke. The two other women made sympathetic noises, and Mrs Horton croaked back.

'You're right, it's something you just have to get used to,' said Margaret. 'But you're fortunate having a nice nephew to take you out and about.'

Mrs Horton uttered a sequence of sounds which I could make nothing of, although her intonation gave them a meaning for Margaret and Janet.

Then their odd exchanges continued and I was left standing beside them with nothing to contribute. Mrs Horton offered incomprehensible sing-song rejoinders and friendly pats to her companions as they chatted away. My guess was the two friends were largely conversing with each other in mind and were happy to have Mrs Horton interject from the side-lines. But unnoticed by the two sightless women her eyes were roving around the room. This weird conversation was a cover for something else ; it was a sort of camouflage that gave her an opportunity to scrutinize the other residents without anyone knowing what she was doing – least of all the pair of unseeing women.

I decided to move away, and took up a position beside the window. I felt less self-conscious there, and could pretend to be admiring the view outside while waiting till my 'aunt' was ready to leave. But I could also watch Mrs Horton stare at each of the three men in the room. That was obviously what she was here for. While she continued to converse huskily with Janet and Margaret as if the three of them were old friends, her eyes surveyed the stooped, isolated figures ensconced in separate corners of the lounge. She glanced back and forth, pausing on one, then passing to another before returning to the first, looking him up and down then moving on to the third. Eventually her gaze came to rest on the broad-shouldered, bald-headed one. I could see one reason why she had taken a while : if she knew him years ago – and by now I was as sure as she was – he had had a full head of hair back then. And I wondered how long he had had a moustache : it was big, white, bushy and wide and drooped over his mouth, concealing the expression on his lips. His eyelids sagged too, giving him a weary look as he stared down at the carpet. He was dressed in a baggy cardigan which had seen better days, over a shirt without a collar. He gripped the arms of his chair with solid, square hands.

I saw Mrs Horton draw herself up in her wheelchair. She turned to me and cocked an eyebrow. I began to make my way across the room towards her.

Suddenly the double doors burst open and Sheila came bustling in. She was a bit breathless, as if she had finished something else in a hurry in order to deal with us. She took a moment to get her bearings. I stopped in mid-stride.

At first Mrs Horton was lost to her in the midst of the residents, so Sheila addressed me over the heads of the others between us.

'Well, have you found things to your liking, Mr....?' her words trailed off as she realised she didn't know my name. She scanned the room uncertainly, looking for Mrs Horton, while vaguely directing words at me. 'Do you... think... your aunt... will feel... at home here?'

I nodded, and shot a glance over my shoulder at Mrs Horton. She had propelled herself forward till she was in front of the bald man, and she coughed to catch his attention.

He raised his downcast eyes.

His chair was higher than hers, so as he lifted his head he saw her staring up into his face.

Her face meant nothing to him. But she reached out and touched one of his hands. It was surprisingly muscular for one so old.

He did not react, and I wondered for a moment whether he was beyond understanding her gesture – a gesture whose meaning was plain to me.

It was plain to Sheila too – or so she thought.

'Well, well, we've made a friend already!' she cried as she crossed the room towards them.

'Found a friend,' I suggested. The idea that Mrs Horton had propositioned this old man out of the blue struck me as vaguely indecent.

Oblivious to the woman bustling in their direction, Mrs Horton was stroking the back of the man's hand and murmuring indistinctly. His eyes flickered as he listened, but he didn't seem to recognize – still less understand – her. She turned one of his hands over and placed her fingers in his palm. He looked down, then into her face once more. She murmured again.

By this time Sheila was on the scene. I approached behind her.

'I see that Dom is working his charm again – aren't you love?' Sheila said, patting his shoulder.

The man looked up at her blankly, then looked down at the two hands intertwined on the chair arm.

'Keeps himself to himself, does our Dom,' she said. 'But he appreciates a bit of company – doesn't get many visitors.'

'Hmm,' I said, and nodded. Dom stared at me, and then at Sheila, uncomprehending.

Eyes glued to his features, Mrs Horton continued to murmur.

Sheila was beginning to show signs of impatience.

'Well…,' she began.

Mrs Horton turned to her, and then to me. She lifted her hand from Dom's palm and used it to take out her notepad. She wrote:

'Speak to him - mention the name "Marion Halstead".'

Sheila interrupted. 'I don't think we should upset him…' she said. 'It's nearly time for his medication.'

I stepped forward, to do as Mrs Horton had asked.

'Marion,' I said. 'Marion Halstead.'

Sheila couldn't contain her impatience any longer.

'Look,' she said, dropping her voice so as not to be heard by the others in the room, 'I'm afraid we can't allow visitors to interact with residents unless they have prior permission.'

Mrs Horton gazed into Dom's face again, hoping he might react to the name – her name.

'Ariung,' she said. 'Ariung.'

Dom remained impassive, but a look of bewilderment crossed his face.

'I must ask you to leave now, please,' said Sheila.

That was when Mrs Horton was suddenly taken ill.

12

I felt myself slump forward in my chair. To this day I don't know if I was taken ill or whether I actually faked a funny turn. One way or another something welled up inside me – emotion, shock, a rush of blood to the head, I couldn't say – and then my strength just drained away. That much I'm sure of. Then I fainted.

Of course Sheila was within her rights to try and get us to leave. They hadn't a clue who we were and we could have been up to no good. Perhaps we were. In all honesty I didn't know what I was doing. The moment I thought I recognized 'Dom' the ground seemed to give way underneath me.

When I came to, I was stretched out on a cot in some sort of side room. I had no idea how I had got there. Graham was standing back in bewilderment while Sheila peered down at me. She was looking for signs that something serious might be wrong. Naturally my face offered no clues. She held up a finger and moved it to left and right, and I had the presence of mind to oblige her by following it with my eyes. This seemed to reassure her.

'My word, we thought we might have lost you there,' she said. 'Now you just lie here and rest until the doctor can come to check you over.' She turned to Graham and dropped her voice. 'She might have to stay here overnight. Is there anyone we need to inform?'

He panicked for a moment, then shook his head. I had a vision of the sitting room at the guest house, and the reactions of the residents when we failed to return that evening. It gave me a queer sort of satisfaction.

The door opened slightly and Doreen's face appeared. She caught Sheila's eye and called her over for a whispered conflab. I imagined she was miffed at the prospect of having an uninvited guest to put up for the night.

I couldn't tell them anything about what had happened to me. I couldn't even write – my fingers were trembling still. I glanced at Graham and I managed to shrug my shoulders, in an attempt to put his mind at rest. I wasn't feeling poorly, but was content to stay where I was for the time being. I had plenty of food for thought.

It was simple curiosity that had led me here. I definitely felt emboldened by the fact I had got one over on Hilda Woodrough since I recognized her and she didn't know me. That sort of superiority came as a small compensation for the way she had teased and humiliated me at school (to say nothing of what happened afterwards). I suppose it went to my head. And when she mentioned she had a relative here in the care home I had an urge to... what, exactly? Gatecrash her family? I was just misbehaving on an impulse, to get my own back on Hilda. It was like coming across a house with an open door – I was tempted to peek inside. To peer *behind the composed façade of that self-satisfied woman and her impostor partner.*

So what was I expecting when we arrived here? I couldn't say. When we used to go stealing apples as children, it was the thrill of being naughty, not apples, that we were after. And then there's this : when you're an invalid, looking helpless serves as a disguise – no one thinks you're capable of misbehaving. So we could get away with our mischief, and that's a heady feeling. It was a sensation I hadn't experienced in years.

In the heat of the moment all thoughts of Hughie were forgotten.

I got my comeuppance soon enough though, when I glimpsed the man in his high chair. There were cushions propping him up and he wasn't slumped like most of the others, so his face drew me right away, even though it was expressionless. He was just staring into space. I moved forward, into his line of vision, but his eyes didn't refocus at all. At first I wondered if he was blind.

When I reached out and touched his hand he started slightly, looked down at my fingers, and then his gaze rose to me. So he could see me after all. But his expression didn't change – not even that little flicker of shock most people can't repress when they first catch sight of my sorry features.

I concentrated on staring into his eyes, to distract him from the rest of my face. It works with many people.

I had the sensation you get when you look into the eyes of an animal and are startled by a spark of intelligence. His iris was the blue-grey I remembered, with little flecks of brown, and I saw his pupil contract, as the skin around his eyes puckered slightly.

He was staring back at me, and my heart skipped a beat: and that was when I began to come over so strange. All of a sudden I was in a sort of delirium, and I can't remember exactly what happened.

When Sheila called him 'Dom' my first impulse was to correct her, then I thought better of it. But in that moment a wave broke over me and drowned out my consciousness.

The doctor felt my pulse and checked my blood pressure, looked into my eyes with a torch, and listened to my chest through his stethoscope. Then as he packed his things back into his bag he pronounced me quite well and reassured those around the bed that I had not had another 'small stroke'. Sheila and Doreen exchanged glances and I could see them breathe a sigh of relief. They even accepted with good grace the doctor's recommendation that I might spend the night at Faircroft just in case. I was happy with that. I didn't feel ready to get up and travel back to Cottsea.

More to the point, I had some unfinished business here.

As for Graham, he was watching the episode from a chair in the corner, confused and anxious, occasionally glancing at the clock on the wall. Now that he was over the shock of having a casualty on his hands, I could tell he was worrying about getting the van back to Mr Witscombe. I should put him out of his misery and free him to go. I leaned towards him from my semi-recumbent posture in the cot, and I was able to convey to him that it was safe to leave me, and he should get back to the guest house.

'I'll let them know what happened,' he said.

I gave him my best cockeyed expression and shook my jowls. I wrinkled my forehead to suggest he shouldn't make a fuss about it, and he twigged. We were getting good at communicating.

Doreen had left the room by now, and Graham spoke to Sheila.

'I have to get back,' he said. 'Is it OK if I come to collect my aunt tomorrow afternoon, when I get off work?'

She nodded, and asked him to write down the telephone number of the guest house .

He stood by the door looking uncertain. Then, as if making up his mind, he crossed the room towards me, and leaned down to kiss me on the cheek.

'Bye bye, Auntie,' he said, and with a wave he opened the door and disappeared.

*

I was glad to get away. I mean, I was reassured when the doctor said Mrs Horton was going to be fine, and when Doreen agreed to take care of her overnight that relieved me of another worry. But all the time I was thinking there was going to be trouble with Mr Witscombe if I got back late with his van.

As it turned out the old chap didn't make a fuss – in fact he was very understanding when I explained that Mrs Horton had been taken ill. Admittedly I embroidered a bit as to the circumstances – and while I was about it, got round to asking if I could borrow the van again to go and bring her back from the nursing home where I'd had to leave her. He agreed right away, and I surprised myself on my smooth talking and my powers of persuasion.

Looking back, I think that acting as Mrs Horton's go-between made me a more confident speaker. She had had to prompt me, putting words into my mouth, but saying things on her behalf made me fluent on my own account – with the fluency that she had been deprived of.

Just as well : I needed a way with words when I arrived back at the guest house. The people sitting in the bay window saw me coming and by the time I got in through the front door and showed my face in the lounge, all eyes were on me.

Where was the wheelchair? What had happened to Mrs Horton?

Mrs Smith was the first to speak.

'Well my dear, did you have a pleasant little outing? Did Mrs Horton enjoy herself? ... Where is she, by the way?'

Her words were dripping with something more than the usual condescension, as I was soon to discover.

The news had got through to the kitchen, and Mrs Dugdale scurried into the lounge. I offered my explanation to her, but spoke so that the rest of the room could hear.

'We... she bumped into an old acquaintance and was invited to stay overnight. I came back to return the van to Mr Witscombe...'

Mrs Dugdale murmured that she was glad she hadn't lost her lodger for good, but her remarks were overtaken by a stage whisper from Mrs Smith:

'For a moment I thought she might have disappeared down a rabbit-hole with Dr Storth...'

It was rude even by Mrs Smith's usual standards. The other guests shuffled in embarrassment. They normally acknowledged Mrs Smith's pronouncements with a deferential silence, but on this occasion I sensed a quiet mutiny, as if she had pushed their patience too far.

Mrs Dugdale caught my eye and gave me an urgent 'Pay no attention' look.

But in spite of myself I couldn't help glancing at Mrs Smith. I noticed immediately that she wasn't her usual well-groomed self. She was sitting ramrod-straight in her chair, but strands of hair had come loose from her normally tight bun, and her lipstick was askew. The powder on her nose was flaky and her stockings were in wrinkles at her ankles.

Mrs Dugdale took my arm and steered me out into the hall.

'She's been at the gin again,' she muttered.

I didn't know what to say to that. I was not aware that Mrs Smith sometimes fell into bouts of drinking. Either she kept it well hidden and I hadn't noticed the signs, or her last spree had occurred before my time.

'Nothing to worry about,' Mrs Dugdale went on. 'She gets a bit unsteady on her feet, that's all, and she can be more cantankerous than usual for a day or two. But she soon comes round again. She'll be back to stealing the cream before long. In the meantime, just pay no attention and carry on as if there's nothing out of the ordinary.'

This wasn't easy, because I admit I was curious to see what Mrs Smith was like when she unbuttoned and let herself go. Her day-to-day demeanour, her strait-laced manner, always struck me as too contrived to be natural, and I had sometimes wondered what the real Mrs Smith might be like.

I was to find out that night.

After my eventful day, I was glad to get to bed. I had to be up with the lark the next morning. I had agreed with Mrs Dugdale that I'd do the early breakfast shift so that I could collect Mrs Horton and bring her back from Faircroft in the afternoon. In my garret room under the eaves I stretched out beneath the blankets and began to doze off.

I was half-asleep when I became aware of a shuffling sound on the landing and heard my bedroom door creak. I opened my eyes to see Mrs Smith standing in the doorway, a finger on her lips. She was wearing her red silk dressing gown and satin pyjamas ; her hair was undone and a long tress, trained over her left shoulder, hung down in front of her. Her slippers made no sound as she stepped forward towards me.

For a grotesque fleeting moment I thought she had died and was calling in on me as she ascended to heaven. But she was carrying a small electric hand-torch to light her way, and I had to accept that she was here, in person, standing over me as I lay in my bed.

She dropped her eyes and swayed slightly, and I smelt the gin on her breath.

I felt groggy and something told me I should not react. I lay still, for fear of provoking her and creating a noise, and waited to see what the tipsy old lady would do next.

She came closer and leaned down.

'My poor boy,' she said softly, reaching out to touch my cheek. 'It must all be too much for you.' She sounded like a sentimental aunt, far removed from the stiff-backed overseer of the sitting room.

My instinct was to recoil, but I found I was unable to move as her fingers stroked my skin. I looked into her eyes, which were bloodshot and pouched. She had removed her make-up and her face was pale, her wrinkles and big nose more pronounced than ever. But her expression was full of a grotesque tenderness.

'Dear Graham,' she murmured, continuing to stroke my cheek. Then she leaned in further and kissed it. I smelt alcohol and felt a cold moisture on my skin as she drew back.

There was a chair under the attic window and moving unsteadily she pulled it forward and sat down. There was more to come, obviously. I sat up in bed, ready to defend myself.

'Is there something wrong?' I asked uncertainly.

She gave one of her smoker's sighs, midway between a croak and a cough.

'My dear boy, that woman is taking advantage of you,' she replied. 'And I can't stay silent any longer.'

I didn't respond.

'She thinks no one knows who she is. She believed she could leave everything behind after her stroke altered her face and put an end to that strong regional accent of hers – poor woman, it was very distinctive and try as she may, she couldn't shake it off... She's been relying on people not recognizing her. But I've known all along.'

'I don't know what you mean,' I said. I couldn't be sure she was making sense. She was slurring her words and her garbled speech could well have been the gin talking.

'A double life,' she mumbled. 'Her past. It will catch up with her.'

It occurred to me to check that she was talking about the old lady I had left in the care home and was due to bring back tomorrow.

'You mean Mrs Horton?' I asked with a smile intended to convey scepticism.

'You think I'm not serious,' Mrs Smith said. She laboured to draw in breath before continuing in that ponderous, deliberate way that drunk people have. 'Mark my words, there's more to her than you realize.'

Mrs Smith's lips writhed as they prepared another tirade. The pupils in her bleary eyes had a piercing intensity ; her slurred words were heavy with conviction. There was something manic, even distraught, in her expression. Was it to do with the resentment she had been nursing since Dr Storth showed a preference for Mrs Horton? The drink must have soured this petty rivalry.

I glanced at the darkness beyond the net curtains, and wondered how long it was till daybreak. How could I get rid of my intruder without waking the entire household? I needed to get some sleep.

Mrs Smith held up a hand, her fingers trembling as she took me further into her confidence.

'She wrote nice things about you in her book,' she said, and let her hand drop onto my arm.

I stared at her, dumbfounded. How had she –?

'I think she sees you as the son she never had,' Mrs Smith continued, ignoring my unspoken question. 'She's always on the lookout...' Then she gave another heavy sigh, and her face fell. 'I never had a child either,' she continued. 'Reginald and I...' Her hand squeezed my arm. 'My Reginald...'

Now her tone was decidedly maudlin. I began to fear that she would break into tears.

Two lonely women, vying with each other for the attentions of chaps young enough to be their son. First Hughie – and now me. That was something I didn't want to dwell on.

Mrs Smith was lost in her mournful thoughts.

'How do you know about her book?' I asked.

She roused herself after a fashion, but answered distractedly.

'I couldn't sleep. I knew she wasn't in, and when I tried her door it was unlocked.'

Her shoulders fell and her whole body appeared to slump into a wretched heap. I gazed at her in disbelief. So prim and upright, but she had been reduced to snooping on her fellow resident... I wondered if Mrs Dugdale was aware that the respectable Mrs Smith had a tendency to roam the house when drunk.

As I considered her in silence, she must have sensed that I was judging her. Suddenly, gripped by a kind of indignation, she was provoked to defend herself:

'I only read a few lines... Couldn't make out her handwriting...' She waved her hand in a half-hearted gesture. 'Some cock and bull story about Dr Storth and a manuscript... don't believe a word of it.' Her brief protest left her deflated, as if it had drained all the energy out of her. Then she made another effort to pull herself together, to regain her dignity. She struggled with one final outburst. 'The bench on the sea wall... that's another matter. As for that old acquaintance she's found... Don't let her draw you in.'

13

Mrs Smith was virtually walking in her sleep as I guided her back to her room and gently deposited her on her bed. I left her there in her dressing gown and slippers and hoped she would remember nothing of what had passed between us – for her own sake. I tried to imagine her hangover, made worse by remorse at having abandoned her usual aloof decorum. But what exactly had passed between us? Had she been trying to unburden herself about something she couldn't put into words while sober?

It took me a while to get back to sleep. At first light I woke and lay still for a few minutes, trying to string together what she had said. It had been so incoherent, I decided she had been in an alcoholic haze, spilling out a stream of disjointed thoughts prompted by some personal unhappiness.

She was absent from breakfast, as usual, so I could make up the tables, do the service and clear away without having to confront her. I imagined her up in her room, pale and chastened, sipping her tea as she recovered her grip on reality.

As for me, I had to put aside thoughts of one old lady as I set about retrieving the other one. I had pulled on my jacket and was on the point of slipping out of the door when Mrs Dugdale came after me ; by the look of her it was an urgent matter.

'Phone call for Graham Rawcliffe,' she said, her hand on my arm as if to stop me from getting away.

'Who would phone me?' I asked, mystified and a bit nervous.

'Some lady,' she replied, 'who seems to think you can answer for Mrs Horton.'

I wasn't used to speaking on the telephone, so I picked up the bakelite receiver with some trepidation.

'Hello,' I said.

'Hello?' said a voice. 'Is that Graham? Mrs Horton's nephew?'

It was Mrs Beaumont.

'Erm, yes,' I stammered.

'I had to ask for you since there was no point in expecting your aunt to answer my call,' she said, a smile in her voice.

'Erm, no,' I replied.

'The thing is,' Mrs Beaumont went on, 'we were wondering – Thomas and I – if we might drop by and see her again. Take her out for a cup of tea together somewhere. Carry on catching up where we left off.'

'Oh, yes.' I said. 'I mean – '

'Just a little outing,' she added. 'I imagine Marion doesn't get many opportunities to enjoy the fresh air.'

I was in a fix, tongue-tied. I couldn't say Mrs Horton had spent the night at Faircroft and was still there, since we had no business being there in the first place. If I said she had been taken ill Mrs Beaumont would be likely to insist on coming to see her... And I needed to get her back to the guest house first.

Then a new-found fluency came to my rescue.

'The thing is,' I said, becoming positively voluble, 'I'm sure she would love to see you again, but I'd have to check with her first. And as a matter of fact she isn't here at the moment... She is erm... out... with a friend who visits from time to time.'

There was a silence at the other end of the line.

'Oh. Oh well. Perhaps we could visit another time. Will you tell her I called?'

'Yes, of course,' I said. 'I – '

'Goodbye,' she said.

The line clicked and went dead, leaving me to wonder at the abrupt way she had ended the conversation.

But I didn't have time to dwell on the matter since I had to go and get Mrs Horton.

Mr Witscombe was happy enough to lend me the van again, though he made a point of suggesting I might 'put some petrol in it' when I brought it back, which I assured him we would do. (I confess I was counting on Mrs Horton to provide the cash.)

Now I knew the way, it was a pleasant drive through the countryside to Neatby, so I was in a good frame of mind when I arrived at Faircroft and drew into the parking area. The door with its coloured glass insert was waiting to meet me as if I was a regular visitor. I pressed the bell-push confidently.

The space behind the glass was empty, and remained so for several moments. I was about to press the bell again when I heard hurried footsteps approaching inside. I stood back.

The door opened and Doreen stood before me. Her face was expressionless, though her eyes flickered and it was evident that she recognized me right away.

'Oh hello,' she said.

'I've come for my aunt,' I said.

She nodded. 'You'd better come in,' she said, and pulled the door open so I could step past her.

As I did so I was aware that something in her manner had changed from the brisk and businesslike woman she had been the day before. She seemed preoccupied. I was soon to discover why.

'Would you come with me to my office?' she asked as she closed the door.

She led the way along the corridor. I followed on behind, misgivings rising in me.

Once inside her office, Doreen closed the door and gestured me to a chair while she sat behind her desk. She took a breath.

'Your aunt's not well. She seems to have had a relapse.'

My first thought was 'she's not my aunt'. Then the sense of what I was being told hit me.

'Is she... is it serious?' I asked.

Doreen glanced down at a notepad on the desk in front of her.

'The district nurse happened to be visiting at the time. She checked her over and could find no obvious cause for concern. But her behaviour... You'll find she is rather vague in her responses to people. And of course she can't describe what she feels, what's happened to her...' She paused. 'Though to be fair, many of the other people at Faircroft have that problem. It comes with ageing, of course.'

I was torn between wanting to see Mrs Horton right away and wanting to know more about the state she was in. I was scared I'd find her changed from the person I had come to know.

'How did it happen?' I asked.

Doreen shifted in her chair.

'Well, after a night's rest she seemed fine when she got up. She joined our residents for breakfast and then moved into the sitting room with them. She was chatting, after her fashion, with Margaret and Janet – the two partially sighted ladies she met yesterday. She even had a cup of tea with them. But shortly afterwards she seemed to get agitated and we didn't know what about. Sheila says it began with her trying to speak to other people in the room – as if she wanted something from them – and no one could tell what it was. This went on for a few minutes, while we tried to understand her... Then without warning she went quiet. And we realised she had gone into a sort of trance – she didn't faint like yesterday, but she seemed to sink into herself as if she had lost touch with her surroundings.' She raised her eyes. 'And that's the way she is now.'

'Can I see her?' I asked.

'Yes, of course,' she replied. 'I just wanted to prepare you.' She paused. Then, in a slightly strained tone, she went on, 'I have to say it seems advisable to keep her under observation here. It might be unwise to take her back with you.'

I nodded, imagining how Mrs Dugdale would react if I was to bring Mrs Horton home in a serious condition.

I got up to go and see for myself. Doreen led the way to a side-room.

'She couldn't remain in the day room... the others were rather upset about her.'

It was where Mrs Horton had been taken when she had blacked out earlier. Doreen went in first and I peered nervously round the door before following her.

Mrs Horton was in her wheelchair alongside the cot she had been lying in when I last saw her. Now she was slumped sideways, her palsied cheek sagging and drool running from the corner of her mouth. This didn't strike me as a mere trance, as Doreen had put it. Her eyelids were drooping, and I couldn't tell whether she was taking anything in or just staring blankly towards the floor.

Doreen took a napkin and wiped her wet lips, then stood back so I could approach.

There was a metal chair nearby and I drew it up to sit beside her. She did not react at all. Her hair was odd. Perhaps whoever had helped her get up that morning did not know how she wore it normally.

Hunched in the wheelchair with her arms clenched to her sides, she had one hand on the chair arm. Her fingers were going into spasms, clenching and unclenching. It could have been a mechanical reflex, but it might have been a signal.

I put my hand over hers and stroked the fingers. The convulsions calmed down. I murmured some comforting sounds. Mrs Horton gave a very slight, barely perceptible nod of the head.

'She seems to be responding,' said Doreen.

I leaned in closer to Mrs Horton. She was still bowed towards the floor and I had to bend down and twist my head in order to examine her face. Immediately her eyes rolled up to meet mine. Though they were foggy and unfocussed, it was a sign that she knew who I was. But it was just between me and her as we huddled together.

Her lips began to move, and indistinct sounds came out of her mouth.

'Ngek ngee owk.'

I sensed Doreen moving nearer, to listen in. I turned towards her before she could get close.

'She's trying to say something,' I said.

'Hmm,' she said, keeping her distance.

'Ngek ngee owk ogh heey,' Mrs Horton said.

Get me out of here.

It took a couple of seconds to register the full sense of the words she had struggled to pronounce.

I turned to Doreen.

'She wants to go home,' I explained.

Doreen gave a grudging smile. 'It helps when you're used to the way she speaks,' she said – through gritted teeth, I thought. She was shamefaced, as if she was embarrassed that Mrs Horton could fall ill on her watch. I continued stroking Mrs Horton's hand as her head slumped once more. 'You know,' Doreen went on, 'the patient may not be the best judge of what's best for her.'

Mrs Horton seemed unaware of Doreen's words, but I felt a tremor run through her arm. I gathered that was the only reaction she was capable of in her condition. It was enough to confirm what I had just heard her say.

I stood up, keeping my hand on Mrs Horton's shoulder. 'My aunt has trouble making herself understood at the best of times,' I began. 'But as you've just seen, I'm used to the way she speaks. And she just made her wishes clear to me.'

Right on time, Mrs Horton managed a croak to back me up. Doreen let out a sigh.

'It's not for me to go against her wishes,' she acknowledged. 'After all, she isn't one of our registered residents. And when all's said and done I can't prevent her leaving with her next of kin.'

I nodded, reluctant to commit myself in words.

Twenty minutes later, after thanking Doreen and Sheila for the hospitality they had afforded my 'aunt', and having apologized for the trouble she had caused, I had stowed the wheelchair in the van. The three of us managed to slide Mrs Horton into the passenger seat and we said our goodbyes. They had made a show of concern for her, but I suspected they were glad to have her off their hands.

Mrs Horton still seemed drowsy as we drove off, but I was in no doubt I was doing what she wanted.

I kept glancing sideways at her while driving, though. She was inert, eyes closed, her head nodding at each bump and turn in the road. I was worried she might become unconscious and slip out of her seat or slump across onto me. I drew up in a layby, jumped out and went round to her side of the van. I managed to move her into a more upright position so she could breathe more easily, and adjusted the seat so I could prop her firmly in place. I wound down the window to let the fresh air blow over her face.

We set off again. I was wondering what could have happened to make her like this. I took it that she was not ill as such – otherwise the district nurse would have had cause for concern and Doreen would surely not have agreed to hand her over to my care. But she wasn't responding to anything I said. Glancing across at her again, I saw that though her eyes were open now, she was simply staring straight ahead, oblivious to the countryside flowing by and the breeze ruffling her hair. She seemed withdrawn, even trapped inside herself. I racked my brains trying to think of something I could do to bring her round. I couldn't face taking her back to the guest house in her present state.

I checked my watch. I had an hour or so before I had to return the van and get back to work. How best to use it? Sea air might help revive Mrs Horton. I decided to get her to the shore by the quickest route. I knew of a cart track that led down to the beach, and turning off the main road I steered us along it. It was unsurfaced and full of potholes that made the van lurch from side to side. I drove as slowly as I could but Mrs Horton was repeatedly jolted and shaken. So much so that I noticed slight reflex movements as she reacted to steady herself. The uncomfortable ride seemed to be helping her regain some kind of awareness.

The track petered out at an opening in the sea defences. The gap was sometimes used by farmers, and occasionally by those with trailers carrying sand yachts onto the beach. Today there was no one else in sight so I pulled up directly in front of the opening that offered a view over the sea. I turned off the engine and we sat in silence.

Mrs Horton was still directing an unfocussed stare in front of her. The smell of salt and seaweed, and the occasional cry of a gull, floated in through the open window. Suddenly her hands began to twitch and she started scrabbling at the door handle. Clearly she wanted to get out. I hadn't bargained for this, because her limbs had been so unsteady that it had taken three of us to get her into the van and I couldn't imagine getting her out of it on my own.

Her efforts became more fevered and I was afraid she might work herself into another fainting fit or worse. So I got out, came round to her side and opened the door. Immediately her hands reached out to me, and a groan like a cry for help came from deep in her throat. I had to do more to pacify her.

Reluctantly, I went to get the wheelchair out of the back of the van. But as soon as she saw me do so, she began to wave it away frantically and uttered a series of staccato grunts. I thought of a child refusing to go along with its parent's wishes. If her legs were in better shape, I thought, she'd soon be stamping her feet.

I would have to try moving her despite my misgivings.

'I'm going to shift you round,' I said. I pulled back the door, reached in and put my arms across her legs, hoping she would understand. It was a manoeuvre we had carried out before, getting her in and out of the wheelchair and moving her between the wheelchair and the passenger seat. The operation had become second nature to her and fortunately she went along with it mechanically now. I soon had her sitting sideways in the seat with her feet on the ground outside.

I had hoped that might be enough, apprehensive as I was about her ability to stand and move without using the wheelchair. I stepped back to see how she reacted.

She was still not herself, though part of her seemed determined to drag the rest of her out of the stupor she had been plunged into. Her upper body leaned forward in an effort to get to her feet, and I had to rush to stop her from falling onto her face as her legs failed to follow suit. I caught her under her arms ; and at that point I had no option but to heave her to her feet. Her body was not particularly heavy, but she had no coordination in her limbs and at any moment I felt she might go limp and slip out of my grasp. I held her tightly up against me, using my own body to prop hers up. Her feet were on the ground now and I sensed that her legs were beginning to take her weight. For the moment, I just needed to steady her.

After a minute or so during which I murmured encouragement to her and felt her fragile body stiffen to support itself, I edged away slightly, keeping a grip under her armpits.

She moved one foot forward. Then the other foot. She was coming back to life.

Her face still lolled from her skull, unable to form an expression. But a glint had come into her eyes. She was determined.

I took up a position alongside her, my right arm round her waist and my left providing support for her left arm, so we were facing in the same direction. She took two steps forward and I moved with her. She gasped with the effort it cost her.

There was a bench up ahead. I stared into her face and found I could catch her eye : she was registering my presence in her line of sight. I nodded towards the bench and her eyes followed mine.

'Hungh!' she said. That was all I needed. Gingerly, as if on a tightrope together, we crossed the intervening distance side by side, and as she tightened her grip on my arm, I felt her muscles learning to flex once more.

We sat down together, the sound of the tide rolling in our ears while the breeze prodded our faces and plucked at our hair. I stared out across the waves. Mrs Horton remained motionless.

'Ah!' she said finally.

I turned to her. Her arm reached across uncertainly, and she patted my hand. I wanted to ask her how she felt, but had to make do with a 'Yes / No' question. Yes, she nodded in response : she was beginning to feel better.

'That's a relief,' I said. 'Doreen had me worried when she told me what happened.'

'Heugh!' she replied, the rough syllable dripping with scorn.

Did she mean Doreen's version of events wasn't to be believed?

Mrs Horton cocked an eyebrow : 'What do you think?'

'Well, I don't know,' I said. 'I wasn't there, naturally.'

Mrs Horton breathed in deeply, then let out a sigh as her hands fell into her lap and her shoulders drooped. It would be complicated to explain and she couldn't begin to try just now.

The gutsy spirit glittered in her eyes but the frail flesh had still to recover.

But recover from what?

14

When I was young, people used to tell me they could read my face like a book. I would blush furiously on the slightest pretext, blink uncontrollably when people asked me questions, and had a compulsion to chew my lip when I felt flustered. None of these things bothers me any more.

I used to have a nervous stammer when I spoke. Nowadays that doesn't trouble me either.

Naturally it took a while to recover from my stroke and get used to people giving me funny looks on account of my face. But as time went by I found a sort of satisfaction in being able to deny everyone access to my thoughts and opinions. My face is my mask.

The tongue-tied girl might have been comforted by the fact that I am no longer expected to express myself at all.

There were moments when that girl would have welcomed a chance to hide behind the mask I wear all the time now, however grotesque.

Young Graham suffers from some of the inhibitions that used to plague me. Fortunately, he's learning to overcome them. I think he likes using me as a cover when he's called on to speak to other people. He told me the other day that he sometimes sees himself as my glove puppet : he can't be held accountable for what comes out of his mouth, and that helps him to speak unselfconsciously.

However, as we were about to drop off the van at Mr Witscombe's, he had to brace himself before telling me we needed to make a contribution for the petrol we had used. Fortunately I had some money in my purse and that settled that. But for future trips out, we'll need to make other arrangements.

Approaching the guest house, I touched his hand and pointed to the front bay window before putting my finger on my lips. He got the message and nodded : keep it simple and don't go into detail over what happened to me.

The sea breeze had cleared my head and sensation was returning to my arms and legs. I had done some speculating about events in the care home, but as ever I kept my own counsel while Graham wheeled me into the sitting room and heads turned to greet me. Geraldine Smith was particularly solicitous, I noticed ; she raised her eyebrows enquiringly and smiled at Graham. I couldn't help thinking she was positioning herself to be next in line if I should turn up my toes.

'My dear Mrs Horton how are you?' she asked, fully aware I was in no position to respond myself. I gave her a friendly little wave and tipped my eyes back over my shoulder at Graham who was standing behind me.

'She's much better thank you,' he said – a bit more uncertainly than I would have wished, I must admit. 'She was just a little ... tired after our outing.'

Ruth came in with afternoon tea, accompanied by Mrs Dugdale, eager to check that I was still in possession of all my faculties. Satisfied at what she saw, she exchanged glances with Graham and he murmured that he would have to leave me, as he was late for his shift.

So I found myself alone with my thoughts, though very much aware of all the questions that hung in the air as I surveyed the room. I nodded now and then in response to enquiring glances, but discouraged attempts to engage me in conversation. Geraldine surprised me again with a kindly expression, and an ingratiating smile meant to assure me that between us, explanations were not needed.

As far as I was concerned, explanations weren't easily forthcoming.

I had slept well at Faircroft, which at my age is rare. I was half-awake when a member of staff looked in on me during the night, but sank back into sleep almost immediately. So I was refreshed when a uniformed young woman came to help me get up and dress, before giving me breakfast and taking me through to the day room where I was to await Graham's return.

But in the meantime I was expecting someone else to reappear. The person they called 'Dom', whom I had been trying to communicate with when I passed out, was not among the dozen or so others in the room. I wheeled up alongside the two partially-sighted women I had struck up an acquaintance with, in the hope that we might resume the kind of half-conversation we had had yesterday.

It was Margaret who greeted my reappearance and told Janet I was back.

'Are you feeling better now dear?' Janet asked.

I croaked as reassuringly as I could manage.

Margaret spoke up. 'We all get funny turns from time to time, don't we?' She patted my hand, and I gave her fingers a squeeze.

'Naturally I didn't see what happened,' Janet said, 'but it did seem rather sudden.'

Margaret spoke up again. 'So far as I could tell, you were trying to speak to Dom,' she said. 'Is he someone you know?'

I managed an intonation I hoped would sound non-committal : Hmm, well...

'Poor man,' said Janet, eyes directed at the floor. 'He sits there, day after day, and barely makes a sound. I can only tell he's there when Sheila speaks to him by name.'

'He's not with us this morning,' said Margaret. 'When he has visitors, they prefer to meet with him in his room.'

I lifted my chin : oh, I see...

'Some people like privacy,' Janet chimed in.

Could the visitors be Hilda Woodrough and the man she called Thomas? They certainly wouldn't learn from 'Dom' that he'd been accosted yesterday... I imagined that my fainting fit might be the talk of the place, but on the other hand professional carers don't gossip about such matters – do they?

I dropped that line of thought because Sheila came in with a trolley, dispensing elevenses to those who wanted tea and biscuits. I helped her serve Margaret and Janet, placing their cups and saucers where they could reach them by touch, and then she handed me a drink for myself. The tea was sweeter than I like it, but I drank it down as best I could and I watched Sheila move on, manoeuvring around the room, pouring the brown liquid from a large metal pot and distributing biscuits which she took from a plastic box on the bottom shelf of her trolley. Some residents chose to add milk and sugar for themselves, but others were happy to let her do it ; she seemed to know each one's preferences. A clipboard on the end of the trolley had a list of what I took to be names, and she would consult it from time to time. On the lower shelf there was also an array of bottles and tubes from which she would take pills, evidently corresponding to prescriptions on the clipboard. Most of the residents were as accustomed to medication as they were to biscuits, and simply washed both down with the tea. Occasionally a man or woman seemed reluctant and Sheila would insist, placing a pill in their palm and murmuring to them until they agreed to swallow it, then standing by while they took a sip of tea. I became intrigued by the approach she took to the different residents, and found myself following her progress round the room.

One man in particular was very wary, and she made reassuring noises as she approached him. He sat back in his chair, pursed his lips, and turned his face away, like a child refusing food. Sheila was obviously used to him and pretended not to notice, busying herself with the milk jug ; but while he was arching away she slipped two pills into the cup before pouring in the tea. Then she added a teaspoonful of sugar, gave the drink a good stir, and held out the cup and saucer to demonstrate that he had nothing to fear ; eventually he took it from her, studied the contents for a moment, then gulped the tea down.

I pondered which category of 'patient' (as I began to consider these residents) the one they called 'Dom' fell into. He had been so listless and detached that I couldn't imagine him either resisting the medication – or taking it of his own accord. I had to assume Sheila practised her sleight of hand on him too.

In fact his unresponsive state must be the result of sedation. What could have happened to make that necessary?

And what about the visitors he was currently closeted with? What did they make of his condition? Did they drop by in the hope there would be some improvement – that a time would come when they could reduce or stop his medication so he might become himself again? I caught myself wondering what his old self would make of the sorry figure he cut at present...

That was when I sensed the first symptoms. My limbs had become heavy, and I found it hard to hold my cup and saucer steady. When they slipped from my hands and smashed on the floor, I knew. I tried to grab Margaret's hand, so she could see what was happening to me. I couldn't make my arm reach out, so I gurgled as best I could to catch her attention. I saw her turn towards me, her eyes searching for something to see. Then my head dropped and I could only look into my lap as my thoughts drained away and my mind closed down again.

So, I told myself as I contemplated the lounge of the guest house, I too had been sedated. Could it have been a mistake? I supposed it was possible that Sheila had confused me with one of the other residents at Faircroft. Could she have doctored the tea of a habitual recalcitrant and given it to me in error? My name wouldn't have been on her list of usual recipients.

Unless it had been added for some reason.

I was beyond having melodramatic reactions to the thoughts that this gave rise to. I was too old to get worked up over pure speculation. I could feel resentment at the thought that I might have been misused in some way, but I was accustomed to existing from day to day, not dwelling on either slights or triumphs. Events had demonstrated what happened when I let myself get agitated.

At the moment I was feeling OK.

So : considering things as calmly as I could, I reflected instead on what Graham had told me as I sat with him on the sea wall and struggled to gather my wits. I was following the motion of the waves, but I sensed he was observing me, watching for signs that the fog was lifting from my brain. He shifted his position and when he saw that I was able to swing round towards him he couldn't contain himself any longer.

'By the way,' he said suddenly, 'Mrs Woodrough phoned the guest house while you were at Faircroft.'

He was expecting a response, so I tried a pout. It's a risky manoeuvre since my lips don't sit together properly and tend to wrinkle up each in its own way, resulting in something more like a snarl.

'She wanted to know if they could come and visit you.'

I nodded to confirm that I had understood his words, and was considering their implications.

I wondered why they should be eager to see us again. Did they have so few acquaintances that they valued visits from strangers? Or was Hilda so taken with the idea of meeting a school pal from the old days that she wanted to continue catching up?

I recalled her self-assured manner. She had evidently led a charmed life since the days when we went to the same school. I had to remind myself that she didn't even know who I was. How could she be sure I'd have anything interesting to tell her about her past? Or that she wouldn't discover something she'd rather not be reminded of?

Ordinarily I would have explained her apparent eagerness as the sort of nostalgia that afflicts all old people. We would meet over a cup of tea and reminisce aimlessly even if we only had in common recollections of favourite songs or dances – or maybe teachers and mutual acquaintances.

But I had difficulty accepting that her motives were innocent. Hilda must have learned about the stranger who had visited Faircroft and been overcome at meeting 'Dom'. An elderly lady in a wheelchair accompanied by a young man. She would have had no trouble in identifying us.

I was prepared to bet that she had her own connection with the unfortunate man. I was convinced he was the 'cousin' she came to visit. And she may well have been the person he was closeted with when someone administered a sedative to me.

They wanted to come and visit me. To do that they'd need to know where I lived. And if I told them...

They would discover that I lived at the same address where Hughie had been staying.

Or would they?

I cast my mind back to the strange letter Hughie had sent to Mrs Dugdale, explaining his sudden disappearance in such a way that no one would come in search of him. And into which he had managed to slip a surreptitious note pointing me towards the place he was writing from.

Then I remembered the bizarre mistake he had made in writing the address on the envelope. Or had he? On reflection, it seemed likely he had deliberately sent it to Mrs Wormold's boarding-house, trusting that she would know to forward it to Mrs Dugdale. And he had thereby avoided revealing his true address to the Woodrough woman, though she (and her partner, presumably) had compelled him to write the letter in order to allay suspicion about his disappearance. This meant that so far as she knew, there was no connection between Hughie and me (and Graham) ; and if I told her our address that would be giving nothing away.

But she did have the phone number of Mrs Dugdale's establishment. We hadn't given it to her.

Graham had given the phone number to the Faircroft people, so they could contact him if my condition got worse.

Assuming Hilda had a particular connection with 'Dom', they may have felt duty bound to get in touch with her when 'Dom' was accosted by an unannounced visitor. The more so as the visitor promptly fainted in front of him. And it would have been natural for them to pass on the phone number we left there, in case Hilda wanted to check on us herself.

Graham said she had phoned the guest house while I was still at Faircroft. Doreen had presumably got in touch with her as soon as Graham left.

But Graham also said she had phoned to speak to me, as if she didn't know I was actually at Faircroft. But she couldn't have got the phone number without being aware that I was there as she dialled it.

So why had she placed that call, in full knowledge that I wasn't at home to take it?

15

I made my way to Mrs Horton's room, where she had taken to spending the mornings. She had more or less recovered from her bad turn, but found that she still needed a nap after breakfast. So our new routine consisted of me gently rousing her at eleven with tea and biscuits on a tray. I had finished reading the latest entry in her journal, and took the opportunity to return it to her.

I knocked and entered, to find Mrs Horton sitting in her low armchair by the window. It faced onto the side street, though from where she sat she had a view of the sea and sky. I put the tray down on a table beside her, and handed her the journal. She nodded by way of thanks: then arched an eyebrow at me, clearly waiting for my opinion on Mrs Woodrough's phone call. I could only shrug. Her speculations had left me puzzled. The call hadn't struck me as out of the ordinary ; perhaps I was just too slow-witted to appreciate that it might seem odd. But if Mrs Woodrough did call Mrs Horton while Mrs Horton was at Faircroft, and Mrs Woodrough could only have got the number from the people at Faircroft, it *was* odd that she didn't know the person she was trying to reach was actually at Faircroft as she dialled.

Unless she had wanted to create the impression she didn't know Mrs Horton was at Faircroft.

I blurted out this thought as soon as it occurred to me. And then something else struck me.

'Where was she phoning from?' I wondered out loud.

Mrs Horton gave one of her 'Humph!' sounds.

Then she reached over to a small desk across from her armchair, pulled open a drawer, and lifted out some sheets of paper which she handed to me. They were covered with the familiar handwriting. I imagined she had written on these loose leaves while I was reading the latest chapter of her journal. In fact, as I contemplated them I realised they were the same format, ruled with the same lines, as the pages in the journal I had just given back. She must have torn them from it before she left it to me to read. She must have done so very carefully, since I hadn't noticed any traces.

I glanced down at these sheets, and then up at Mrs Horton. She made a gesture which I took to mean I should read them. I murmured 'OK', and prepared to fold them so I could slip them into my pocket. Mrs Horton made a series of urgent squawking sounds to stop me, and gestured at the pages again with both hands, palms upwards, pushing at me.

'You mean I should read them here, right now?'

She nodded.

I gave a sigh and pointed to my watch. I had work to do.

Mrs Horton looked deflated. She was obviously impatient for me to read what she had written.

'If I could take them away…' I said.

'Mm-mm-mm-mm,' she replied sharply, and shook her head.

I thought for a moment.

'Tell you what,' I said, 'I finish my shift after lunch. I could visit you then and read these.'

Mrs Horton took a deep breath and let it out resignedly. She pursed her lips and nodded her head.

'OK,' I said, handing back the manuscripts as I rose to go about my business. 'I'll see you later.'

*

When the guests had finished lunch and my shift ended, Mrs Horton and I both retired to her room. I hoped no one else noticed us leave together ; it felt odd.

I helped Mrs Horton into her armchair and while she took the manuscript out of the drawer once again, I sat down on a straight-backed chair. She obviously wasn't happy with the positioning of the chair : she gestured to me to move closer, and to put my chair opposite her so that we were face to face. Then she handed me the papers.

At this point I realised she was going to watch me as I read what she had written.

She must have been waiting for my predictable reaction when I read the opening words:

'Tom Beaumont and I were childhood sweethearts.'

The manuscript went on to describe their childhood together. Their families were close ; she was friendly with Thomas's sister. Her father was a dentist, Thomas's father was a solicitor ; they moved in the same circles. The two young people attended the same primary school. They had other friends of both sexes, but they were known to be inseparable even as infants. They played together in each other's house and garden and in the nearby woods and fields. When they reached secondary school age Thomas went to a nearby grammar school while Marion won a scholarship to Greenhalgh Girls' High. But their social life continued in the same way. They could be seen together at the local recreation centre, they joined in dances at the village hall, were part of the choral society, attended chapel together. They played tennis in mixed doubles, took part in ramblers outings, went on cycle rides and picnicked in the open countryside.

Though an athlete and a sportsman, Thomas wasn't a boisterous young man. He had the self-assurance of an accomplished male at ease with his physical prowess, but belligerence was not in his nature. In the heat of the moment, when others would be excited or provoked during a football match, for example, he had the ability to remain calm and self-possessed. He tended to avoid rough and tumble and horseplay, the crude after-effects of adrenalin-fuelled exertion, and would smile as he declined invitations to join with 'the boys' in riotous post-match rituals.

To Marion none of this was exceptional. She was accustomed to his tranquil steadfast temperament ; she loved him without question for what he was, without asking herself what bound them together, what set him apart from the other young men who might have caught her eye. They had always been comfortable together ; and would continue to be so.

One day when they were sitting on their favourite bench by the sea-wall, looking out over the bay, Thomas asked Marion if she would marry him, and they agreed to become engaged. They had no reason to envisage a future where they would not be united, companions and spouses. They were both eighteen years old, at the point when Thomas entered Medical School to train as a doctor. Marion stayed behind, considering the possibility of becoming a primary school teacher before becoming a mother, but content in the meantime to occupy herself with housework in the family home, providing a helping hand to her mother. Thomas would return at weekends, and during the holidays their life would resume its habitual path, except when Thomas was posted to work placements in neighbouring towns, then appointed as a junior in a number of local hospitals.

All of this struck me as unremarkable, if a little old-fashioned. I turned the page, coughed to clear my throat, and I glanced up to see Mrs Horton's eyes lost in smile-lines as she watched me intently.

This placid existence and prospects of a serene future remained untroubled through to Thomas's final year at Medical School.

One afternoon Marion was out in the garden, dead-heading roses, when she heard someone passing in the lane behind the house. A face appeared above the gate.

'Excuse me, I'm looking for Foxglove Cottage. I understand it's around here.'

The face was tanned and sculpted ; muscles rippled along his jaw as he spoke. The cheek bones cast shadows down to the lips. The eyes too were in shadow, but gleamed with reflected light from the garden.

Marion was quick with her reply.

'Yes, it's the third house down the lane from here. Just a hundred yards along.'

'Thank you,' he said. He was not local. He spoke with an accent she did not recognize.

'Are you looking for someone in particular?' she asked.

'No, not really,' he replied. 'I've been called to do a job there.'

His teeth glinted.

He was the kind of person you would want to be nice to, *wrote Marion*.

I glanced up. She was watching me carefully, expectantly.

He was a surveyor. He had recently set up a practice in the village, and had been asked to carry out an inspection of a neighbour's house. He went on his way, and she watched him as he headed off to his appointment. Then she finished dealing with the roses, and returned to the kitchen.

Not long afterwards, gazing out through the window as she stood at the kitchen sink, she saw that he was at the gate again. He waved to catch her attention, and she dried her hands and went out to see what he wanted.

She had taken off her engagement ring while she rinsed the pots, *she wrote*.

'Sorry to bother you,' he said, 'but there's no one in. I'm not sure what to do. I've completed an external inspection and I've left a message in writing, but could you tell them I'm sorry I missed them?'

Marion explained that the neighbour often popped out to the greengrocer's after lunch, and she would probably be back soon.

'Oh well then, I think I'll go back and wait. It'll save arranging another appointment.'

'Would you like a cup of tea?' Marion found herself saying.

'That's very kind of you,' he replied.

So they sat together on a bench in the garden and sipped tea. He asked her about herself and she told him her name but found there was little else to tell that would be of interest to him. He told her he was called Joshua, was from Devon, and had moved into the area a few months previously. He asked her what he needed to know about the region, how he could become a part of the community – he needed to make contacts for his business. He wore his hair long and brushed it from his brow as he spoke. With hindsight, Marion wrote, she would describe him as 'raffish'. But she didn't know the word then. In the space of a few minutes she came to realise there were many things she did not know, and most of them centred on this man. He had the kind of charm she had not encountered before.

By the time the neighbour came down the lane, saw them over the gate and interrupted their conversation, an attraction had already grown up between them. When Joshua took his leave and followed his client down the lane, both he and Marion understood they would see each other again.

When Thomas returned from his latest stint as a junior hospital doctor, Marion found he was like a stranger to her. Or rather, *she wrote*, she realised she was a stranger to him. Joshua had made her aware of things in her nature which Thomas had never awakened – or even suspected.

I wasn't the most worldly of people myself, but I couldn't help noticing, as I read Mrs Horton's story, how her language became quaint, prim and proper when she tried to describe the effect Joshua had on her. He was a different kind of man from the clean-living fiancé she had naïvely committed to sharing her life with. She had known there were other men – hobos and tramps, itinerant labourers and beggars – but they lived in the margins of her awareness and she had paid them no mind. Now she sensed in Joshua something of their wayward manhood that stirred dormant instincts in herself.

She didn't go into details, but even I could understand what she was getting at when she wrote: 'I was seduced.'

It took her a while to find a way of breaking the news to Thomas. He stared at her uncomprehendingly when she told him she had 'met another man'. She met other men all the time, he stammered. No, she replied, this time it is something different.

Her written account passed over the subsequent details, except to say that she and Joshua were married within the year. They were shunned by most of her friends, and her parents were very cold towards the couple. Marion and Joshua left the area and set up home in a town some distance away. They were very happy, apart from the fact that a first child – a boy – miscarried.

And then the outbreak of war took Joshua away, never to return.

This brutal sentence stopped me in my tracks. Knowing that Mrs Horton was watching my every reaction I didn't dare raise my eyes, so I read it a second time. Then I steeled myself to look Mrs Horton in the face. Her disfigured features suddenly seemed the image of desolation. In that moment I knew that even before she had lost the power of speech she would never have been able to tell this story to anyone, least of all to someone like me. And for my part I could only feel relief to have been spared the ordeal and embarrassment of listening and watching her voice the intimate details.

The habit of writing had enabled her to overcome such inhibitions ; and the written version allowed me to relive her story in a sort of privacy. Without direct eye contact, frank admissions could be offered and received less awkwardly.

That said, I was conscious she had been monitoring my responses closely. All the same I wasn't sure it would be appropriate to say anything. I stared at her with wide-open eyes, and she nodded gently.

I couldn't help myself. I said, 'You mean in the space of a couple of years you lost two men you... loved, *and* a baby?'

Her paralysed face was like a mask of tragedy. She was a player marked by irreversible calamity.

I flinched from the pain in her eyes. I looked down and continued reading. There was one final paragraph.

Thomas, heartbroken, did not lack admirers. He had long been considered the most handsome man in the area, and eligible young women began to circle as soon as they heard the news that Marion had jilted him. One of these was Hilda Woodrough, who for years had envied Marion's relationship with Thomas. At school she had led a spiteful group of girls who gossiped and giggled behind their hands and teased Marion, saying they didn't know what Thomas saw in her – all the while spreading rumours about other young men she had supposed dealings with, long before Joshua came on the scene. Now Hilda applied her wiles directly to Thomas, pointing to Marion's infidelity as confirmation of the rumours. She was herself undoubtedly beautiful and attractive, and he turned to her for comfort in his grief at the loss of his sweetheart. Barely six months after the marriage between Marion and Joshua, Thomas married Hilda – on the rebound, wrote Marion in conclusion.

I ended my reading and let the papers fall into my lap.

'And this... Thomas Beaumont is the man we saw at Quainton Lodge?' I asked.

Marion didn't offer an answer. Instead, she held out her hands, and beckoned impatiently with her fingers, as if she finally regretted having let me see what she had written. Dutifully, I gathered up the papers and gave them back to her.

She shuffled them together. Then she grasped the top edge of the thin sheaf, tore it into two, put the halves together and tore them across. I made a sound by way of objecting, as she tried to repeat the operation ; her gnarled hands hadn't the strength. The clump of torn pieces just twisted in her fingers. Finally she offered them to me and I ripped them up once, twice more. Then she held out a waste paper bin and I dropped the tattered fragments into it.

16

So now the cat is out of the bag...

I could see that Graham was taken by surprise. I felt a little guilty about forcing him to share my secrets like that. Over the decades since Joshua's death I had never confided in anyone. The fact is that though brief, our married life had been enough to make me regret Tom's qualities. Josh was mercurial, given to mood swings. I was taken aback by his sudden, fierce impulses and I found it hard to deal with the darker elements in his nature. Meanwhile I had become a pariah to those I had been close to previously, so there was no one I could turn to for help or advice as a young wife adjusting to marriage with a man I still had much to learn about.

Our marriage might have lasted, after all. But I had to admit to myself that the first rush of grief was soon followed by a certain consoling relief. I had been spared what might have been a lifelong struggle to keep us together... – and who could say whether Josh would have been faithful to me? In all likelihood that cocksure character of his that had swept me off my feet would never have been content with my mousey temperament. So on balance, learning to live with Josh might have proved more difficult than learning to live without him.

There were other consolations, of sorts. As a war widow I had a certain status as well as a small pension, and by returning to my parents' home and duly acting out my bereavement I regained some sympathy and respect in the community. It was as if the tragedy that had befallen me mitigated the shame and scandal attached to me since my betrayal of Tom.

None of this helped me reconcile myself to having lost Tom. Indeed, in some quarters I was subtly made to feel I deserved my misfortune for wounding him so deeply. There were those who claimed they could still read the hurt in his eyes, even though on the face of it he had made a 'good' marriage. Of course our two newly-wed couples had gone separate ways, and by the time I was widowed my part in his life was over and done. Now and again, though, a mutual acquaintance would let fall some details of their married existence. Apparently, flighty Hilda Woodrough was proving to be a wayward spouse too. Among the many things that Tom and I had had in common, it seemed we shared a weakness for lovers we were unsuited to. I have to admit that as rumours of his predicament accumulated my feelings were mixed. There was no question of him coming back to me – though there were moments when I let myself speculate on that possibility. But on the other hand the humiliations he was apparently putting up with in his marriage made *him seem pitiable, and I confess that diminished him in my eyes.*

As a newly-qualified doctor, Tom was eligible for 'reserved occupation' status and exempted from military conscription. But one day, about a year after Joshua's death, I learned that Tom had volunteered for service as a Medical Officer on the Western Front. I couldn't help but imagine this was his way of escaping from a difficult marriage.

The villagers also made what they could of the news, and so far as I could judge they reached the same conclusion as I had done. Hilda – Mrs Beaumont – had driven her husband to risk death on the battlefield rather than endure marital life with her.

Hilda reacted by letting it be known how proud she was of her husband's heroism. Her behaviour apparently changed overnight. She took to visiting the shops more frequently than she had been accustomed to, eager to exchange the latest news with other wives who were running households on their own. Her demeanour invited their sympathy rather than scorn. She informed them that her husband was currently serving at a Regimental aid post located near the front. She declined to say what manner of casualties he was having to deal with, explaining merely that his duties involved organizing clearing stations from where wounded soldiers were transported on stretchers to a field hospital some way behind the lines. Commiserating with those who had actually lost their menfolk to the fighting, she proposed the creation of a voluntary organisation to support women 'on the Home Front', as she liked to put it. Her reputation as a wayward wife or a domestic shrew melted away as she became a pillar of the local female community.

Then came the news that her husband had been reported 'Missing in Action'. He had last been seen under heavy artillery fire while attempting to treat soldiers wounded in the field.

No further information materialised. Hilda resigned herself to a long period of uncertainty, and kept her spirits up by redoubling her work with the voluntary group. She was to be seen organising collections for food parcels and medical supplies for the war effort, and rallied her fellow widows and wives with spirited lectures on the theme of 'they also serve who only stand and wait.' Meanwhile I experienced a personal bereavement more acute and complicated than when Josh died. I had lost Tom for a second time, and ached again with regret for my own folly. On the other hand, now he was lost I felt I had a prior claim to mourn him since Hilda had treated him so badly. I relived my memories of Tom in sleepless nights and painful grey dawns. It seemed to me that she was play-acting as a war-widow; the real grief was mine.

I was being unfair, obviously. It soon became clear that Hilda was stricken. Her activities in the community began to flag, and then she stopped attending public gatherings. There were reports that her health was failing, that she was suffering from melancholia. Apparently she had shut herself away and was spending her time writing letters to the Ministry of War, the Royal Army Medical Corps, the regimental commanders and medical officers who had reported the last sightings of Tom.

Weeks went by and eventually Hilda appeared in public again – wearing the uniform of a Red Cross Nurse. The news from France was bad :

fighting had intensified, the Germans were using poison gas, the numbers of casualties were overwhelming and military hospitals had sent out requests for special assistance from volunteer nurses. Hilda had made up her mind to answer the call. She had completed training and enrolled for 'special service' in a so-called Voluntary Aid Detachment which had been assigned to a casualty clearing station close to the front line in Picardy. She let it be known that it was her way of getting close to Tom.

That was the last I heard of her. Her parents had taken refuge in Scotland and she had no family to write to in Cottsea, so that once she had left for France, there was no way news of her could percolate back to the village. I concluded that she had gone out to drown her sorrow in the mud of the battlefields. Perhaps she had ended her days there ; later I was to read stories of VADS and other medical auxiliaries who had died of typhus caught from soldiers they were treating, or septic poisoning due to contact with infected wounds.

That chapter of my own life ended there. I moved away from Cottsea, took up a post as a Primary School teacher in the Midlands, and put all this behind me. The war preoccupied the country for two more years and then life returned to normal. I got used to teaching other people's children while having none of my own. I was a single woman among many during the post-war years, contented myself with having a career, and grew to enjoy my independence.

If it hadn't been for my stroke, I would probably never have seen the seaside village again.

It happened one day in the classroom. I was leaning over a pupil's desk, examining her work and offering encouragement, and as I stood upright I began to feel light-headed. Then I blacked out.

When I came to I was in a hospital bed, unable to move my left arm and leg and with no feeling in my face. The doctors made it clear that my working days were over – and I began to fear my independence was at an end too. Fortunately I was referred to a specialist unit which had been formed towards the end of the war, to deal with the upsurge in patients suffering from neurological disorders. The consultants were not the type to give up on cases like mine. With sympathetic treatment and supportive doctors I began to feel I could still have a life of sorts. It would not be easy, but fortunately I had built up a financial nest-egg during my working years. And my mother, who had stayed in the family home after the death of my father, was eager to take me in and help me recover as best I could. We tacitly agreed that I would be likely to die before she did, from a further stroke, and that I would never be left to fend for myself. The prognosis was not promising, but we were lucky enough to have the resources that provided for my needs and eased the burden on my mother.

When I came home after my stroke, at first I hardly dared look at myself in the mirror. I saw a deformed face that on one side hung down like a wet flannel. There was no feeling in the skin of my cheek ; my lips were numb and didn't respond to my attempts to move them. I struggled to will my features into shape, but the only force that would work on them was gravity. They fell and stayed fallen. The best I could manage was to have them sway or swing a little this way and that when I moved my head. Eventually I found I could shift my lips a little, and blink and wrinkle the skin around my eyes. I sat there in front of my mirror for hours on end and by dint of practice, gradually managed to compose a limited repertoire of facial expressions – lop-sided tremors and palsied twitches – that I hoped might serve to communicate some meaning. However, though my face drooped more or less permanently, from time to time an involuntary spasm would take hold, creating an unpredictable smile I couldn't control : I would find myself beaming without reason, often while nodding as someone commiserated with my misfortune or spoke earnestly about a serious matter. My face hid my own embarrassment but the confusion of others was painfully apparent. It even put some people off talking to me at all ; and made me nervous of going out whenever my mother or one of our helpers offered to wheel me to the park, for instance. I became increasingly uncomfortable at the prospect of being a speechless gurning witness to conversations about me between passers-by and whoever was pushing me along.

To my (and her) surprise, my mother pre-deceased me, leaving me by myself in a fairly large house I could not negotiate alone. My mother and I had had few friends, content with our own company, and now the district nurse became my sole visitor. She tried to persuade me to move into a care home, but the prospect of sitting in a room full of people like me did not appeal at all. Though my own social skills were now non-existent, I thought I would find it more agreeable to watch others interact even if I couldn't take part. And so after a brief interview with Mrs Dugdale, who accepted the nurse's reassurances as to my self-reliance, I was able to install myself in the guest house, paying my rent from the sale of the family home. The other guests quickly grew accustomed to my gormless smirk in response to their greetings, and we all got on perfectly well – with the possible exception of Mrs Geraldine Smith. But even she, latterly, seems to have mellowed and accepted my idiosyncrasies. I suspect her motives, but that is another matter.

And that brings me back to the present. I let myself stray into more autobiography in the event that Graham should ever show an interest in my past ; but I expect that in the end I'll tear up this sequel to the previous pages that I am now mortified to think I let him read... whatever made me imagine they might hold any interest for him? Whatever could have possessed me?

Who am I kidding? This sudden outpouring is prompted by that encounter with 'Dom'... which I have to admit has shaken me. Could it really be true that he is Tom? In the heat of the moment I felt convinced, but after two woozy turns, I begin to have doubts. I need to see him again if I am to be sure. But that will be difficult : I won't be welcome at the care home.

However, it does seem likely that if we are ever to get to the bottom of Hughie Storth's disappearance, further visits to my own past may be in order.

Meanwhile, we need to prepare for our next encounter with Hilda Beaumont and her supposed husband. She phoned again, and invited us out for a ride. I think I can justify insisting on being accompanied by Graham, but I shall have to school him in what to say – and what to avoid saying.

I have to assume they know I was at Faircroft. It seems reasonable to suppose that Sheila noticed my interest in 'Dom' and Doreen alerted them to the strange visitor who accosted him. To judge by the fact that Sheila drugged me (assuming that to be the case), she takes instructions from them. They might well have been there behind the scenes at the time, directing her to deal with me. Perhaps they wanted to put me out of action, and hoped that at my age, in my poor state of health, it wouldn't take much to do so permanently.

All this because I showed an interest in 'Dom'. That's what they wanted to put a stop to. Why?

I have agreed to let them take me out for a drive to who knows where. I have decided to play the unsuspecting victim. I can reinforce that impression by putting on the act of a helpless invalid. That might persuade them that they have nothing to fear from me, and they may drop their guard.

But I'm aware that I'm putting myself at their mercy, with only Graham to defend me.

17

Mrs Smith had warned me about getting *drawn in,* as she put it, to whatever past Mrs Horton seemed to have stirred up. Mrs Horton's journal made it clear there was something mysterious, and maybe sinister, about Mrs Beaumont. So as I braced myself for an excursion with two of the old ladies, I didn't know who – or what – to be most wary of. And with the enigmatic Mr Beaumont at the wheel there was no telling where we might find ourselves.

Mrs Horton was cautious enough, that much was certain. She made it plain I should be careful about what I said. If in doubt, she scribbled on a piece of paper, tell them you don't know and look towards me. Given what someone had tried to do to Mrs Horton – if she could be believed – she hardly needed to forewarn me about the dangers of loose talk. Up to a point I was well-rehearsed, but what worried me most was that I hadn't much of a clue as to what was going on. This drama – if that's what it was – went back to a remote era before I was even born.

However that may be, Mrs Horton and I both knew that in getting into their car we had little prospect of escape if their intentions turned out to be hostile. Mrs

Horton could hardly run away, and I couldn't just up and leave her if matters turned nasty. Could I...?

On the day we had agreed over the phone, I arranged to take the afternoon off. I had cleared away the lunch service and done my share of washing-up when the doorbell rang. Though I knew it would be for us, I hung back and let Mrs Dugdale answer. Into the hall came Mrs Beaumont, wearing a camel-hair coat and high-heeled shoes, her hair freshly permed. She exuded expansive cordiality and I could tell from the posh accent Mrs Dugdale put on that she was flattered to receive a visit from someone of her standing.

'Mrs Horton will be with you shortly,' she grovelled. 'Would you care to sit down in the parlour?'

Mrs Beaumont demurred, saying she was expected and would wait in the hall. I put my head around the door and Mrs Dugdale virtually bowed as she took her leave. I explained that Mrs Horton would be along in a moment, then went to bring the old lady out to join her visitor.

Mrs Horton had made an effort to spruce herself up. She had on her best tweed coat over a bright yellow cardigan, and she had even put powder on her face. She walked into the hall on my arm and steadied herself on the dado rail, nodding as Mrs Beaumont greeted her while I went to bring out her wheel-chair. We had agreed that I would help her walk down the steps and she would make her way to the car on foot. She insisted also that I must put the wheelchair into the car before helping her get in ; that way there was no chance of her being driven off leaving me behind on the pavement fiddling with the wheel-chair. I thought she was being overly mistrustful, but had second thoughts when Mrs Beaumont explained that the car was round the corner – out of sight of the guest-house, I noted – as parking on this part of the promenade was not allowed.

I carried the wheelchair out to the pavement but before I could go back to help Mrs Horton, Mrs Beaumont had offered her arm and the two elderly ladies came down the steps and shuffled along the pavement together. We turned the corner to see a dark-blue station wagon parked at the kerb. Mr Beaumont – if that was his proper title, which by now I was unsure of – sat at the wheel. Seeing us approach, he jumped out and offered to help Mrs Horton into the rear passenger seat. This was my cue.

'Mrs Horton likes to see the wheelchair properly packed away,' I said. 'It's a bit complicated, and she's very particular about how it's done. Can we see to that first?'

I thought I saw Mr Beaumont exchange a brief glance with his wife before he passed behind the car and opened the tailgate. Mrs Beaumont stood tight-lipped beside Mrs Horton and watched us load the wheelchair.

Then there was more hesitation as to who would sit where. I explained that I should take a back seat alongside Mrs Horton so that I could help her communicate. Mrs Beaumont looked disappointed. I said, 'It helps if I can see her lips move.' Mrs Horton nodded.

So in we got, and pulling away from the kerb, turned onto the promenade to head out of the village. As we passed in front of the guest-house, I noticed Mrs Smith, in her green twin-set, standing in the bay-window watching us. She caught my eye and saluted with her cigarette-holder. The gesture seemed ironic. All the same, feeling slightly apprehensive as to what would happen next, I found it comforting to know that she had seen us leave.

'Now then,' said Mrs Beaumont over her shoulder, 'we thought it might be nice to take a little ride along the coast road, and perhaps stop for tea at a pretty little spot we know.'

Mrs Horton volunteered a grunt of approval and I felt I should voice agreement while being seen to translate. 'That sounds very nice,' I said.

Leaving the village behind we headed inland for a while, then took a road that wound between fields and hedgerows, briefly followed a meander of the river Lyre, and eventually led us back to a stretch of coast further round the bay. Here the incoming sea sometimes covered the road at high tide, and I caught myself wondering if this was a week when cars ran the risk of becoming marooned on the low-lying lanes.

'Do you know this part of the area?' Hilda Beaumont asked, turning in her seat. Mrs Horton stared out of the window, pursed her lips, and nodded. *A little.*

'It's been some time since she was able to go sightseeing,' I volunteered, and added, 'she's enjoying this trip.'

'So your visit to Quainton Grange was a rare exception?' asked Hilda innocently.

I felt Mrs Horton's elbow in my ribs. *Beware of careless talk.*

'Oh, erm, it was my idea,' I said.

'Ah,' said Hilda, and lapsed into silence. I got the impression that for the time being she didn't feel the need to pursue the subject. Not with me, at least. Mr Beaumont remained as taciturn as ever, his posture as stiff as his bristling hair while he coaxed the car along the narrow roads.

After a while though, the silence became oppressive and Mrs Beaumont, evidently accustomed to making conversation, tried to lighten the atmosphere with occasional remarks about the sites we passed on our way : here a windmill that dated back to medieval times, there an old coaching-inn, and up a lane to our right a manor house that was mentioned in the Doomsday Book…

Mrs Horton would respond with an 'Ooo' sound, drawing it out and modulating it to show how interesting she found Mrs Beaumont's comments. For my part, I had ridden bits of this route on my bike when I was a schoolboy, and had never found anything of note in the flat terrain with its distant horizon and occasional clumps of trees.

So when Mrs Beaumont finally said, 'We're nearly there now,' all I knew for certain was that she was taking us to a place some way off any route I was familiar with.

'Do you know Gleeson Creek?' Mrs Beaumont asked.

'Hu-uh,' went Mrs Horton, over my reply : 'I don't think so.'

'Very pretty,' said Mrs Beaumont. 'Away from the beaten track... peaceful and secluded.'

The narrow lane ahead of us was like a tunnel beneath the foliage of the trees growing up on either side of it. But as we drove into the shade, we began to see an opening up ahead, beyond which masts and rigging were visible. Back in the sunshine, I caught a glimpse of the sea in the distance ; but directly in front of us was a narrow inlet which curled in from the bay and provided sheltered moorings for a handful of sailing boats. Most were drawn up on muddy sand banks, since the sea was at low water ; it was only possible to set sail at high tide, evidently.

Mr Beaumont steered us along the narrow quayside past bollards, coils of rope, nets and flotation buoys. We drove by a row of cottages overlooking the creek and the mud flats beyond. Above the door of one of these cottages was a sign indicating that there was a tearoom inside. Just past it, Mr Beaumont drew into a patch of parking space. Bleak calls of curlews greeted us as we got out of the car, while seagulls circled and squawked overhead.

Inside the café, globes of coloured glass dangled from netting suspended across the ceiling. Stuffed seabirds and fish perched or floated in display cases. On a corner shelf stood a storm lantern on a brass base. A barometer and framed navigation charts filled the walls. Arrangements of seashells, pebbles and artificial flowers occupied the window ledges.

We took a table in a quiet corner, alongside a cartoonish mural of an undersea scene with grinning fish and barnacled rocks draped in technicolour seaweed. A partition of webbing featuring sailors' knots curtained us from the half-dozen other tables in the room. The waitress smiled patiently while we manoeuvred Mrs Horton's wheelchair into position at the head of the table and took our places on banquettes around the other three sides.

'Cream tea for four,' said Mrs Beaumont in a tone that brooked no opposition. The waitress wrote down the order and moved away to the counter. Mrs Beaumont inspected the table-top for traces of previous customers, and satisfied there were no left-over crumbs, placed her hands palm-down on the formica, leaned across to Mrs Horton, and said : 'Now we can continue our conversation. Catch up on old times.'

Mrs Horton murmured and nodded.

'Ellen Keighley. I can't believe we were at the same school, at the same time, and I have no recollection.'

Mrs Horton nudged me and made sounds I was primed to interpret. 'At that age, a small difference in age meant being in a different year group and that can keep pupils separate,' I volunteered. Then I allowed myself to improvise on my own account : 'I hardly knew anyone in the year below me.'

Glancing at Mrs Horton I could tell she approved.

'Hmm, that's true,' Mrs Beaumont conceded. Then after a pause : 'And you say she volunteered as a nurse in the Great War.'

'That was the last my aunt heard of her,' I said.

'She may have been a VAD,' she said.

I eyed Mrs Horton. I remembered that Mrs Beaumont herself had joined the Volunteer Aid Detachment – supposedly to console herself for the loss of her husband... A certain Mr Beaumont, who was supposedly sitting with us just now...

Except that it wasn't him.

I was tongue-tied by this turn in the conversation. And I could tell that Mrs Horton hadn't anticipated it either. Why would Mrs Beaumont mention this detail that had a special significance for her while neither of us might be expected to understand the reference?

Unless she was testing us for a reaction. Our invented school-friend seemed to have triggered something. A thought occurred to me : was it possible that 'Ellen Keighley' held up a mirror to her own career as a nursing auxiliary on the Western Front? Was Mrs Beaumont angling for more reminders of her past?

Mercifully the waitress provided a diversion by bringing our order on a tray. It took her a few moments to lay everything out and by the time Mrs Beaumont was pouring tea the awkward silence was behind us.

Mrs Horton was going to have trouble with her scone. To spare her embarrassment I took her plate and prepared it for her : jam first, cream on top.

'I see you have Graham properly trained,' said Mrs Beaumont with a smile.

Mrs Horton managed a little pout, then put one hand in front of her mouth to hide the messy way she was obliged to eat.

A look of concern crossed Mrs Beaumont's face. 'I'm so sorry, how thoughtless of me,' she said.

Having managed to push a crumbling portion into her mouth and smoothed away the traces of cream on her lips, Mrs Horton nodded contentedly as she chewed.

'Oh, it's all right,' I said. 'Aunt Marion enjoys scones.'

Mr Beaumont was concentrating on his scone. I noticed he applied cream first, then jam on top.

'I was taught to do it the other way round,' I said, attempting a light-hearted remark. 'Perhaps you're a Cornishman, used to having clotted cream on the bottom?'

Mr Beaumont's knife slipped from his fingers and clattered on his plate. He was flustered.

'Sorry, I didn't mean to be rude,' I said.

He quickly recovered his composure.

'Not at all, I was chust doing what came naturallee,' he said, and smiled.

Definitely a foreign accent. I was sure of that now.

'That's Thomas's contrary streak again,' said Mrs Beaumont. 'Always has his own way of doing things.'

I smiled, but when I glanced at Mrs Horton she was staring at the man. She may have lost the power of speech for herself, but she was evidently an acute observer of the way others exercised it. And I could tell that she was keen to hear him talk again.

Without warning she addressed – or rather, barked – a flow of incoherent sounds in his direction.

It was obvious that she was questioning him, but it came as a surprise to all of us. And the vehemence with which she spat out her unintelligible phrases left him bewildered. He gasped slightly, on the defensive, lost for words. Even I couldn't make out what she was saying, so I wouldn't have known how to respond either. Mr

Beaumont looked at Hilda, panic in his eyes. His mouth hung half-open but still he was silent. And then all at once, under his breath but audibly, he let slip a brief burst of speech. I put it like that because although he was saying something, he was not making sense – at least not to me.

Mr Beaumont fell silent again, evidently embarrassed by his lapse. I wondered for a moment whether Mrs Horton understood what he had said. I glanced at her and caught a brief nod of her head, but whether it was for me or herself I couldn't tell, nor what she meant by it.

Hilda stiffened visibly, before forcing herself to relax. With a drawn smile on her face, she gave a nervous giggle and spoke up in the silence.

'Well, Marion, you certainly caught him off-balance there...' She turned to me. 'What exactly does your aunt want to know, do you think?'

She was speaking through pinched lips, and I felt the sting of her irritation as she addressed me.

I shifted in my seat.

'I don't really know,' I replied. And on the spur of the moment, I allowed myself an attempt at improvisation. 'She sometimes has these involuntary outbursts. It's a feature of her condition.'

Mrs Beaumont paused as if to weigh my words.

Eventually, looking askance at Mrs Horton, whose face was as inexpressive as usual, she said, 'So I don't suppose we'll ever know what she meant – or if she meant anything'. For a moment Mrs Beaumont slipped into assuming that on account of her disability Mrs Horton couldn't hear or understand what was being said.

For my part, I couldn't see why the lady might be irritated, if that's what she was. She evidently didn't like her husband to express himself as he had ; and she resented Mrs Horton for having provoked him into doing so. As for 'Thomas', he was looking abashed as Hilda took her feelings out on me. She noticed this, and seemed to take pity on him. She reached out and patted his hand.

'Whan caught off-guard he does sometimes revert to the language he was… brought up in,' she explained.

It had been obvious to me that Mr Beaumont had a foreign accent, so when he slipped into this other language, that didn't tell us anything we didn't suspect already. Except that those of us – me at any rate – who didn't know any foreign languages were left wondering exactly what it was he had spoken in.

I forced a smile in my turn.

'And there can't be many situations more unsettling than taking a broadside from Aunt Marion,' I said. 'But I'm sure she meant no harm,' I added quickly. 'Sometimes she can't keep it bottled up when she feels the urge to join in a conversation.'

I turned my smile to Mrs Horton, who let me get away with it.

18

I came down early for the morning shift, and was laying the breakfast tables when I heard shuffling feet on the stairs and Mrs Smith appeared, heading for the kitchen and her pot of tea with the top of the milk. Normally I avoid looking at her since I'm not sure she's comfortable being seen in her dressing gown, without make-up and with her hair down. To be honest I don't find the spectacle particularly appealing myself. But she reached the bottom of the stairs and turned into the hallway just as I was coming the other way with a tray full of crockery. She stood with her back to the wall to let me by and as I passed in front of her I heard her say softly, and without the usual rasp in her voice, 'Good morning, Graham.' I nodded and murmured in reply, glad that I had the tray to focus on.

When I returned to the kitchen a few minutes later, she was setting out her breakfast tray while she waited for the kettle to boil. Steadying her cigarette-holder between clenched teeth, she prised the foil cap off the milk-bottle and decanted the cream into her jug, making little grunts of satisfaction as she did so. I tried not to catch her eye as I busied myself with cruets and cutlery but I began to feel her staring at me. Eventually she took her cigarette-holder from her mouth and said sweetly, 'Did you and Mrs Horton have a pleasant outing yesterday...?'

'Yes,' I said. 'It was... –'

'I'm so glad,' she replied. 'It's nice to see her enjoying the company of people of her own generation.'

I didn't know what to make of this, so said 'Hmm-hmm' as I counted out paper napkins.

'I mean,' she went on after a pause, 'I know she appreciates all that you do for her...'.

I said, 'Oh, I just push the wheelchair.'

'You're very kind to her,' she said. Then : 'Do you enjoy working here?'

'It's all right,' I said.

The kettle came to the boil and she filled her teapot. She picked up her tray and made her way towards the hall.

She paused as she approached the doorway, peered along the hall to make sure no one else was around, then dropped her voice and said,

'I owe you an apology for my behaviour the other evening.'

I froze. I had hoped all that was forgotten. It was an embarrassing memory for me too.

In the silence, Mrs Smith pulled back her shoulders and took a breath.

'I think I may have spoken out of turn, and an explanation might be in order.'

She was having difficulty preserving her dignity ; she needed a response.

'Oh that's all right...' I began.

'No it's not,' she said stiffly. 'There are some matters we need to clear up. I'd be most grateful if you could meet with me to talk. Please,' she added.

I was stunned. This was so unlike her usual manner that I hardly knew how to address her, or what to say. At the same time a number of images flashed through my mind. The last thing I wanted was to be seen knocking at her door, let alone going into her room. Not even Millicent was allowed that privilege.

'Well... erm, if you like,' I stammered at last.

'Thank you,' she murmured, and became her brisk self once more. 'I have an appointment at the bank after lunch. Shall we meet in the tea room round the corner from there?'

We agreed that I would join her at three o'clock, when lunch had been cleared away and the residents had gone back to the parlour. It started raining in the mid-morning, which ruled out any possibility of taking Mrs Horton for a walk. In any case she had made it clear that I was under no obligation to her, and she was at pains not to impose on my free time. But she would be bound to wonder what reason I had for going out in the rain on my own, so I decided I would simply slip away to avoid an explanation. I couldn't help feeling guilty though, as if it was disloyal to arrange a meeting with her arch-enemy.

The tea-room was a modest establishment, set back at the top of an alley off the side-street, and I had never been there before. The entrance was in a small paved courtyard, alongside a bow-window with prim lace curtains, and I couldn't see if Mrs Smith was already there before I stepped inside.

A waitress approached me, and I had the presence of mind to announce that I was there to meet someone. She had been told to expect me and guided me through a narrow doorway into the adjoining room where Mrs Smith was seated at a table beside an inglenook fireplace. She waved her cigarette-holder at me and gave the waitress a nod as I sat down opposite her.

'I ordered for the two of us,' she said as the waitress headed for the kitchen. 'I thought it might be a treat for you to be waited on for a change.'

'I hope you won't be making comparisons,' I said.

'I have no complaints about the way you do your job,' she replied, with a gracious smile.

Silence. She was waiting for us to be served so she could say what she had to say without being interrupted.

'Was it a pleasant spot you visited the other day?'

I told her about Gleeson Creek and she nodded.

'Charming place,' she said. 'My late husband moored his boat there for a while. But the creek used to silt up, so he said, and could be difficult to navigate when the tides weren't high.'

'Did you go sailing with – ?' I began, but the waitress returned with our order and we sat back in our chairs while she served us. When she had gone, Mrs Smith smoothed her napkin over her lap and poured us some tea, urging me to help myself to a cake.

'This is very kind of you,' I said as I did so.

'Oh, it's nothing,' she said. 'My banker tells me my investment portfolio is performing healthily, so I can afford it.' She gave a husky laugh, which triggered her smoker's cough.

Stocks and shares were a closed book to me, but I was surprised to hear her speak about her money. It struck me as unladylike, particularly from someone who cultivated such airs and graces ; I had imagined she was above such matters.

'Yes, my husband left me well provided for, bless him.' She sighed as she caught her breath. 'But I still miss his company.'

Now I was being invited to share in the state of her emotions. This was not like her at all.

'Sometimes,' she went on, 'I take a little comfort from the gin. As you have cause to know.'

I was completely at a loss in the face of this unexpected flow of confidences. The more so as she was speaking of things I had no experience of and I had no ready response.

'I can't imagine what it must be like...' I began.

'To be lonely?' she responded. 'Yes, it gets me down sometimes. I do have Millicent for company. She's a bit simple, but kind-hearted and very loyal. Fortunately she has never seen me when I'm the worse for wear, and that encourages me to be at my best when she comes to call.'

I had often wondered what motivated Millicent to drop in and keep Mrs Smith company. I had heard that her husband was too ill to leave their home, and assumed her visits to the guest-house were the only change of scene she could allow herself. Once again I groped for something to say.

'She does seem... attached to you,' I said. 'Are you related?'

'Oh no,' Mrs Smith said. 'To tell the truth I feel rather sorry for her. She has no companions of her own age. She sometimes suggests we go on excursions together, and I have to find tactful ways of declining. A little of her company goes a long way.'

I was going to have to revise my opinion of this lady I had come to think of as fastidious and strait-laced. I had already discovered that gin could loosen her tongue but here she was, stone-cold sober, taking me into her confidence as if we were on familiar terms.

Then she gave the conversation an unexpected turn.

'But to return to your trip out with Mrs Horton and... what are her friends called?'

The small-talk had been a prelude to this. She had been softening me up and now she had wrong-footed me.

'Erm.... Mr and Mrs... Beaumont.'

'Ah,' she said. 'I thought I recognized her.'

I recalled Mrs Smith had been standing in the window, watching as we drove off.

'Oh,' I said. 'That's interesting. Do you know her then?'

'I did. But not the gentleman who was driving the car.'

'Oh,' I said again, lamely. 'When did you know her?'

'When we were young,' came the reply. 'Very young.' She scrutinized me with what I could swear was a touch of devilment in her eye. 'But I didn't know she and Mrs Horton were acquainted. I wonder how they got to know each other?'

I felt under pressure to provide an answer of sorts, but I offered one that gave away as little as possible.

'We... bumped into Mrs Beaumont when we were out walking.'

Mrs Smith had become pensive.

'Mrs Beaumont,' she murmured. 'Well, well.'

'May I ask how you knew her?'

'She was a war widow,' Mrs Smith replied. She looked at me and made a concession to my youth. 'The Great War. Her husband was reported missing in action.'

I needed to watch my response to this. In effect, what Mrs Smith was implying confirmed what Mrs Horton had said to me. 'That's not Mr Beaumont.' And it was obvious Mrs Smith drew a number of inferences from the fact, though I couldn't read her expression.

'So, did you know her well?' I asked.

'Not exactly. When my late husband was called up, I joined a women's voluntary group to do my bit on the Home Front. And Hilda... that is her name, as I recall?...'

I nodded.

'...Hilda became one of the leading lights when her husband... disappeared. So she was well-known as a personality, you might say, though I don't remember anyone being particularly close to her. Then she went off to join a nursing contingent in Flanders, I believe.'

'And you lost touch with her after that?'

'Well, as I say I never had any real contact with her at any point.'

I nodded. I had the impression Mrs Smith had not said all she wanted to say, so I kept silent. She had finished her cake and was fitting a Craven 'A' into her cigarette holder. She clicked a silver lighter and applied the flame. Sweeping the smoke aside with a wave of her hand, she turned to me.

'You might say that Mrs Beaumont was better known from local gossip than in person.' Then she dropped her voice. 'But I had the advantage of being married to the man who helped manage her affairs. Her financial affairs, that is.'

'Ah,' I said. 'Your husband was the bank-manager.' It seemed best to pass over the evident breaches of confidence she was hinting at.

'Yes. He and I were engaged at the time, and my husband-to-be advised her, while her husband remained unaccounted for. Her situation was difficult when she could not yet call herself a widow.' She paused. 'So long ago. And suddenly there she is ; large as life and twice as...' Her words trailed off and she stared into the middle distance. Then she spoke again, in an afterthought. '...Being driven around by a certain Mr Beaumont.' She put her cigarette holder in her mouth and her teeth formed a fierce grin as they gripped it.

I had to say something but there were so many details I must take care not to let slip. I must give the impression I had nothing to say. I put my best naïve face on.

'So was her husband eventually found safe and well?'

Mrs Smith took her cigarette-holder from her lips and blew out some smoke.

'Who knows? The man driving her car certainly seems hale and hearty.'

I pretended to be uncomfortable. She was obviously being ironic. In those days it wasn't done to talk openly about irregularities in people's private lives. I let silence settle between us. Then, to break it, I tried a change of subject.

'How long have you known Mrs Horton?'

She tapped the ash from her cigarette.

'Oh dear, that brings us to what I really wanted to say. I rather hoped we might be able to forget my regrettable behaviour. But since you ask that question, I have to apologize and explain myself before I answer it.' She put out her cigarette, returned her cigarette-holder to her handbag, and then raised her eyes.

'None of that would have happened if I had not drunk too much.' She sighed. 'Living on one's own can be difficult, you know. I don't have much in common with the other residents, as you will have noticed. Oh, I can talk to them if I choose to, of course. But it's more like holding court than having a conversation, and it's very far from having someone to confide in. I act a part with Millicent, since for reasons beyond my comprehension the poor woman seems to look up to me. And that gives people the impression that I have no need of more company.'

She crossed her hands on the table in front of her.

'I am aware that Mrs Horton sees through me. And that makes me self-conscious when she is in the room. Understandably enough she has no sympathy for me – she has sorrows of her own – but what I find unsettling is the fact that while I know she is passing judgement on me, I cannot tell what is going on behind that woebegone expression of hers. And of course I can't draw her into conversation and get a grip on the thoughts in her head. Her eyes look out as if a strange being is at the controls inside. I try to dismiss her as a mere invalid whose opinions have no importance, but that wretched mask of a face really torments me. It seems to take everything in but gives nothing back.' She stared at me. 'I wonder if this makes any sense to you?'

I nodded. I had observed various versions of the unnerving effect Mrs Horton's inscrutable features – and her wordless presence – could have on people. But I hadn't heard it explained with this level of intensity.

'So, as I was saying, she has me constantly on edge and there are days when I find myself simply overwhelmed by this feeling. And it drives me to be rather rude, I know. That's when I seek comfort in the bottle. Usually it remains a private affair, between myself and the gin. But when Mrs Horton, simply by being helpless, manages to make a conquest of the likes of Dr Storth... or yourself... and my attempts to be sociable prove fruitless, well, that can be hard to bear...'

Then to my astonishment, she took out a handkerchief and dabbed her eyes. It seemed so stagey and out of character that I could hardly believe what I was seeing. Was she putting it on for my benefit? Or was she really about to burst into tears?

I moved my hand across the table towards her. She sniffled and put her handkerchief away.

'You're very kind to listen to my ramblings. It's humiliating to find myself talking to you in this way – it goes against my nature. But in the years since my husband died, I find my nature is just not up to the task of living alone. Things were so much easier when we had a proper social life together.'

She reached out and patted my hand briefly.

'If we had had children....' Then she sat up, cleared her throat, and called for the bill. 'I'd be most grateful if you could forget what I've just told you – and please, I beg you, wipe the other night's untoward lapse from your memory. I don't know what I can have said, but I assure you it was merely the drink talking.'

I was only too ready to do as she asked. But then she put a question to me.

'Tell me,' she said, 'How exactly did Mrs Horton and Mrs Beaumont become acquainted? You said they bumped into each other. Did they know each other before that, I wonder? Did either of them recognize the other?' She paused, then added, 'Did you get the impression Mrs Horton knew Mr Beaumont?'

' Oh, er...' I said, flustered. This was a lot of questions and called for careful responses. 'So far as I could tell, they didn't know each other, though Mrs Horton thought they might have had an old school friend in common. Mrs Beaumont had lots to say about mutual acquaintances – classmates, teachers and so on. Mr Beaumont didn't say much. I don't suppose goings-on in a girls' school are very interesting for him.' I stopped. Mrs Smith did not respond, evidently waiting for more. I concluded : 'But strangely their paths don't seem to have crossed at the time.'

'Strangely indeed,' said Mrs Smith as the waitress appeared.

And as she paid the bill I realised that in all she had said, Mrs Smith had not actually answered the question I had asked her. She put away her purse and took out her compact case, and as she touched up her nose with powder I decided to try a little improvisation of my own.

'I wonder...,' I said tentatively. Then : 'How well do you know Mrs Horton? Have you been... acquainted for long?'

My tone was an attempt to suggest that they would get on better if they got to know each other properly. I realised I was making a big assumption : for all I knew, their mutual antipathy could have been fermenting over years. But I was hoping to play on those other emotions that I had just been given a glimpse of, beneath the surface of Mrs Smith's starchy exterior.

She snapped shut her compact case. She eyed me directly as she slipped it back into her handbag.

'I knew her when she could speak,' she said.

19

Well, we got past that awkward moment, resumed harmless conversation to conclude our outing, and despite everything they delivered me and my chaperone safely back to the guest-house. As we came out of the café there was a moment when I felt they might push my wheelchair into the dock with me in it ; but Hilda's a stickler for etiquette, and behaviour like that would never do.

I must say Graham showed great presence of mind when he stepped in to calm things after my gaffe. Cheeky devil, inventing some compulsion or other that supposedly made me prone to blurting out strange yelps and groans... But I have to give him credit too for bringing the discussion back to innocuous subjects after patting me on the back as if I had choked on my vowels. Our little excursions are turning him into quite an urbane young chap.

Hilda is rather good company when it comes to small-talk, and once she started reminiscing about teachers and school trips at Greenhalgh High everyone was able to relax and I just nodded along, with an occasional interjection that Graham contrived to interpret, bless him. At that age, life at school is the whole of life, after all, so there was lots to converse about, even if Hilda did most of the talking.

I say 'most', but tutored in the social graces as she is, Hilda did make a point of bringing Graham into the conversation . She asked him about his own school days. That caught him unawares : he is obviously someone for whom school was little more than an inconvenient prelude to getting on with a proper life.

'I couldn't wait to leave,' he answered.

'Did you have a job to go to?' asked Hilda.

'Oh yes. I went to work on a poultry farm,' he replied.

Hilda struggled to find a response. Finally she said,

'And what did your Mother have to say about that?'

'Oh well, my Mum and Dad were killed in a road accident when I was fourteen, so I had to learn to take care of myself.'

Hilda glanced across at me.

'I imagine your aunt...' she started ; and then she paused, having second thoughts as to whether someone in my state could have had a role to play in rearing the young man.

Here Graham demonstrated once more his developing gift for improvisation. Cool as a cucumber, he responded:

'Well, as you may know, Aunt Marion has been... disabled for some time – since before I left school, in fact.'

Hilda nodded sympathetically, and looked to me. I did my best to project a little emotion through my eyes. At this point I couldn't tell whether everything he said was untrue, or just some parts of it.

'So it was just me and the chickens, really,' Graham concluded.

'Hmm,' murmured Hilda, in the manner of someone who had never found herself alone among feathered creatures. *'And... do you still do that work?'*

'Oh no,' he answered. *'Hens are nasty beasts, especially when they're cooped up in battery cages. And then the farmer built a broiler house. It was my job to shovel provender pellets at thousands of broiler fowl to fatten them up. After a couple of months shut up with them I decided I really didn't enjoy the company of poultry.'*

I felt like complimenting him on the aplomb with which he delivered this autobiography – fake or not. I was anticipating with interest how he would move on to the next chapter.

'As it happens,' he went on, *'Aunt Marion had just moved into the guest house and she tipped me off about a job that was available there. It's a live-in arrangement, so that saves me paying rent.'*

Fact or fiction, his tale revealed to me a side to Graham I would never have suspected.

Hilda eyed him, then me, and then she smiled.

'Yes,' she said, *'that IS very convenient.'*

"Thomas" (I have decided the inverted commas are henceforth obligatory) stayed largely silent throughout, though he smiled now and again at Hilda's anecdotes and occasionally showed signs of taking an interest in things Graham said. Setting aside his faux pas that discouraged him from making further contributions, his silence was probably due to the fact that he had no experience of English secondary school, and any attempt to draw parallels with education abroad would

obviously not have been welcome – at least not to Hilda.

He's French, no doubt about it. Though Hilda can't know for certain that I know : I showed no sign of understanding his reaction to my little sally (I couldn't if I wanted, of course). Among her anecdotes from our school days she didn't touch on language classes. And to be honest I don't recall much about them. But I do remember being amused when I learned that the French use the word 'charabia' for 'double Dutch' when actually it derives from Arabic. Even at that young age such exotic etymology seemed the stuff of crossword clues to me. 'C'est du pur charabia' he said, emphasising that last word, which was a fair reflection on my attempt to put the question to him. Those bloody intractable consonants! But to be fair, if I'd been able to pronounce what I wanted to say I wouldn't have dared say it. I like being able to stick my face in anywhere, knowing it won't be recognized, and the same goes for my words. My impairment means I can get away with doing or saying what I like without fear of repercussions.

'Who are you anyway? And what have you done with Dr Storth?' I was asking. Funny how he intuited something about the nature of my utterance – that it wasn't just meaningless noise coming out of my mouth. And it was striking how it intimidated him, put him on the defensive. He's obviously not comfortable speaking English – I gather he's taciturn at the best of times – and as far as he was concerned I could have been just another jabbering native in this foreign country he currently lives in, God knows how or why. I might have been saying something straightforward that he simply couldn't grasp – and that would have

been a giveaway. Hence his panic, that made him lapse into French.

'The language he was brought up in,' Hilda said. Which left open the possibility that he has lived his adult life in England. But for my money he's not been here for all that long. So we may have got a step closer to answering one of the questions I threw at him in my fashion. But a lot remains unexplained. And I don't suppose he will be the one to do the explaining.

As for Hilda's remark about the VADS... I don't think it was mere nostalgia that made her raise the subject. I'm sure she was testing us, to see what WE might know about HER involvement – had 'Ellen Keighley' brought back any gossip about her time among the wounded troops? Any gossip that might have pointed a finger at Hilda Beaumont?

I mustn't let my imagination run away with me. And none of this is getting us any closer to finding Hughie.

But what I'm not imagining is an odd change in Mrs Smith's behaviour. I had the impression earlier that she was actually being quite pleasant towards me, and now I'm sure her attitude has changed. But I don't know why.

She greeted me quite cordially when the residents assembled for dinner that evening. She gave me a full-toothed, crinkle-eyed smile and asked if I had had a pleasant outing. I nodded of course, and she remarked how agreeable it was to have acquaintances to take one out like that. I thought I noticed a slight pause for effect before she said 'acquaintances', as if she would like to know more about who they were. Naturally I wouldn't have gone into detail with her even if I could have done, but I did try to make my eyes glint in a neighbourly way, and she went off contented, to take up her place at her table and wait to be served.

Granted it's not much to go on but compared with her behaviour since Hughie arrived, this certainly represents a thaw in our relations.

And then, as she got up to leave, she wished me a good evening on her way out. I shall be sure to reciprocate as best I can, if only to see what her ulterior motive might be.

*

'I knew her when she could speak,' she said.

That took my breath away, I must admit. I couldn't imagine a world where Mrs Horton was capable of having ordinary dealings with those around her. I needed a moment to respond, and even then the question that came into my head surprised me.

'What was she like before she became… ill?'

Mrs Smith smiled.

'The first thing to bear in mind,' she said, 'is that she was a lot younger than she is now – we all were…'

By this time she was standing and I got up too. I led the way to the door while Mrs Smith said goodbye to the waitress – she was evidently a regular here. I held the door open and she stepped out into the sunshine, where I joined her. Suddenly she took my arm.

'Now, young man, for the price of tea and cake I think I am entitled to expect you to accompany me on a brief *promenade*,' she said, giving the word a French inflection.

Taken unawares, I mechanically fell into step and let her guide me up the street, wondering what further plans she had for me. We found ourselves heading towards the foreshore.

She resumed her story as we walked.

'I met Marion in college. We were trainee teachers. It was a strange time, as we women were suddenly being asked to take on professional roles in the war – so many men had died and lots of jobs needed to be filled. Up until then girls were mainly groomed to be discreet and docile in preparation for marriage. Even as professional women in the making, our role was to be self-effacing, not assertive. Still like children, you know? But... Marion didn't come from the same background as most of the other students. For instance, many of us had been brought up on elocution lessons, so we had been taught to express ourselves correctly. At first that made Marion quite timid, afraid to draw attention to her Northern accent. But she did become rather truculent at a meeting on votes for women, as I recall – and as a result she got into trouble over what was referred to as her "unbecoming" conduct. That experience transformed her. She was indignant at having her behaviour judged by old-fashioned principles, and spoke out to defend herself. Which got her into more trouble, as you might imagine. But it didn't deter her at all, and from that point on she became the spokesperson for anyone too shy or deferential to stand up for themselves against the restrictions imposed on young women – often by old men, of course.' She smiled and shook her head. 'And my, how she could speak.'

Mrs Smith exchanged greetings with a passer-by while I wondered what Mrs Horton might have sounded like in full flow.

'How did you come to know her?' I asked when Mrs Smith turned back to me.

'To be honest I didn't really get to know her very well. I was in my second year, and was appointed her mentor when she joined as a fresher. It was my responsibility to explain the rules, to see that my protégées followed the guidelines regarding dress, behaviour, all that kind of thing. And that is how I became aware of Marion, and why I remembered her. But I can't say we were close at all. She resented the pettiness of the regulations and didn't hide her views, which made my task – such as it was – somewhat tricky. I once heard her say, within earshot of a gaggle of students with upper-class accents, that the purpose of training women to speak properly was to stop them speaking up for themselves when it counted. Naturally it didn't help our relations that she viewed me as just another posh girl. And of course she was a widow, and I wasn't yet married, so she didn't take kindly to my telling her what to do, as she saw it.'

She paused, glanced left and right as if fearing she might be overheard, and dropped her voice for effect.

'In fact she acquired something of a reputation as having a… rather free lifestyle… "No better than she should be", as people used to say…' She pursed her lips, obviously pondering whether she could say more. 'On my bad days I feel her disability serves as the perfect disguise for a person with a past…'

Here were hints of a lurid story from a world some twenty-five years before I was born, a world where everyone was stuffy and respectable – weren't they? Mrs Horton? Was it possible she…?

Meanwhile Mrs Smith, having cleared her throat, continued her story.

'As a matter of fact I didn't know her for very long. During that year I became engaged to Reginald, who felt that I need not have a career of my own, since in any case that would mean denying a job to a widow or spinster who had no one else to provide for her. So I dropped out before qualifying and didn't feature in Mrs Horton's life beyond that year. I imagine she was happy to see the back of me – if she ever noticed my departure…'

We had arrived at a spot where we could look out over the foreshore. A blustery breeze coming off the bay plucked at our clothes ; Mrs Smith shivered, pulled a headscarf from her pocket and tied it under her chin, then tugged up her coat collar.

'Ah!' she said. 'Fresh air!' and was immediately overcome with a fit of coughing. 'I've never really been one for the outdoors,' she gasped as the coughs subsided.

There was a bench nearby, and she let herself slump onto it until she could breathe steadily again.

I recognized it as the one Mrs Horton had told me about. I took a seat alongside Mrs Smith and for a minute or so we both contemplated the beach without speaking. Mudflats stretched for miles before us. The sea was a thin ribbon on the horizon.

Eventually I put into words some of the thoughts I had been turning over in my mind.

'So you left college, and you and Mrs Horton went your separate ways?'

'That's right. I admit I would like to have known her better, but we didn't have much in common at that time and had no reason to stay in contact. I did learn on the grapevine that when she qualified, she moved away and took up a teaching post – in the Midlands, I think it was.'

'And yet here you are, living under the same roof.'

'Yes, who would have thought it?' she replied. 'Quite by chance. I had been living in the guest-house for a while when she... turned up. After her mother died, I believe.'

I was still pondering.

'Did you recognize her?' I asked at last.

'No,' she replied. 'But one wouldn't, would one?' She brushed a speck of sand from her coat sleeve. 'Of course, the name "Horton" rang a bell, but this was more than forty years after we had been together at college. And I would hardly expect this to be the very same person I had known then. Added to which, her present... condition sadly renders her unrecognizable to anyone who knew her as I did. And even without that, who can say what effect ageing would have had on her appearance?'

'But... perhaps she recognized you?' It seemed the obvious thing to say.

'She's never shown any sign of doing so. It's only to be expected, coming across me outside the setting in which she knew me before. Being married to Reginald changed me too, of course – and not only my name.' She examined my face. 'And in any case, as you will come to realise, young man, it can be surprising what a difference several decades or so can make to some sets of features.... Even without the kind of mishap that befell poor Marion.'

I had to ask. 'You mean... the way you look now...' the words died on my lips as I realised how impertinent they might sound.

She giggled at my embarrassment – a girlish reaction, I thought, and for an instant, yes, I could imagine her as a different person from the arch and upright figure she cut in the parlour of the guest house.

'Faces are like fashions, they can change immensely,' she said. 'For instance, I never had this colour hair until my natural colour gave way to grey. And my lipstick... And the wrinkles! The nicotine doesn't help, I'm afraid. My complexion has suffered over the years. I stare at the mirror these days and try to make sense of this withered fizzog... – No, no,' she said as I made a small gesture of protest, '... it's kind of you, but there's no need to be polite.' She paused, then directed her gaze across the bay. 'In a word, there are times when I'm a stranger to myself – as, apparently, I am to Marion Horton.'

I was beginning to sense something wistful in her tone.

'And yet… you did realize who she was, despite what happened to *her* face…'

'Well, yes, one day it dawned on me…' she said after a pause. 'I noticed she was left-handed and that drew my eyes to the way she held her pen. She has a very odd way of pinching it between three fingers, with her thumb steadying it. The other girls at college used to remark on it, and when I saw her doing the same thing as she filled in her crosswords, it came back to me right away. Once that happened I began to watch her more closely and came to recognize little mannerisms I wouldn't have noticed otherwise. She has a way of sitting forward with her elbows on her knees when something catches her attention, for example.'

I'd seen these tics but attached no importance to them. I suppose that meant I was unobservant. But once I had registered Mrs Horton's face I wasn't paying attention to any other peculiarities she may have. I told myself I should watch people more. And what would Mrs Smith's quirks be? I wondered as Mrs Smith watched me absorb her explanation.

'Oh, I see,' I said. 'And yet she doesn't recognize you.'

'If she does, she isn't letting on.'

No wonder Mrs Smith felt uneasy in her presence, suspecting she might be aware of her identity but choosing not to acknowledge the fact. It must feel like a monstrous snub, I thought.

'Look,' I said, aware that I was about to sound presumptuous and naïve again, 'could you not… just… introduce yourself?'

She shrugged her shoulders and said 'Hmm!' which brought on another brief bout of coughing. When she got her breath back, she said, still with a slight croak in her voice, 'It's too late now.'

'How can that be?' I asked.

'Oh, it's a silly story, I suppose. To begin with, right from the start when she was just another newcomer, at the first "Hellos" I was referred to by my married name, which of course made me a stranger to her. I didn't feel comfortable adding any more. How would she respond? I even thought she might be mentally defective by the look of her, and that made me shy away from engaging with those gabbled sounds she makes. I mean, those eyes in that face seemed lacking in proper intelligence, which discouraged me from making real contact. Then later on, when I realised for certain who she was, I thought I might try to open up to her ; but I would have had to acknowledge my failure to do so earlier and that would have been mortifying. And then I must confess there was a peculiar thing that put me off. Should I speak to the disabled face, or speak to the eyes? The face doesn't move, which inhibits conversation, and yet one's eyes are drawn to it. And her eyes register that. Even worse, there are days when those eyes actually seem to be mocking me from behind their mask. I find this...' – she paused, searching for a word – '... disconcerting. So eventually I gave up thinking I should make an effort, and got into the habit of accepting that communication wasn't possible.'

In the light of everything she had just said to me, it suddenly occurred to me that Mrs Smith may well have lived much of her existence as a habitual onlooker. Knowing what I knew about Mrs Horton, this all seemed pretty silly – and having seen how readily Mrs Horton and Hughie struck up a relationship, the thought of Mrs Smith sitting paralysed – and tormented – on the sidelines was almost tragic.

I couldn't help saying so. 'I must say, that strikes me as a very sad misunderstanding.'

'Well, we've been going on with this pretence of not knowing each other – me her, at any rate – for so long that it would be too awkward to confess the truth now.'

20

'A person with a past,' Mrs Smith had said. I couldn't imagine what she meant by that. I only knew about living in the present. All around me a new era was breaking out, and for my generation the past was merely a sketchy, repressed precursor to our swinging age of openness. But the deeper I stumbled into the stories of Mrs Horton, Mrs Smith and Mrs Beaumont – force of habit had me still thinking of them in these formal terms – the more I began to perceive the possibility of previous existences that were not so remote after all. That's not to say I understood what kind of world I had happened upon. There were moments when I felt like an archaeologist deciphering the inscriptions on ancient stones while a trio of elderly lady spirits watched over me.

I was brought back to the present when it came to serving lunch the next day. With Mrs Smith at her usual table and Mrs Horton set back at hers, I was made aware that I now had divided loyalties. Mrs Horton was evidently quite glad to see me, as usual, though only I could read the signs in her puckered eyelids.

Mrs Smith was positively effusive.

'Good morning, Graham,' she breathed softly as I put a plate down in front of her. She leaned towards me, evidently to confirm our new-found intimacy.

I smiled but didn't speak, and glanced back over my shoulder towards Mrs Horton. The old lady seemed intent on buttering her bread. I was glad to be able to busy myself with serving the other residents. Moving back and forth between the dining-room and the kitchen, I concentrated on the dishes I was carrying and avoided catching either woman's eye.

While the guests got on with eating, I retreated to the kitchen and pondered how to manage the situation I found myself in. It was going to be uncomfortable, caught between two mutually hostile old ladies. I had no wish to distance myself from Mrs Horton, obviously – we still had a good deal of business to sort out with Mrs Beaumont – but neither could I revert to being merely polite towards Mrs Smith. Behind her off-putting manner there was another person with... well, with 'a past', but also with a present she was entitled to enjoy more. I didn't exactly see it as my vocation to cheer old ladies up, but I couldn't just ignore her.

When I went back into the dining room to clear away, I steered past both women by going straight to the tables in the window. But that seemed to act as a signal to Mrs Smith. She lay down her napkin and got up from her table, but just as she was about to leave the room, she turned towards where Mrs Horton was sitting. I froze as she crossed the space between them.

'What a lovely sky there is today!' she said with a smile.

Mrs Horton raised her head, but her face remained completely expressionless, as usual. I felt a pang for Mrs Smith. The blank look that responded to her greeting had the air of a deliberate snub.

Then Mrs Horton nodded her head, growled a low indistinct sound, and a slight crinkling at the corner of her eyes gave Mrs Smith to understand that her words were appreciated.

I took this as my cue to approach Mrs Horton's table and gather up the crockery. I had a pile from the other tables balanced on my arms, and needed the help of both ladies to add Mrs Horton's plates to the stack. This involved a flurry of interaction, smiles on everyone's part, and an exchange of pleasantries that left me at least feeling much more relaxed as I headed off to do the washing-up.

Whether this was to be the start of a thaw in the two women's relations I had no way of knowing, but a part of me registered some relief at the prospect of them getting on together – and leaving me to get on with my life, such as it was.

However, my thoughts began to wander as I tackled the washing-up,– and I found myself wondering, not for the first time, what could have happened to Dr Storth. It was a month or so since he disappeared and life in the guest house had resumed as if he had never existed among us. When Mrs Horton recruited me to help her investigate his so-called abduction, I had been sceptical and really just went along for the ride. The strange letter from Dr Storth – if it had been from him – had certainly piqued my curiosity, and our first meeting with Mrs Beaumont and her puzzling husband, followed by the incident at the care home, pointed to some murky undercurrents ; but our most recent encounter with the Beaumonts had left me thinking they were after all just an innocuous couple with no other concern than a nostalgic attachment to the past, like so many elderly people. But there was certainly something foreign about the man, and Mrs Horton was adamant that he was not who Mrs

Beaumont said he was. And on this point Mrs Smith apparently agreed.

That said, Mrs Horton's account of her own past suggested that she and Mrs Beaumont had had more in common than an alleged mutual acquaintance from school days. What about that man who had been Mrs Horton's fiancé and supposedly went on to be Mrs Beaumont's husband? In any case I didn't believe there had ever been an Ellen Keighley – I must see if I could get Mrs Horton to acknowledge that the girl was just a fiction devised to establish contact with the Beaumont couple.

And then I thought : how much of the rest of Mrs Horton's tales could I trust to be true? If I had heard the story from her own lips, would it have seemed credible? Would the tone of her voice, her facial expressions, have made it more convincing? Or more likely might I just have dismissed it as the senile ramblings of an old woman? I would have nodded along until she fell silent, and that would have been the end of that, and I'd have gone back to my chores. I'd been drawn into this business chiefly, I concluded, because a hand-written version seemed to carry more weight.

But why should it? It was just a second-hand – or third-hand – version of a tale of another manuscript, allegedly written by – or for – some novelist whose stock-in-trade, like all of his kind, was fiction and fantasy… and falsehood. Perhaps what I had learned from Mrs Horton had no more substance than those sheets of paper she tore up after giving them to me to read.

This whole saga might amount to very little if it were not for Hughie Storth. Who was he, after all? All I knew about him was what Mrs Horton had written. Mrs Smith's scepticism about him might have been inspired by envy – but there might have been some basis for it after all.

And even then, what really started things off was the scrap of paper that accompanied the letter sent to Mrs Dugdale – at the wrong address, which didn't inspire confidence. That letter itself, of course, simply explained that he wouldn't be back, and paid off what he owed. End of story.

Except for the bizarre note specially written to Mrs Horton. Its authenticity, such as it was, stemmed from the fact that it drew on their shared interest in crosswords. But I had only a loose recollection of its bizarre contents, which with hindsight seemed implausible to say the least. And I couldn't check it out any more than I could re-read Mrs Horton's manuscripts, since she had shut them away – or perhaps even destroyed them?

I didn't think it was feasible to ask Mrs Horton if I could consult her journal. All the same, try as I may I couldn't stop my mind returning to the place that weird note had led us to : Quainton Grange, in Scatcham.

By the time I had dried my hands and put the crockery away, I had decided to go back there on my own and see what I could find. I hadn't taken much in for myself when I was acting as Mrs Horton's chaperone and interpreter, and I was still curious about the place. Without Mrs Horton and her wheelchair, I would be able to move around unencumbered and would draw less attention. Travel was not a problem if I was unaccompanied – I checked the location again on my Ordnance Survey map and confirmed that I could get a bus to Wimberley and walk the three miles or so from there.

Mid-morning on a mid-week day, and I was the only upstairs passenger on the bus. I gazed at the fields dotted with smallholdings. At first we passed through familiar countryside. I had often cycled the back lanes, largely invisible from the main road, that criss-crossed the flat land : from my top-deck perspective I could place the church spires and weather-vanes, the barns, silos and water-towers, even from a distance. But when the bus turned off the main road and headed towards outlying areas I knew of only from hearsay, I was soon having trouble getting my bearings. I had asked the driver to set me down at the closest point to Scatcham – a spot named Hardship Lane as I recall – and from there I would have to climb over a stile and continue on foot.

I had brought my map, and opened it up as I stepped down from the bus, to find that my landmarks were there to meet me. I had no trouble identifying the stile and was soon making my way up a public footpath that ran alongside hedgerows, led through five-barred gates and more stiles, and had me squeezing between stone pinch pillars placed to let only sheep pass through. I clambered over fences, giving cattle a wide berth as my route traversed their grazing land. At one point I found myself crossing a farmyard, eyed suspiciously by a stocky man in shirt sleeves, cap and heavy boots, with trousers tied at the knee. For fear of looking furtive, I called out a cheerful greeting as I passed but he merely grunted in reply. I wondered if he would remember me should word ever get around about an incident involving a stranger in the vicinity.

I reckoned I had walked a couple of miles or more when the track plunged into what was a remnant of ancient woodland, according to the map. The leaf canopy blocked out much of the sky, but patches of sunlight filtered through to the ground. At this point the path disappeared and I had to find my own way through the underbrush, weaving among the tree trunks and taking care not to stumble over exposed roots. I was getting near to Quainton Grange now. I wasn't coming at it from the same direction as last time, so I knew the approach wouldn't be familiar when I emerged from the copse.

Eventually I stepped out gingerly from the shadow into the sunshine and waited for a moment while my eyes adjusted to the light.

A meadow sloped down before me towards a group of stone buildings clustered together among trees. Over and beyond their rooftops I could make out a lane I recognized : it was the one that passed in front of Quainton Lodge and petered out in the farmyard where we had had to turn the van around. So this time I was at the back of the gatehouse. I could get nearer without advertising my presence if I stayed close to the hedgerow, and then I could slip unnoticed behind the screen formed by acacias and box trees lining the garden.

The house actually sat in a hollow at the foot of the incline. From where I was I could not see the ground floor, but three upstairs windows were in full view. If I could see them, I would be visible from inside those rooms – so I'd have to take care not to draw attention. I had not had the opportunity to take in these windows before, and I kept my eyes trained on them as I came closer. They were latticed, and the glass panes winked at the sky and greenery with irregular, flickering reflections. I felt exposed, though there was no sign of anyone who might be peering out in my direction.

Then from round the side of the house, a couple emerged into the garden. I glimpsed their heads before they passed out of view behind the hedging. One was Mrs Beaumont. The other I couldn't be sure about – he was wearing sunglasses and a hat with a brim, though he was not so tall and stooped as the man she had presented as Mr Beaumont. I took a few quick strides and crept up to the box-tree, holding my breath.

I could hear their footsteps behind the foliage. They were in conversation, but in low voices, and I couldn't make out what was being said. It was Mrs Beaumont who seemed to be doing most of the talking – and her modulated words had tones I hadn't heard her use before. There could have been some urgency in what she was saying, as if she was anxious – or agitated. I crept along the hedging to stay with their conversation as they walked, trying to grasp what was being said. But strain as I might to hear, I couldn't distinguish any words. At the corner of the hedgerow I abandoned the effort and came to a halt before taking a cautious peek beyond. Crouching down, I glanced behind me to be sure the coast was clear.

At the opposite corner of the tree screen there stood a man. Arms folded, grizzled head held up, he gave me a fixed stare. As I froze in surprise he raised a finger and placed it on his lips.

I straightened up slowly, trying to project a relaxed air that might belie the shifty-looking figure I undoubtedly cut. He lowered his finger from his lips and pointed it at me.

'Young man, could it be that you were prying?' he said, striding towards me.

'Ah… – oh, hello Mr Beaumont,' I stammered. 'I've lost my way… When I realised I was close to your home I wondered if I might knock at your door and ask for directions.'

'Ah!' he said, 'I see who you are – it's Graham, isn't it?' The slight difficulty he had in pronouncing the 'h' in my name reminded me he was a foreigner, and this had the effect of making him less intimidating.

I nodded.

'And you've lost your way…' he paused. 'But where was it that you were headed for?'

'Well, I set out from Wimberley for a walk, and was, erm, just exploring the countryside when I realised I had misread my map…' I took the map out and waved it at him in support of my story.

Mr Beaumont rubbed his chin.

'Exploring, eh?' he said. 'Well, perhaps you'd better come inside and we'll see what we can find for you.'

He gestured to me to accompany him, and after a moment's hesitation I followed warily in his footsteps. He rounded the corner of the hedge and made his way through a wicket gate into the garden.

It was deserted. Mrs Beaumont had evidently gone indoors with the man she had been talking to. Mr Beaumont led me across to the entrance and I braced myself for a meeting with the people inside.

Then I heard the sound of a car driving off along the lane. I wondered briefly who was in it, as Mr Beaumont ushered me along the corridor and into the sitting-room where we had talked together on my previous visit with Mrs Horton.

'Do sit down,' said Mr Beaumont with an insistence that might just carry an air of menace and a formal politeness that marked him out as a foreigner.

I settled into an armchair. He remained standing and asked if I would like some tea ; and when I said yes he excused himself and went off to make it. If he had any hostile intentions he would be unlikely to leave me alone in the room, I thought.

I took the opportunity to inspect my surroundings. There were pictures on the walls – no photographs, just paintings, several landscapes, one of a seashore, one of horses, one of a dog.

Last time we had been here I had noticed bookshelves beside the fireplace, and I got up to take a closer look. I'd never been much of a reader, but some of the books had handsome bindings, with gilt tooling on the spine, and I had never had a chance to handle volumes like these before.

The authors were mainly classics : I recognized the names of Jane Austen, Charlotte Bronte and Charles Dickens. There were some foreign authors I can still recall : Friedrich Hölderlin, Wolfgang von Gœthe, Honoré de Balzac, Gustave Flaubert. I took down one volume after another to weigh it in my hand, stroke the leather, open the cover and smell the paper.

I couldn't make much of the books themselves. At that time the only name I had vaguely heard of was Flaubert, and I knew he was French. I opened a volume by him and saw that it was not a translation. I put it back on the shelf. I got down one of several books that had 'Gœthe' on the spine. It wasn't in English either, so I was unable to make sense of even the opening lines. But I could tell that it was in French, like the one by Flaubert – though Gœthe was surely a German name. Hölderlin, with those two dots over the 'o', was another German-looking name, so I took that one from the shelf and opened it. I could tell right away that this was a translation into French. Then I took down a book by Dickens, and found that it was in French too. Whoever owned these books did their reading in French – was probably French. And this would explain Mr Beaumont's accent. Mrs Horton had made her suspicions clear, but here was further proof.

21

Well he hasn't come back – yet. Could it be he's gone the same way as Hughie? I could tell there was something amiss when he disappeared after his shift, without even nodding to me. It gave me a bit of a pang, I must admit. I assume he was too embarrassed to tell me to my face that he'd grown bored with our little saga. After all, it's only to be expected that a youngster like him would tire of my company, such as it is. He has a life of his own to live, a future to pursue, and excavating the past of superannuated widows can't possibly compete with such attractive prospects.

Fortunately, surprisingly, Mrs Smith has taken advantage of his absence. I was taken aback, although I had seen something like this coming. When she noticed I was on my own again, she promptly set aside her snooty disregard and actually took to bidding me good morning and good evening, with unaccustomed warmth, whenever our paths crossed.

Obviously the matter of when our paths crossed has rarely been mine to decide, since even indoors my mobility is limited – and without someone to push me, indoors is where I remain. I'm happy enough with my crosswords, of course. But this morning, as I was poring over the clues, I glimpsed from the corner of my eye that Mrs Smith was rising from her chair with a noticeable sense of purpose. She had evidently set her mind on something, but it took me a few seconds to realise that I was the object of her intentions. I lifted my face to her, which is a tactic I sometimes adopt to disarm incoming advances. As a rule they look into my eyes and conclude that my face is at the mercy of a pilot baffled by the dashboard.

I expected this to deter Mrs Smith, but there was resolve in her manner. I had the distinct impression that she had steeled herself to... what? Confront me?

She stood before me, clutching her handbag as if it were a talisman.

'Good morning Mrs Horton,' she said. 'I trust I'm not disturbing your concentration?' She gestured towards the crossword page that lay before me.

I shook my head.

'I wonder if I might sit with you?'

I made a sound in my throat and gestured at the empty space beside me. She brought a chair over from the next table – as Hughie used to do. I experienced a stab of resentment but the moment passed when she placed a hand on my arm.

'Do you mind if I smoke?' she asked.

Normally I would have minded quite a lot, but by this time I was too intrigued to object. I watched as she extracted a Craven 'A' from her cigarette case, and fitted it to her cigarette holder. Her hands were trembling as she lit up ; evidently she had set herself this task to calm her nerves and put us both at our ease.

She gave a sigh as she breathed out her first lungful of smoke and wafted it away with a hand.

'Such a lovely morning, don't you think?'

I murmured in agreement.

She stared out of the window at the bright clouds that scudded over the incoming tide.

'I do think it would be a shame to stay indoors,' she said, and turned to me to see if I was disposed to interpret this as an invitation.

I made a sound intended to convey diffidence : I can't go far without my wheelchair, and...

She smiled. I noticed a smear of lipstick on her front teeth.

'My dear,' she said, waving her cigarette holder at the view, 'I enjoy fresh air as much as you do. Why shouldn't we share some together?'

I pushed the crossword away. This was an offer I had no cause to decline.

We met up in the hall twenty minutes later : me in my hooded anorak and Mrs Smith in a fur-collared coat and bright red cloche bucket hat, the colour of her lipstick. If anyone noticed us passing by she would be the one they remembered, I thought as I huddled in the wheelchair.

Once we had been helped down the steps and onto the pavement, Mrs Smith's spindly legs proved more vigorous than I had imagined. She pushed me along briskly, and chatted as she did so. Graham can be quite laconic, saving his breath for the effort of propelling me forward, and he rarely volunteers to speak unless he judges my gargarisms require some kind of reply. Mrs Smith was positively garrulous by comparison. The breeze carried away most of what she said, and I didn't feel compelled to provide responses, though I did appreciate her one-sided version of conversation. It was quite enjoyable to bathe in the flow of gossip that makes for good company between women.

We made our way along the promenade with the breeze in our faces, and I could sense that Mrs Smith was beginning to flag by the time we came within sight of the shelter that affords a view of the beach. I gestured towards it, and I think Mrs Smith was grateful to steer us under its roof out of the wind. She parked my wheelchair, and took a seat beside me on the bench that runs the length of the shelter.

An odd silence descended on us when the sound of the breeze was no longer in our ears. Mrs Smith sat with her hands crossed demurely in her lap, and side by side we gazed at the beach. The enclosed space made for a peculiar intimacy. It reminded me of being in a station waiting-room. I thought how glad I was that there was no one else in there with us, to make the atmosphere even more awkward.

Mrs Smith gave a slight cough to clear her smoker's chest. Thinking she was about to speak, I unbuttoned my hood.

'Hm-hm,' she said.

'Hmm,' I responded.

Here we were, both reduced to inarticulate sounds.

I had an excuse – there was no way I could break the silence. So I waited.

'Well,' she said, and cleared her throat.

'Mmm,' I agreed.

'I don't think we have had an opportunity to talk properly before,' she said.

I raised my eyebrows : Me? Talk?

She was flustered. 'Oh, I'm so sorry,' she said. 'I didn't mean....' She swallowed, and pinched her lips together. 'What I mean is, I've always felt rather self-conscious about trying to start a conversation with you. Even in normal circumstances it can be an intrusion, but with you ... if you don't mind my saying so...'

How out of character she seemed, this stand-offish woman suddenly at a loss for words, committing one gaffe after another as she struggled for a diplomatic way to make contact. I almost felt sorry for her. I did what I could to show I appreciated her efforts : I rewarded her with my most friendly grimace.

'You see, I imagine that conversation is hard work for you,' she said.

I shrugged : I've learned to live with it.

She thought for a moment.

'Tell me,' she said, '– oh I'm so sorry, there I go again...' she sighed.

I opened my eyes wide : Never mind that, do go on.

'Did I recognize the lady who took you out for a drive the other day?'

I tipped my head quizzically : How should I know?

I can allow myself blunt responses without causing offence : my limited collection of facial reflexes doesn't stretch to tactful. It does however serve to camouflage give-away reactions that others would be prone to when a leading question is sprung on them.

Was she saying she knew Mrs Beaumont?

'She reminded me of someone I used to know slightly,' she went on.

I raised my eyebrows : surprise, puzzlement, query.

'Was her name Mrs Beaumont, by any chance? Hilda Beaumont?'

I might just have blinked. Well I never, I nodded as non-committally as I could manage.

Mrs S took this as a Yes.

'I can't say we were properly acquainted, but I seem to recall she was once a client at my late husband's bank.'

Oh really, I grunted, my saggy lips doing the nearest thing to a pout.

'Wasn't she widowed at the outbreak of the Great War?'

I had a flashback. I hadn't encountered insistent probing like this since the occupational therapist put me through a set of questions designed to elicit evidence that my stroke had not damaged my brain functions.

Brain functions in perfect working order, I raised my chin and gave a slight nod to create the impression that Mrs Smith had given me food for thought. I tried to appear unsure. What a pity I didn't have Graham to delegate responsibility for answering. The more so as Mrs S seemed determined to press on.

She tucked a stray strand of hair under her hat.

'Have you known her for long, I wonder?'

I drew a breath, to give me time to think. I couldn't tell whether we were still in the realm of gossip, or whether her show of new-found cordiality disguised an ulterior motive.

I decided to open up a little.

'Hghooo,' *I gurgled.*

She furrowed her brows and eyed me with a pained expression intended to convey sympathy.

'I'm so sorry... I...'

'Hghooo,' *I repeated.* 'Hghooo.' *I tried it again with a final consonant of sorts.* 'Hghooong.'

She tried a version of what I was saying, but it came out even less like what I intended.

I managed a hissing sound from the back of my throat. 'Hhh...khoo.'

'Sss...' she echoed. 'Ssskooo'

I nodded encouragement.

'Ah, now I have it : SCHOOL,' she said with an air of satisfaction.

I made a raucous noise, half gurgle, half sigh, expressing relief.

It had been a minute or so since she asked her initial question and I feared that by now she may have forgotten what it was she wanted to find out.

'So you knew her at school,' she said.

I nodded.

I think she deliberately avoided asking me which school because she foresaw another struggle to understand my reply...

'A local school?' she asked.

Yes, I nodded.

'So you both grew up in this area?'

Hmm-hmm.

Mrs Smith took a moment to contemplate a spot on the horizon. The tide was advancing across the sandbanks towards us. Eventually she turned to me and placed her fingertips on my gnarled hand.

'But you haven't always lived here, have you?' she said softly.

I shook my head. That 'have you?' reverberated in my mind.

'I imagine you had a career before your...' Now she was very cautiously – but unmistakably – bringing forward a proposition.

I nodded my head and wrinkled what I hoped would be a regretful eyebrow : yes, my ... interrupted my plans.

Now she lifted my hand in her palm and placed her other hand on top of it.

'Didn't you go away to train as a teacher?' Mrs Smith was whispering now.

She stared into my eyes. And I realised my eyes are the one vulnerable thing in this carapace of a countenance I've got. The one chink in my armour. I tried to blink, but couldn't stop them welling up. Where did it come from, this sudden regret for the life I might have had? I'd long since come to terms with the consequences of my stroke, but something in the way she asked her question brought a part of the past flooding back.

Mrs Smith was evidently as surprised as I was by my reaction.

'Oh, my dear,' she said as she watched my eyes fill with tears. 'I didn't mean to distress you... I'm so sorry...'

She reached into her bag for a handkerchief and proffered it to me. I took it from her, dabbed my eyes and blew my nose. She fell silent and turned towards the foreshore, giving me a moment to compose myself. Then, still staring out to sea, she spoke again.

'You must forgive me for upsetting you. I really should have known better. But the fact is I've been wanting to...'

She turned to face me, – and suddenly it dawned on me who she was. Geraldine, yes, but who? What was her maiden name?

I tried to give expression to my thoughts.

'Oooh aahh ooo?' I hooted pathetically.

'Yes,' she said, 'Geraldine Clarkson. We met at Training College. Do you remember?'

She gave me a look of entreaty I would never have thought her capable of. I teared up again, cursing my inability to control my feelings.

She noticed my hands become fists as I struggled : not just with my emotions but also with the overwhelming urge I had to assail her with questions I was unable to put into words. She reached out again and covered my hands with hers.

Leaning in to me, she said,

'To begin with I didn't know it was you. After all these years, and then the... effect ... of your stroke...'

She patted my forearm.

'The fact is, when I first moved into the guest house I was not myself. My husband's sudden death, and the realisation that he had left me with barely enough to live on.... I was grief-stricken, and wrapped up in my own misfortune... resentful at the way life had treated me...'

We were face to face now.

'I had a score to settle with... what shall I call it? Fate? And I was so consumed with bitterness I had no sympathy to spare for the feelings of others... I walled myself up...'

I nodded. I recognized some of the symptoms.

'And when I began to suspect who you were, I was too set in my ways to lower my defences ... the more so as...'

I stared at her with watery eyes. Now it was my turn to entreat her.

'Do you remember I was your mentor in your first year at college? I was a senior trainee, deputed to help you settle in.'

I nodded, and tears ran down my cheeks.

'You were full of spirit, I remember, and had firm ideas about what you wanted to do with your life.'

She found another hankie for her own use.

'From time to time I had my work cut out keeping you out of trouble...'

She blew her nose and took a moment to fold up her handkerchief, then continued.

'I was aware we didn't see eye to eye on the new ideas about how women should behave, and I admit I took my duties rather seriously when it came to following the traditional rules.'

At this she smiled, no doubt remembering some of the scrapes I'd got myself into and the lectures she'd had to administer. In spite of myself that smile softened my heart : she could still see a young thing in need of guidance who was – and was not – me.

She breathed in, and there was a tremor in her sigh as she breathed out.

'We were never very close, of course. We had no reason to be. I was in the year above you, we didn't study or do our practice sessions together. A brief glance was the best you could manage if ever we passed each other in a corridor.'

I had to acknowledge it : I'd had little time for her and our acquaintance, such as it was, had been a distant one at best.

We nodded at each other. This much we had to agree on. But there was some regret in our agreement.

'You were making your own radical way while I dutifully toed the line and conformed to expectations...'

I suspect that my inability to sustain a proper dialogue, to keep up my end of the conversation, was actually inducing her to say more than she might have intended. I decided that in the circumstances, the best I could do was to be a good listener.

Then she shut her handbag, closing the fastener with a firm click. For a moment I thought she had finished what she had to say after all.

'And then...' she resumed speaking, 'I terminated my studies. I dropped out of college to get married. I had all the right reasons for doing that – a husband who would provide for me, and so on – but I knew what you and your group would think... We had had our discussions on the topic.'

At this point I had to avoid her eye. I knew what was coming.

'You made it known that you disapproved, and despite the distance between us, the message reached my ears. After all, the college was a closed little world. Of course I was indignant. What business was it of yours? But I had to admit I carried your disapproval away with me...' She breathed in again ; I did the same, and let out a sigh of regret by way of apology. She held her breath for a moment longer. 'And then,' she concluded, 'when I realised that our lives had crossed again, I think that was the main reason why I found it hard to... to... renew our acquaintance.'

I was mortified. To think that my brash, youthful, dogmatic judgement might have impinged on her awareness at all came as a surprise, but the thought that it had stayed with her for almost half a century filled me with something more than regret.

If only I could have explained the state I was in at the time. Married, widowed, bereaved twice over for a man I had misused and then lost... My shoulders sagged and I let my hands fall into my lap. I shook my head.

Then I took her hands and she responded by squeezing mine.

We sat in silence, bonded by nostalgia and contemplating this strange meeting-place our separate lives had eventually brought us to. And I felt a great surge of mutual fondness envelop us both.

22

I heard someone coming along the corridor, so I put back the book I had been holding and turned my attention to the picture on the wall nearby. It was a seascape, but I couldn't tell where. I stayed in front of it, feigning interest, as I heard the door open behind me.

'I see you're admiring my wife's water-colour,' came Mr Beaumont's voice from across the room. I turned to watch him put the tea-tray down on a low table beside the armchair. I had expected Mrs Beaumont to come in with him but he was alone. I felt a slight apprehension as I understood this was to be a man to man conversation.

He stood upright, briefly massaged the small of his back, and took a few stiff steps towards me. 'She used to paint a lot. In the early days we would go out for drives taking a *pique-nique* lunch, with her easel and equipment in the boot, and she would paint *en plein air* while I read my book.'

'I don't seem to recognize the view,' I volunteered.

'It was new to me at the time,' he said, standing beside me. 'It was painted at a spot on the coast, with a view across the bay...' he gestured vaguely into the distance beyond the window. 'The site had once been part of the family estate, so the painting is by way of being a souvenir.'

I let a moment pass in silence, as if absorbed in the work. But I was wondering : was this an unguarded indication that Mrs Beaumont had felt the need to tour the landscapes of her childhood with this man ? After all, if he had grown up around here too, he could be expected to be familiar with them already...

'So... are there many more like this?'

'One or two,' he confided. 'But she keeps them stored away. She doesn't like to have her past on display, she says.'

A woman with a past, I recalled, though I nodded noncommittally. In spite of himself his words carried admissions ; his stilted English left him ill-equipped to manage nuances. He was in foreign territory here, not alert to its pitfalls.

But I couldn't be sure that gave me any sort of advantage in this conversation.

Mr Beaumont – whose actual name I didn't know – touched my arm lightly and invited me to sit down. I resumed my place on the sofa and he proceeded to pour tea. He lifted the milk jug and raised his eyebrows ; I shook my head, recalling that Mrs Horton may have been the victim of a drugged drink. I found myself watching the man's every move, and was relieved to see that he added milk to his own tea.

He placed the cup and saucer on the table in front of me. 'How is your aunt?' he asked. As I was about to answer he added 'Sugar?' and offered me a bowl and teaspoon. I murmured 'Thank you,' and mechanically helped myself. It was only as I began stirring that I realised I might have self-administered some substance aimed at making me speak more freely than I ought – or perhaps pass out completely. The effect on me was immediate – I was on my guard before I absorbed anything at all. I lifted the cup to my lips, let them barely touch the meniscus of the hot liquid, and put it down again, pretending to swallow as I did so. Then I offered a response to his question.

'She's quite well,' I said.

He nodded.

'She seemed somewhat agitated when last we met,' he said.

'Oh, it was just a momentary thing,' I answered. 'I'm sorry she caught you unawares.' I gave him a smile.

He nodded again.

'So,' he said, 'as you must have noticed, I sometimes struggle a little bit with your language. There are even moments when I think everyone sounds like your aunt.'

I gave him a sympathetic smile. He had opened the way to questions I wanted to put.

'Well I'm no good at all when it comes to foreign languages,' I said. 'So I'm sorry if you find my English difficult to understand…'

'Oh no, most of the time I can manage,' he said. 'I've had lots of practice, after all.'

'I understand you were brought up to speak French as a child,' I said.

'Yes, that's right,' he said.

I took another pretend sip of tea.

'So were you… born in France?'

There was a silence. I had a sense that we were at a tipping point.

'Near Antwerp,' he said, and was about to continue when we heard the sound of a car engine outside. Mr Beaumont stiffened, and glanced towards the window.

'Ah, I think that will be my wife,' he said.

In an instant he had pulled back from the brink. Another implicit admission hung in the air. To unfreeze the moment I picked up my tea again and went through the motions of drinking. Over the lip of my cup I noticed him watching me.

Footsteps came along the path and together we listened in silence to the sound of a person entering the house. Mr Beaumont was about to get up but before he could do so the door of the parlour suddenly swung open and Mrs Beaumont strode in. For an elderly lady she moved briskly, and with considerable vigour. He opened his mouth, presumably to explain my presence there, but she cut him short with a torrent of words.

She spoke in French. Though he flicked his eyes to signal my presence, she continued as if I wasn't there. She'd evidently decided she could speak freely because I couldn't understand a word. He responded in kind, the two of them conducting an animated dialogue under my nose. It was an argument, that much was clear : she was telling him off and he was defending himself. To my ears her French was as fluent as his, so she could more than hold her own in what was evidently a difference of opinion between them.

Happy to be ignored, I tried to be as unobtrusive as possible. I switched off and directed my gaze towards the water-colour beside the bookshelves. From a distance the composition impressed itself on me. And suddenly I recognized the spot : it was the view from the bench on the sea wall at Cottsea. I remembered this was a special place for Mrs Horton – and it featured in the manuscript Dr Storth had been investigating. But I had no time to digest the fact : I sensed that the altercation had passed its peak. The whole episode had lasted less than thirty seconds, I suppose. While waiting for things to settle I reached out idly for my cup and saucer.

At the soft sound of the chinking porcelain, Mrs Beaumont broke off what she was saying and rounded on me.

'How much of that have you drunk?' she asked pointedly.

'Erm, well, not very much,' I said, glancing apologetically towards Mr Beaumont.

Mrs Beaumont peered into the sugar bowl.

'How much?' she asked again.

'None,' I answered, shame-faced.

There was a rush of air through her nose and she said something in French, that ended in '…merci'.

Mr Beaumont had a hang-dog expression on his face : so much so that I felt sorry for him, even though it seemed he had tried to drug me. Of course I wasn't supposed to know this and tried my best to appear mystified.

He shifted in his seat. Mrs Beaumont said from the corner of her mouth something in French that might have meant 'think yourself lucky'.

'I'm sorry,' he mumbled.

I stuck to my air of ignorance.

'No,' I said, 'I'm sorry. I didn't want to seem rude. I wasn't very thirsty, that's all.'

'It's not that,' Mrs Beaumont said. 'There is… something wrong with that batch of tea-leaves.' She laughed nervously. 'I had told Thomas that he mustn't use them, and had meant to throw them away, but…' her words trailed off. Then she put on her mannered smile, the hostess confirming that the episode was closed, and declared crisply, 'Anyway, all's well that ends well, eh?'

I returned her smile, while Mr Beaumont got to his feet, picked up the tray, and headed for the door.

'Excuse me,' he murmured.

As he left the room Mrs Beaumont offered an explanation.

'He's not used to dealing with visitors – as I'm sure you are aware. He can get rather flustered.'

'It's all right,' I replied. 'As a matter of fact we were having a pleasant conversation. About your water-colour painting, among other things.'

While I was speaking, footsteps could be heard above our heads. I glanced up at the ceiling. They were uneven steps : step-halt, step-halt. Someone with a limp, I thought.

Mrs Beaumont followed my gaze and spoke firmly to cover the sound.

'Oh, that old thing. It only has sentimental value.'

'I didn't recognize the place where it was painted.'

'Ah yes, I gather you got lost while exploring this area. I imagine Thomas wasn't much help... So you're not familiar with our neck of the woods?'

'No... well, I think I must have cycled around some of the back lanes when I was still at school, but without knowing exactly where I was. I've never actually walked the footpaths over the fields. That's why I lost my way. You have a completely different perspective when you're in the heart of the landscape... But Mr Beaumont said you painted the picture from a spot on the coast.'

She glanced across the room, taking in the picture, evidently wondering what else Mr Beaumont might have said.

'Yes, that's right,' she said distractedly.

I decided to take the plunge.

'I understand Mr Beaumont was born in France – near Antwerp, he was saying....'

She drew herself up, as if bracing herself to counter what I might be about to say.

'... and – you speak fluent French,' I stammered.

She gave a sigh.

'Yes. I'm sorry about that little exchange.'

'Did you learn French when you served as a ... what was it? A VAD? In the war?'

She seemed reluctant to answer.

'Umm – hmm.' She paused. 'So long ago.' She studied me for a moment. Then she said, 'I imagine you were a war baby – the Second World War'.

I nodded.

'Mine was a long time before you were born.'

'The First World War?'

'Yes,' she answered. 'When I was about your age, I suppose.' She gave me a smile: this thought seemed to make her warm to me. She fell silent again, then went on : 'I volunteered at a time when I felt my life was lacking in purpose. I thought I ought to "do my bit", as we used to say.'

I thought I knew what it was to have a life lacking in purpose. Two generations of my elders had told me how their young years were taken up with wars, and none could tell me what to do with my youth in peacetime.

I took a moment to clear my throat.

'I feel as though people like me have never been put to the test like your generation was,' I blurted out.

She gave a little gasp, cupped her right fist in her left hand and propped her chin on them, elbows on knees, considering how to respond.

'Think yourself lucky you weren't!' she said eventually. 'Young you may be but you're mature enough, I'm sure, to see the folly of that temptation – confronting danger and death to prove you're a grown-up. There are better things for a man like you to do.'

I felt duly chastened by her words ; but noticed her eyes glisten with something like affection as she addressed me.

'It must have been hard to be a nurse in the war,' was all I could find to say.

'A nursing auxiliary,' she corrected me. 'Yes, when we joined we could never have imagined how brutal and gruesome it was going to be. We were warned, of course, and put through the necessary training, but…'

Suddenly she changed tack.

'Which is one reason why I was so interested to learn from your aunt that a fellow pupil from Greenhalgh Girls had also signed up.'

'Oh, that… I really don't know much about her. Aunt Marion – ' I pronounced deliberately – 'had never mentioned her before we had that conversation with you.'

Mrs Beaumont nodded. 'After all, Ellen What's-her-name may well have passed on by now. I sometimes ask myself how I survived – to live on for so long…'

I cast around for words.

'Did… Did the nurses actually come under fire during the war?'

She shrank into her chair. She folded her arms across her chest, hugging herself, and closed her eyes.

'If I were to tell you what it was really like…'

She seemed to be at a kind of threshold, a hinge in our encounter ; she could go back or she could press on. She stared at me, appraising me, assessing my likely reaction to what she might find herself saying.

'Young men, just like you… mutilated, disfigured, frightened, crying out…'

I listened. Perhaps in her old age she was losing the capacity to keep her nightmares to herself. Perhaps my being there was serving to revive them. Perhaps I could have found a way of diverting the visions she was calling up. Instead I did a cruel thing : I hung on her words, transfixed, and willed her to say more.

She looked down at the carpet, and her voice dropped to a murmur.

'We worked in a Field Hospital, treating wounded men brought from the Casualty Clearing Stations just behind the lines...' She paused. 'I can still remember the first time I was called on to pick up an amputated arm and dispose of it.' She shook her head to banish the recollection. 'We were within earshot of the artillery fire,' she said, returning to my question. 'Normally we were safe from the shelling, but nurses died of illnesses they caught from injured soldiers : typhus, pneumonia, septicaemia ... If the front line shifted towards us the hospitals had to be moved ..., some nurses were killed by direct hits...'.

Her eyes were following the pattern in the carpet, as if it mapped out her memories.

She lifted her gaze and stared at me again, measuring me up once more. She was about to test me – by passing on her experience of war.

'When the battle was at its height, we were having to deal with scores of wounded at a time. We had no time to think, and mostly we acted mechanically, following the doctor's instructions as they came at us thick and fast... Day after day, night after night, until we were merely going through the motions, exhausted, barely able to distinguish one patient from the next.

I remember one casualty we lost during an operation. A piece of shrapnel that lodged in his throat had partly paralysed him. And the x-ray showed the fragment was wedged alongside the cerebral vertebrae, so it had to be removed. It was an emergency and I was put in charge of administering chloroform – not through the nose, but via the gaping hole in his larynx. The patient was so weak that it only took two drops of chloroform to sedate him. Suddenly the fragment gave way, and the surgeon was able to extract it ; but at that very moment blood came spurting out of the opening where I had applied the gauze mask. It splashed up everywhere, I was drenched from head to toe. One last choking sound, and the wounded man was dead. All in the space of five minutes. The shrapnel had penetrated the front of his throat and struck the carotid artery, but it had been pressing it against the vertebrae, blocking the flow of blood ; as soon as it was dislodged there was nothing to stop the haemorrhaging. I wept and wept, with no thought for changing out of my uniform, or washing myself. The next day I couldn't stop crying, and the next... I tried to carry on, but my strength had gone, my hands would tremble if I tried to help with moving a patient, and whenever I was called on to comfort a soldier in pain, my eyes would fill with tears...'

Her voice died away and she looked down at the carpet again. The colour had gone from her face. There was nothing I could say that wouldn't seem clumsy, so I held my breath, waiting for her to recover her composure. Eventually, as if rousing herself from a trance, she sniffed and said:

'That was the end of my career in a Field Hospital. I had what people today would call a nervous breakdown. There was no name for it then –' She shrugged ' – this was even before they came up with the term shell-shock to explain the impact of trench warfare on the soldiers. So a woman in an emotional state was hardly deserving of a second thought.'

'Did you come back to England?' I asked hesitantly.

'No. I had my reasons for remaining in France. I managed to get myself seconded to a new hospital for Belgian casualties that had been created on the coast, close to the border with France. Most of Belgium had been overrun by the Germans and huge numbers of refugees had to be evacuated to England early in the war.

Many wounded soldiers too... the Red Cross set up a hospital with proper facilities so that fewer displaced Belgian casualties needed to be ferried across the Channel for treatment. A call went out for English nurses and since I was already in the region I found myself working there. It was hard, as you might expect, but in fact it gave me an opportunity to recover from my experience closer to the front line... And I perfected my French, as you might say, among the Belgians.'

A question came into my mind : was this near Antwerp?

But there was a rustle in Mrs Beaumont's demeanour, a shift in her posture, signalling that her mind had moved on.

'Enough of that,' she said. 'Tell me... The other day you were talking about the work you do. You said you had tried several jobs, but I got the impression that you were not really... wedded to anything one might call a career.'

I sat up, taken aback by these remarks. I hadn't been comfortable being the subject of conversation last time, and had merely tried to bluff my way past her questions. And now to find she had actually paid attention and remembered what I'd said made me distinctly uneasy.

'Er, well, I suppose not,' I responded.

'Hmm,' she murmured. 'What would you say to a job that could lead you to a proper future?' she asked.

23

The tide wasn't going to reach the sea wall today. And I think we both sensed that our conversation wasn't going to go much further for the moment. But our emotional reunion had done its work.

Geraldine released my hands she had been clasping, gave my fingers a pat, and began buttoning up her coat collar.

'Now then, should we head back to the house?' she said briskly. 'If we get a move on we'll be home in time for afternoon tea.'

I nodded, and soon she was wheeling me back along the esplanade. I was feeling wistful about the past that had surged up around us, about the possibilities that fate (and our own folly) had denied us. But the arc that had first separated Geraldine and myself, and then brought us together again, seemed to mark a fundamental continuity in our fragmented lives.

Why did I fail to recognize Geraldine? I can only put it down to the simple fact that I had never given her any thought in the forty years or so since she left the Training College. Like everyone else in the guest house, I was introduced to her as 'Mrs Smith', and there was nothing in that name to jog my memory. And though she had been spared the grotesque transformation that had been my lot, the passage of time had done her features no favours either.

Geraldine and I didn't have much in common even when we were briefly studying alongside each other. The few friends I made at college were among the students who completed the course with me ; and once Geraldine Clarkson had dropped out early to get married, so far as I was concerned she was swallowed up in the anonymous morass of dutiful wives.

I think it was her current appearance that misled me. Her very person defied such memories as I had retained. The young woman I remembered from college was a colourless conformist. She had mousey hair in a bob, wore no make-up, dressed in muted shades with severe skirts and blouses, and everything about her bearing was orthodox, predictable, chosen to blend in with her surroundings.

Here in the guest-house she was anything but self-effacing. She had taken her grey hair as a pretext to become a red-head, and had adopted makeup with evident relish. Her green sweaters and crimson lipstick ensured she would never go unnoticed ; but by way of a final touch to her flamboyant persona, that cigarette-holder she brandished at every opportunity left no one in doubt that she was determined to be mistress of ceremonies on all occasions.

I wondered : was it married life that had changed her? I couldn't imagine that her current character fitted the self-effacing role of a bank-manager's wife. Perhaps she had reacted to widowhood by adopting a new identity. Stylish and distinctive, her affections, irritating though they sometimes were, might be a response to grief, anxiety, insecurity...

She was much more interesting than I had been giving her credit for. By the time we got back to the guest-house I was determined to sound her out some more.

*

Still no sign of Graham. Mrs Dugdale seems to have given up hope of seeing him again : she has recruited a lumpish niece of hers to take over his functions. Predictably enough there has been a decline in the quality of service, and Mrs Smith – Geraldine – is making no effort to conceal her dissatisfaction. Her disapproving looks terrify the poor girl, which only makes her even more clumsy. So far there have been no major incidents but everyone's patience is under strain as she labours painfully to carry out her menial tasks.

But what can have happened to Graham? He showed no signs of wanting to give up his job. He was good at the work and got on well with the residents and staff. Could it be that he had grown fed up of having to deal with me? He may have felt under pressure to take me for walks and in the end had found it burdensome to be my carer – it wasn't what he was paid for, after all. I thought we had developed a sort of acquaintance that didn't impose any moral obligations on him, but you never know. I suppose it was to be expected that a young man of his age would hope to find other more attractive females to distract him.

So that's another companion who's abandoned me in recent weeks. As Oscar Wilde might have put it : to lose one young man may be regarded as a misfortune ; to lose two looks like carelessness.

To tell the truth, my liking for Graham has come to overshadow my attachment to Hughie. He possesses a kind of stolid presence that Hughie, for all his urbanity, tended to lack. But I can't help thinking that Graham's disappearance has about it the same air of mystery that Hughie's had. I still don't have any idea what happened to my charming Scotsman ; but I continue to suspect that Quainton Lodge holds the clue.

The clue to what, exactly? Hughie is a grown man and increasingly the thought of him being held against his will by a pair of old-age pensioners seems far-fetched – a figment of an elderly woman's imagination.

But ruminating on my recent sentimental misfortunes triggers a surge of remembrance that still pains me : my record of carelessness extends to another loss, that of the young man I let slip away all those years ago... What might be left of him...?

'Marion?' a voice summons me from my reverie. 'Marion,' it calls in a hoarse stage whisper. It's Geraldine, trying to catch my attention from across the room. 'Do you mind if I – ?'

And she comes over, pulls up the nearest chair, and sits down beside me. I reflect that I have been missing close company, and the reversal in our relations helps fill the gap. I stare at her with a question in my eyes. I would be hard put to it to formulate a precise question, but my disability saves me the trouble.

Geraldine pats my hand as it lies on the table, and leans in with a confidential air.

'I've been wondering...' she says tentatively.

I raise my eyebrows, encouraging her to continue.

'Mrs Beaumont,' she murmurs, and looks around the room to ensure that no one can hear. 'Do you see much of her?'

I shake my head and pucker my lips : not really.

'Do you think we might pay her a visit? After all, if you were at school together she might like a chance to swap more reminiscences. You know,' she adds with a smile, 'discussing memories keeps old age at bay...'

I point to my mouth and roll my eyes a bit : I can hardly hold my own in a nostalgic dialogue.

'Of course I understand,' she responds. 'But I'm sure Mrs Beaumont has lots to say for herself, and all you need do is nod.'

She gives me a sly grin.

'And I think I'm a pretty good chatterbox when the occasion calls for it,' she says. 'I could fill in for you if ever the conversation should flag.'

Then her voice drops further.

'To be honest, I would welcome a chance to talk with someone of her... calibre,' she says, a plaintive note in her voice.

So there it is : the snobbery that dare not speak its name. I can't hold it against her. Living in a guest house represents quite a come-down for a bank manager's wife. And conversing with Hilda Beaumont would be a reminder of the old days when she had a position in provincial society.

As we rolled along, I watched Geraldine out of the corner of my eye. She took the business of driving very seriously. I raised my hands, mimicking hers on the steering wheel, and put a question with my eyes.

'Ah yes,' she nodded. 'I learned to drive in the war. I don't suppose you can imagine me behind the wheel of an ambulance?' she smiled. 'That was my way of asserting my independence.'

She left a silence, in which I recalled how I had dismissed her, during our college days, as a biddable subservient female.

I made a cooing sound to express my admiration.

'Yes,' she said. 'That was the high point of my driving career. After the war, Reginald was in charge of our motor car and he wasn't comfortable at the thought of me driving it. I had no objection to being chauffeured everywhere, so I rather lazily let my skills grow rusty. And when Reginald died, I couldn't afford the upkeep so had to sell the car.' She glanced across at me to check that I was listening, then back at the road. 'And that would have been the end of the matter – except that Millicent's husband still has his motor, though he has been too ill to drive for quite some time. Millicent has never learned to drive, so she suggested I might like to take the car out for a run now and again, just to keep it in good order. I was surprised at how easy I found it to pick up where I had left off...'

She concentrated on her driving, and I watched the countryside go by, looking out for the next turning. I had told Geraldine that I would be able to give her directions and she was happy to trust me. I would grunt or growl from time to time and gesture in one direction or the other : up to now we had not lost our way, so far as I could judge.

She was dressed for a formal event ; she had put on her makeup – rouged cheeks and vermilion lipstick – and was wearing a pearl necklace and earrings. A russet-coloured beret, perched on her *head, set off the red of her dyed hair. I could imagine her in her heyday, sallying forth for a gathering where she expected to shine by virtue of her husband's status and her own social graces. She was more animated than I had seen her before, presumably excited at the prospect of reviving her old aura when face to face with such examples of the county set as our backwater could offer. Quite apart from my other interests in the encounter, I was looking forward to seeing her put on a show.*

To entertain me as the road unfurled before us, she offered bits of tittle-tattle about various residents in the guest house. But this was just a prelude to her real subject : Hilda Beaumont. I soon gathered that her knowledge of Hilda wasn't restricted to what she would have picked up about her as a client of her husband's bank.

'I believe Mrs Beaumont... has a cousin, doesn't she?' she asked.

I paused – then nodded hesitantly.

Then, bluntly, she said, 'I wonder where she picked up that replacement man who carries her husband's name?'

I was glad that my reaction did not show.

I was puzzled at first, but then began to suspect that Graham had been telling Mrs Smith about our dealings with the Beaumonts.

We hadn't announced our decision to pay them a visit. Geraldine would take responsibility for explaining my impromptu arrival on their doorstep. With a sympathetic glance in my direction, she would give them to understand that it was merely a charitable gesture on her part – a brief outing for one whose life was mainly confined to the four walls of the guest house.

On balance, I was confident that her social skills would camouflage my own purpose – her gift for small talk would serve to put Hilda at her ease and perhaps encourage her to open up about her past – which with luck would furnish insights into whatever was going on currently.

Geraldine drew the car up alongside Quainton Lodge, gave the accelerator one last stab so that the engine roared before it died, and applied the handbrake with a determined yank. She took a moment to survey the front of the house.

'Hmm,' she murmured. 'Some Georgian features in urgent need of restoration.'

I noticed that the front windows were no longer shuttered, though net curtains obscured the interior.

Geraldine stepped out of the car and slammed her driver's door shut. I opened my passenger door and lifted out my lower legs so I could lever myself up from my seat. My wheelchair would not fit in Millicent's modest motor car, so I was reduced to a drag-footed trudge as I made my way to where Geraldine stood at the cast-iron gate.

She adjusted her beret and flashed me a wink.

'They'll have noticed that we're here. They'll be expecting us.'

Swinging open the heavy gate, she strode up the path with an imperious bearing designed to place her respectability beyond doubt and cause doors to open at her mere approach.

Sure enough, she had no need to use the bell-push. Before she reached the front steps, the timbered door swung back and Hilda Beaumont emerged from the dark porch. She blinked in the daylight.

She eyed us guardedly and was about to speak when Geraldine launched into her exordium.

'My dear Mrs Beaumont, I do hope we're not intruding. My name is Geraldine Smith – I don't suppose that name means anything to you but in the dim and distant past I believe our paths crossed. Furthermore' – *she gestured to me* – *'we have one or two acquaintances in common.'*

Mrs Beaumont gazed past her and caught sight of me. Her eyes narrowed slightly ; but the courtesy that Mrs Smith's demeanour commanded compelled her to arrange her face into a smile that gave nothing away. Meanwhile Mrs Smith continued her tirade.

'You remember Mrs Horton I'm sure. We were out for a drive, my friend and I, and found ourselves in the vicinity ; and it occurred to us to drop in on you ... I do hope that wasn't too presumptuous of us.'

Hilda was reconsidering what she had at first intended to say, but even as her lips were reshaping themselves, Geraldine cut her off once more.

'I must say, you have a splendid example of rustic Georgian architecture here. Not many people appreciate the distinctive features, do they?'

'Well...,' Hilda began.

'Yes indeed,' Geraldine went on, taking a step backwards and staring up at the masonry. 'But alas, the upkeep can cost a king's ransom, and one has to rely on the availability of skilled craftsmen to ensure the work is done properly...'

A worried expression flitted across Hilda's face and she moved forward to see what sign of deterioration might have caught Mrs Smith's eye. Was this woman here in an official capacity? Was she on a crusade to preserve the English heritage?

Hilda stared at me : was I a party to some design that had brought this inquisitive woman to her door?

Geraldine had fallen silent as she continued to scrutinize the front of the house ; her eyebrows raised, she breathed out through her nose and made a series of throat-clearing noises.

Hilda was compelled to fill the silence, though she was clearly uncertain what words to use.

'Erm... well, perhaps you'd like to come inside,' she said finally. For my benefit she added, 'Mrs Horton, it's a pleasure to see you again... I've been hoping we might continue our conversation.' She kept her shoulders forward and forearms across her body, looking defensive or submissive, it was hard to say. She stepped back, inviting us to cross the threshold, and as Geraldine followed me, Hilda led the way into the room behind the bay window which had previously been shuttered.

Far from having a sinister purpose, all that the blinds had concealed was furniture clustered incongruously, elderly armchairs facing grandiose sofas across a jumble of occasional tables. Deep bookcases lined the walls, leaving footstools and plant stands to jostle for the restricted floor-space.

The descendants of the family which had had to sell up and move out of the big hall further up the lane had evidently brought every last heirloom to the gatehouse with them. In this room the past was preserved and time stood still, immobile as the upright piano that had been pushed into the far corner.

Mrs Beaumont straightened the antimacassars on two button-back wing chairs and gestured to us to sit down. The seat was too low for me and I had to let myself drop into it awkwardly ; Mrs

Beaumont made an apologetic noise. Mrs Smith settled down as if to the manner born and surveyed the room, taking in the bric-a-brac on the shelves.

'Your antiques are rather splendid,' she said. 'I dare say you've had several generations of collectors in the family.'

Mrs Beaumont glanced briefly towards the ornaments. 'Oh, just a few bibelots that survived the Great War,' she said.

Mrs Smith nodded as she prepared her next conversational gambit. Hilda caught my eye but before she could say anything Geraldine cut in.

'Do you have children, Mrs Beaumont?'

'No,' she replied.

'Ah no,' Geraldine responded, and having decided to take the plunge, she went on, 'I seem to recall that you were widowed at the start of the war...'

Mrs Beaumont raised her eyes, gave a slight shrug, and looked at her without responding.

Mrs Smith pressed on. I couldn't tell whether she was oblivious to the reaction her words were likely to provoke, or had decided to go ahead regardless.

'Of course,' she said, 'I didn't know you at the time. It was when you came to prominence as a campaigner among the wives and widows of the war... For a while your name was on everyone's lips. Such a heroic response to your bereavement. That's when I first heard of you.' She paused, leaning towards Hilda. 'I was very moved by a speech I heard you make, urging us young women to play our part in the war effort. Believe it or not, that's when I decided to learn to drive, so that I could help with transport – and ambulances. It was a life-changing moment for me – and I owe it all to

you... You can't imagine how much it meant to me... You were an inspiration to many others too...'

Loquaciousness, as I have learned from observing conversations I could not take part in myself, creates in those who must put up with it an almost unbearable urge to speak. Hilda had pinched her lips and was biting her tongue as she listened to Geraldine's effusive outpourings, and though she didn't interrupt directly, I could tell she could hardly contain herself. I watched in anticipation of how she would respond when the rambling monologue came to an end.

Eventually Geraldine heaved a sigh and announced her conclusion.

'Ah, those were the days!'

There was a pause. Hilda rose and switched on a lamp. She was taking time to consider her response. The half-light seemed to create a sense of intimacy.

'Well, all that is in the past now,' she said, sitting down again. 'But it's strange, isn't it, that those formative years seem to have stayed with our generation despite the passage of time. It's true that the men – those who survived the war – find it hard to give expression to what they went through...' She paused. 'We've seen many examples of men who were robbed of words even when they were not physically impaired. But I can tell you that my time as a nursing auxiliary in the field changed me for ever.'

She stirred in her chair, casting a glance at me.

'So even though we may have memories of schooldays in common... I have to say that my wartime experiences have eclipsed them somewhat.'

I pondered this – as I had the leisure to do, since she could hardly expect a reply from me. From somewhere else in the house I heard a sound like the scraping of a chair on floorboards.

Geraldine evidently felt that a response to Hilda's remark was called for. I was surprised by what she did next.

'I wonder – ,' she asked, 'would you mind if I smoke?'

Hilda welcomed this distraction.

'Not at all,' she said, and got up to move an ash tray to a table beside her guest.

Geraldine drew her cigarette-holder from her handbag along with a packet of cigarettes. She offered the packet to Hilda, who shook her head. We found ourselves both watching as Geraldine went on to insert a cigarette into her cigarette holder and pull out her gold lighter. Before she struck the spark, with the mouthpiece clenched between her teeth she began to speak, from the corner of her mouth.

'It's true that as the years pass and our lives take one direction or another, the possibilities that filled our childhood tend to close down and can get forgotten,' she said.

She lit the cigarette, drew from it, puffed out the smoke, and put her lighter back in her handbag. This business was evidently intended to give us time to consider her words.

'For example,' she went on, taking the cigarette holder from her mouth, 'I was a diligent schoolgirl and decided quite early that I wanted to be a teacher. I even enrolled at the Training College, as Marion remembers.' I nodded, wondering what on earth she was getting at. 'But it was not to be, as I met the man who became my husband and he decided otherwise. But I can't say I have forgotten the potential I turned my back on.'

She took another puff and produced a further plume of smoke, which she swept away, like an orchestra conductor, with a wave of her cigarette-holder.

In some people's world, to talk about themselves is to get to know the other person better. Clearly she had this precept in mind.

Hilda seemed quite taken by Geraldine's words. She nodded and pursed her lips. Something had been conjured up in her mind – something from before her world lurched in an unexpected direction, perhaps?

But it was to me that she turned to put her thoughts into words.

'I have wondered,' she said. 'When we first met, Marion, when you were trying to trace an old school friend – what was her name, Ellen Keighley? – you told me – your nephew told me – that your maiden name was Rawcliffe. I didn't recall anyone of that name. But your first name put me in mind of another Marion whom I do remember from our Greenhalgh School days. Her family name, as I recall, was Halstead. Marion Halstead.'

She paused, let silence fill the space between us, and looked me in the eyes – the only part of my face that might have betrayed a reaction. And indeed, I did blink when she spoke my name. I couldn't help myself. I was once that girl, the one who had been engaged to the man she later married... I had to hope she hadn't noticed, as I took refuge behind my blank expression. I tipped my head to one side, as if searching for a memory, then shook it slowly. Sorry, no...

But at the same time, my right hand rose to my throat in spite of myself, and my fingers plucked at the neck of my jumper, in a gesture that betrayed my real response.

Hilda watched my hand, and stared at me insistently once more. Then she knew. And I knew she knew.

'There we are,' Geraldine butted in as Hilda and I stared at each other. 'However deeply the past is buried by subsequent experiences, a half-forgotten detail like that can suddenly spring up as if from nowhere.'

She gave one of her throaty laughs, and tapped out her cigarette.

'Why, it was just the other day that Marion and I discovered we had been fellow-students many years ago, before we went our separate ways.' In a brusque escape of breath she added, 'Would you believe that neither of us recognized the other, though we had been living at close quarters for quite some time?'

'Really?' said Hilda, wrinkling her brow, and her eyes moved back and forth between Geraldine and myself. 'Well, stranger things have been known to happen,' she commented. I felt her unspoken resentment at the way I had exploited my infirmity to take advantage of her.

Our conversation – which was beginning to feel like a confrontation – was interrupted by more muffled noises from upstairs.

Hilda sprang up, clearly intent on distracting us.

'Well, a fine hostess I am – should I make us some tea?...' She bustled around the low tables, arranging them for trays and cups. 'But my, it's growing dark outside. Perhaps... but we can't part without enjoying a cup of tea, can we?'

The ritual of taking tea, and the small talk that accompanied it, took up an hour and I could tell that Hilda, beneath her urbane manner, was counting the minutes.

Eventually, as tea and talk were running out, she turned to me and adopted a sort of stage whisper which conveyed to Geraldine that this was a matter that concerned just the two of us.

'Marion, I was thinking about our conversation the other day. I wonder if...'

I couldn't think of a recent conversation with Hilda that might account for her tone just now, but I did recognize the invitation to accept a show of complicity between us. I nodded.

'Well,' Hilda said. 'I was wondering, since Geraldine has been so kind as to bring you here, if I might detain you a little longer to deal with those matters before you go.'

Perplexed, I could do nothing but flash a glance towards Geraldine as if to say : 'What about her?'

This was Hilda's cue. She turned, benevolent and gracious, towards Mrs Smith.

'My dear Geraldine, would you think it terribly rude of me if I were to monopolize Marion for the rest of the evening? There are some points – some personal business – that she and I rather left hanging the other day...'

She gave Geraldine her most winning smile. I couldn't do the same but tried a beseeching look. So sorry about this, I sought to convey through my eyes. This is something I can't get out of...

'I shall of course bring Marion back to the guest house later on,' said Hilda.

Geraldine had been put on the spot, she knew. But Hilda's best society manner called for a matching response – that too she knew. So murmuring 'By all means,' she folded her napkin and rose from her chair, delicately brushing crumbs from her jumper, and said unctuously,

'It has been a pleasure talking with you. I hope we might meet again to resume our conversation.'

Moments later, she had put on her coat and all the dignity she could muster, and was marching down the path towards the car that she had brought me in.

24

'My apologies for drawing you into that piece of subterfuge,' Hilda said as the lamps of Geraldine's car receded into the twilight. 'The fact is there are several things I've been wanting to talk through with you, and I couldn't let the opportunity pass... I think we are beginning to understand each other better, and this is a good time...' she added, closing the curtains to shut out the darkness, the damp and the fog. Then she switched on two standard lamps – one behind me and one behind the facing chair, which she seated herself in. Encircled by shadows, we sat beneath two pools of light, isolated from the world outside, and the space between us was suddenly charged with an air of intimacy and expectation as Hilda took thought for a moment, the knuckle of one forefinger on her lips. Then she began to speak.

'When I became engaged to Thomas I felt I was the luckiest girl alive. He was handsome, of course ; clever, gentle and kind, but strong and calm. I knew I could rely on him ; he would be the man I could build a secure future with.'

She paused and glanced around the room, once the setting for the future she had envisaged.

'But to tell the truth, this was only what I came to understand once we married. Up till then I was chiefly aware of my own feelings more than Thomas's many qualities. In the heat of the moment, when I first realised he was mine, I was elated. Because I had won the boy who had caught everyone's eye....'

She stared at the floor, the memory of her childhood folly bringing a rueful smile to her face.

She could not know what expression my face would assume if it hadn't lost the capability ; but my heart skipped a beat and the thud beneath my ribs felt like it reverberated across the room.

As if in response, Hilda raised her eyes. She spoke the next few words softly.

'Of course, he was on the rebound. His heart had been broken by his previous fiancée...'

There was no irony in her words, no bitterness or sarcasm aimed at me : at a distance of almost fifty years, she was simply inviting me to acknowledge the facts. I pinched my lips and gave a slight nod. I avoided her eye : I was in no mood to retaliate with rumours of how she had mistreated Thomas after they were married. Perhaps she had found it hard to live with a man still half in love with another woman. A brief flash of longing coursed through me in spite of myself : suppose that had been so?

'He was much too considerate to let this show, naturally. The way he behaved towards me was everything I could have hoped for. But I could tell that in some sense his heart wasn't in our marriage. He had decided to make the best of things, but I would always be second-best. He set about being a

good husband and making a good marriage, he was conscientious and dutiful. But as time went by, I learned to read the signs of a man resigned to his fate.'

She allowed herself a pained smile. And I understood how misplaced had been my resentment during all the years in which I had hated her for having stolen him away, as I saw it, while I was momentarily distracted by another. The last laugh had been on her, I reflected.

Hilda took a deep breath and continued with a sigh.

'It was obvious that the spark that attracted everyone – not least me – had gone out of him. In the end, I could hardly bear to look him in the eye, because what I saw there was a crippled soul staring out onto an emotional wasteland.'

Then she fell silent. Knowing that I could not reply in words, she examined me for other reactions. I took in a breath that caught in my throat : there came a hoarse sob that was enough to convey some of the pain I was feeling. Not for her, but for me : for the possibilities I had thrown away in a mad rush of attraction for another man.

'I came to hate you,' she said matter-of-factly. 'You captured my husband even before we married.' She turned her face to mine, scrutinizing the wretched mess it had become. 'And he remained your prisoner ever afterwards.'

It was my turn to squirm uncomfortably in my chair. I cleared my throat but could do nothing more.

Then Hilda's tone suddenly changed ; her voice was more assured.

'Oh, I did what I could to retaliate for his not being able to love me as he had vowed to do. I had *my pride, after all. So I tried to suggest that if I couldn't be the one for him, then he couldn't count on being the one for me...' She paused. 'That tested even his good nature... We began to quarrel... Our life together was very difficult.'*

As she spoke I wrestled with conflicting emotions. Guilt towards her, pity for Thomas, profound regret for what I had done to him, remorse for wrecking two lives. And also a deep, wretched gratitude on learning that he had apparently continued to love me in spite of my mindlessly ruining his happiness.

Had this been a normal, two-sided conversation, I could have kept up the momentum by sharing my emotions, cajoling, encouraging Hilda to go on. But hoarse croaks from a hapless face would have been a grotesque way to react. So despite the feelings that flooded through me I made no effort to express myself, and sat motionless, unable to formulate a response.

I needn't have worried. Hilda still had more to say. And I began to suspect that as frequently happened, my lack of reaction, my inanimate features, created the impression that I wasn't taking things in. So my presence, such as it was, didn't inhibit her. I was 'not all there', as they say. Hilda was only half-aware that she was being listened to, and so she was able to speak freely, as if confiding her secrets to no one in particular.

In fact, her next words were spoken as if she was alone with her thoughts.

'If I hadn't been in such a rush to snatch him away, I might have noticed his true state of mind. Once we were married it was too late. We were condemned to make each other miserable. At the time when war was threatening to break out, there

was already a state of open hostility between us. So when war was declared, he took it as an opportunity to escape from a marriage that had become unbearable.'

With this she returned to the present, and addressed me directly.

'Why am I telling you all this?' she said. She took a deep breath. 'Perhaps because I feel I owe you an explanation.'

Of what, I wondered? Did she think she would make me feel better in the knowledge that she gained nothing by depriving me of Thomas? She left me to ponder this for a moment, then continued with her story.

'When Thomas was reported missing, presumed killed in action : what did I feel? Sadness, grief, obviously. Relief, too, that our trials were over – his anyway. Loss? I don't know. But whatever emotions I had been subject to at first, they were soon overtaken by a crushing sense of remorse. I had caused him to go missing. I had been responsible for his unhappiness. I was guilty of having betrayed him while he was alive, and I had to compensate not only for his death but for his ruined life.'

She frowned and bit her lip.

'I had to do penance.'

I shook my head. It was up to her to decide whether I sympathised, or whether I agreed that she was guilty.

In any event, intentional or not this came as a barb in my flesh too. Was it possible that Thomas went off to war and got himself killed because I broke his heart? Which of we two women was most to blame?

'This all seems like emotional incontinence, doesn't it?' Hilda went on. *'With hindsight, the intensity of youth can seem overdone, I suppose. Perhaps I could have settled for a humdrum, day-to-day atonement, and time would have done its work. But there was a war on, and we experienced everything so fervently, didn't we? There was a taste for sacrifice in the air. And I found an outlet for my emotions in volunteering to support the war effort. You might remember I was quite a campaigner, urging women to do their bit on the home front.'*

At this I did manage a nod. I well remembered her fiery, inspirational speeches tinged, I now realised, with a hysterical impulse to purge her remorse.

'But I found I needed more. I had to admit that being in the limelight distracted me from my real motives. I had to go beyond mere patriotic harangues. I felt a compulsion to get involved closer to the battlefield, where Thomas was reported missing. That's when I joined the VADs.

They didn't just accept anyone, but I had connections by virtue of my father's standing... I threw myself into the training programme, which was hard work. But I welcomed the discipline – it was what I needed to drive out the thoughts that tormented me. I still couldn't be sure if Thomas was alive or not : even the War Office insisted I wait for six months before they would confirm him as a 'fatality' and grant me a widow's pension. Can you imagine ?

So I suppose I was clutching at straws when I looked forward to the prospect of being near where Thomas went missing. In the event I found myself at a Field Hospital closer to the Somme than to

Ypres ; but with every push from either side we would have to dismantle our installation and move with the tide of battle.

I have to admit the experience was largely blurs, though in retrospect I can see that we worked at a punishing pace. The casualty rate was often overwhelming, and we worked amidst a tide of the maimed and the mutilated, the dying and the dead, to the sound of soldiers crying in agony. I told myself I had to put myself through this, and even though the most rigorous training couldn't prepare anyone for the horrors we had to confront, part of me welcomed the ordeal as my punishment for having driven Thomas to risk his life in this inferno. After a while I felt inured to the suffering around me, and it was a kind of blessing that the work numbed my personal feelings too. I worked as conscientiously as I had been taught to do, and drove myself to the limit ; but inevitably I found I couldn't function any more.'

She stopped talking, aware that I had been silent throughout all she said, and she looked to me for a response. I raised my hand to my cheek, placed my little finger on my lips, stared at her and shook my head. She took that as the gesture of sympathy that was intended, and inhaled deeply, letting out a sigh as she continued.

'My superiors noticed too... I know I had impressed them by my commitment – I had been commended more than once. But when it became obvious that I was no longer at my best, even they had to acknowledge I was not much use to them any more.

I tried to protest when I was told I should stand down, but to be fair I didn't even have the strength to insist. However, the matron of our detachment did make a concession : instead of sending me back home, she detailed me to a hospital near the border with Belgium. It had been created to treat Belgian troops whose country was occupied by the enemy. It had convalescent wards for those soldiers who could not be sent home, and I was assigned to light duties in these wards, which enabled me to carry on working, after a fashion, while recovering from my experiences behind the trenches.'

I managed to make a sound that I hoped echoed the relief she must have felt at that time. She acknowledged my show of sympathy, nodding for slightly longer than seemed called for. Then she shrugged her shoulders and pursed her lips.

'That was when matters became more complicated than I could have expected.'

I raised my eyebrows as she hesitated to continue. It was the best I could do to encourage her to go on.

'Among the convalescents was an infantryman who had suffered a shrapnel wound in the chest causing haemothorax. After aspiration he had seemed to recover from the initial trauma, but remained at risk of a pneumothorax, and he required close supervision.

So I tended to see a lot of him. He was Belgian by birth, he told me, but had spent the last few years in Paris, where he had been hoping to make a name for himself as a writer. Since he had been invalided from the trenches he had been trying to write a record of his experience. I knew nothing at all about the literary life, but found his manner so charming that when he asked me if I'd like to read something he had written, I found it hard to refuse.

I was somewhat hesitant since at the time I felt my French was still quite rudimentary, despite the best efforts of our teachers at Greenhalgh Girls High. My ability to speak the language had improved through my contacts with French nurses who worked at casualty stations behind the battle-lines. Hence my ease in conversation with Paul. But to begin with, reading was a challenge, though I was pleasantly surprised to discover that my schoolgirl grounding in grammar served me well... that and the fact that Paul wrote in very pure French.'

She paused, and seemed to be considering how to continue.

'I would probably not have gone along with his suggestion, had it not been for the fact that Paul was quite a likeable man, and I felt sorry for him. He had no relations to write to and rarely received mail ; he had lost touch with most of his friends since Belgium had fallen under German occupation. So that while other patients with family and relatives wrote letters home, Paul simply wrote for himself. Others in his position resorted to signing up for official pen-friends, young women volunteers back on the home front whom they were encouraged to call 'marraines' and who referred to their soldiers as 'filleuls' – to discourage any hint of improper communications. Paul told me that in response to his one attempt at that kind of correspondence he had received such a torrent of mawkish sentimentality and cloying patriotic fervour that he had had to give it up.

Initially I began reading Paul's work purely for recreation. It was a way of improving my French and filling those hours between shifts when I would otherwise be assailed by my memories of the front-line casualties and thoughts of Thomas.

Little in what I read by Paul came as a surprise to me. But I was still in a vulnerable state and I had misgivings about being plunged back into the world of the trenches. Many of the wounded in the Field Hospital had struggled to put their suffering into words but most were rendered speechless by their agony. And we who could only watch their pain and hear them cry out had nothing to offer them. We know now that veterans of the war prefer not to speak about it, and with good reason. But Paul's written descriptions cut through the delirium and the numbing anguish to make clear just how appalling an ordeal trench warfare was. He was recreating his personal experience to bear witness on behalf of the inarticulate victims. That's when I understood that he was a natural writer, with a gift for bringing those horrors under control by shaping them through precise and sober prose.

Which makes it all sound very solemn. But the fact is that he wrote with a light touch about every aspect of the soldiers' stories, and could counter the brutal carnage with sharp and witty observations about the ludicrous aspects of military routine.

So, every so often I would retreat to my dormitory with the latest episode of Paul's writing, and read for hours on end. As my reading became more fluent I could imagine I was a friend back home, getting letters from the front ; except that what I read was a far cry from the formulaic paragraphs imposed by the military censor.

These pages were full of life and colour as well as violence and mutilation, and yet at the same time there was a strange equanimity in their style, in the rhythm of the sentences and the mellow voice that spoke through them. One forgot that they were the work of a convalescent, a man who had recently been at death's door. And ... – inevitably, I suppose – as I came to admire the writer I found myself growing increasingly fond of the man.'

At this point Hilda showed signs of embarrassment...

'It was not long before I realised the feeling was mutual. Paul had been very grateful to me for agreeing to read his work ; and since my response to what I read was invariably favourable, he obviously warmed to me. But there was more than that. He would take my hand to thank me each time I gave him back his manuscript, and gradually my hand would linger in his, and it became clear that between us there was a genuine affection.

Of course the war continued to drag on as this... tendresse developed. In the convalescent ward where we spent most of our time together we were at a remove from the storm outside. But this sentimental interlude could not last, obviously. Though Paul had been declared unfit to return to active service, he would soon be discharged as a patient. For my part, I had no wish to go back to the Field Hospital. As a matter of fact I could wish for nothing more than to continue caring for Paul, wherever he was – wherever I was.'

25

Hilda's voice sounded wistful, but her features had become drawn and distant. All this was so remote, her face seemed to say. Certainly such thoughts were going through my mind. We had both become accustomed to living with memories that had dulled with age, losing definition to the point where they might have belonged to someone else – someone we had long ago ceased to be. Nevertheless I could sense that telling the story of her experiences had served to revive them ; and where Hilda's story impinged on my own, to my surprise I found myself reliving emotions I thought I had outgrown.

Hilda understood this, and mused half to herself :

'Talking of a shared past is seductive, isn't it?... You realize that certain events have grown more powerful in the mind with the passage of time.' She raised her eyes to mine. 'I must admit though, meeting your friend Mrs Smith affected me more than I might have expected. Listening to someone who claims they knew you back then although you were completely unaware of their existence – it's *like looking into a mirror that becomes a bottomless pool.'*

She paused and patted her hair, evidently in response to a moment of hesitancy. She plucked at the fabric of the chair arm.

'How far do our actions ripple out?' she continued. 'To think that memories we've forgotten have been picked up and preserved by others... It's as if some don't really belong to us at all... how many surprises might they still hold for us?'

She caught my eye.

'And as for your reappearance...'. Her lips formed a tight smile. 'I thought I had come to terms with what happened. But here you are, back from that dim and distant past we have in common but had both –' she directed a questioning look at me '– both put behind us?...' She paused a moment for her words to register. Then as an afterthought she added, 'I suppose I should resent you for tricking me like you did.'

I managed to make a warbling sound, an apology of sorts. I wanted to say I had been as surprised as she was by the turn of events that had brought our lives back together. I opened and closed my mouth, which fell far short of what I wanted to convey. Actually, Hilda herself put my thoughts into words as she went on :

'Now we're two old ladies, but like it or not we have a debt to our joint past... a shared loyalty, so to speak. And I find there's always more to say about when we were young women...'

There was a silence. Then without warning Hilda threw up her hands and sighed.

'I'm sorry, but try as I may not to let it affect me, your poor face is quite unsettling. What is it that Shakespeare says ? "There's no art to find the

mind's construction in the face." I can't even tell what kind of person you are, let alone what you're thinking as I talk.'

I shrugged my shoulders, took a deep breath and let it out with a gurgle that was harsh and moist, as close as I could get to an expression of regret : sorry, there's nothing I can do about that. But I did appreciate her candour. I leaned forward and extended one hand palm upward. After a moment's hesitation she did the same, reaching across the space between us to take my hand in hers.

'Sorry,' she murmured, 'it's not for me to complain. The fact is...'

She hesitated, searching for words.

'...I sometimes think that everything that's happened since our young days is a bit unreal. The fact is, I've never found anyone I could talk to about what took place afterwards. I've begun to realise that of all the people I have known, you are the one best placed to... to... understand...?' Again her voice lifted and the hint of a query hung on her lips. Then a sceptical note crept in. 'But there again, you have good reason to be hostile...'

I puffed out my cheeks : well I don't know about that ; my own behaviour was not beyond reproach...

Hilda gave a small sigh .

'Thank you,' she said. I wasn't sure what she had to thank me for, but something in her seemed to relax as she evidently decided she could trust me to listen without rushing to judgement.

She resumed her story.

'There we were, near the Belgian border, Paul about to be discharged and me desperate to stay with him. He had no home to return to, since the Germans had occupied his country and their

brutality towards the population was notorious. But the phrase "plucky little Belgium" was on everyone's lips and the country had won a special place in the hearts of the Allies : hundreds of thousands of Belgian refugees had already crossed the Channel and been made welcome here.'

I nodded. Our local chapel had been one of several that had found accommodation for these displaced people. And I could still recall some of the names of volunteers who had invited refugees into their homes.

Hilda had paused to draw breath and scrutinize me. Encouraged by such signs as I could make to assure her I was attending to her words, she plunged on.

'What's more, you might remember it had become common practice for Belgian soldiers to take leave in England. So it wasn't difficult to persuade the authorities that as a Belgian refugee, and a soldier recovering from war wounds, Paul should be permitted to join his fellow exiles who had found asylum here.'

She smiled at the memory. Then pursed her lips.

'The tricky part was convincing my Matron that I needed to take leave in order to recuperate at home. To show willing while leaving the war zone I proposed to accompany a contingent of Belgian stretcher-cases and convalescents scheduled to make the Channel crossing. The idea struck me as a bit transparent, but fortunately Matron agreed.'

She shook her head, still slightly surprised at the success of their ploy. Then she brightened as she went on.

'Once we were back in England, my parents were only too ready to take in this stateless young hero who had been driven from his homeland and

invalided out of his army. I think it presented them with an opportunity to show they were doing their bit in the struggle against the Kaiser. They could hold their heads up alongside the proprietors of the boarding houses on the sea-front who were making quite a ceremony out of having soldiers billeted on them.'

I nodded. This fitted with my recollections of the time. As rationing began to bite, the queues in the local shops had their share of landladies claiming preferential treatment on account of the refugees they had taken in as lodgers.

'For my part, well I took care to be wearing my nurse's uniform when I arrived home with him, which established in their eyes that this was a formal arrangement, a matter of civic duty and nothing more...'

All I could do to acknowledge what she was saying was make a guttural noise intended to sound complicit but which resembled a snigger of sorts. Hilda stopped short when she heard it, and raised her eyebrows. Was I being ironic? I fluttered my hands and a sharp intake of breath served to reassure her. She resumed her narrative.

'Of course we had to be discreet and make sure the wider community understood that things were above board. I took up some volunteer work, distributing rations and clothing to our local war widows, and organising food parcels for our boys on the continent. Not too ostentatiously, you understand. The aim was to camouflage myself by blending in with the general climate of charitable works.

As for Paul, he spent most of his time in the room my parents had allocated to him. They didn't speak French, and his English was restricted, so proper conversations were out of the question : polite exchanges were as far as they went. But being a writer, Paul was used to solitude – and in fact he found the relative isolation of his new quarters rather congenial. He settled down to continue writing his recollections of the war, and when he needed some air we would go for walks together in the countryside.'

She sighed.

'While the war raged on in another world, we found ourselves living a kind of idyll here.'

She gestured around the room and shot me a coy glance that gave me pause for thought. It seemed to cross a line and struck me as insensitive : I couldn't help thinking that this romance banished all thought of Thomas. Was she still expecting news of his fate? Was she one of the women waiting to be officially confirmed a widow by a letter from the War Office? She must have been aware that many who had initially been notified their husband was lost in action had eventually been reunited with him. Did Hilda have this in mind? It seemed not. On the other hand her behaviour would have been under scrutiny by prurient neighbours waiting to denounce any hint of immoral conduct... Numerous genuine widows had been condemned as pariahs and even deprived of their pension for having taken comfort with other men. But perhaps in the heat of passion Hilda had decided to throw caution to the winds. After all, I had done something not dissimilar myself – and changed the course of my life.

Meanwhile Hilda had launched into their story.

'Obviously we didn't mix socially, but I was happy to share in Paul's taste for the studious and solitary life. We were company enough for each

other. Occasionally we went for long hikes together, into the foothills of the Pennines over there.' She waved a hand towards the window, through which we could see the undulating horizon. *'Paul had grown up on the flat plains of Belgium and exploring our fells and moorlands was a novelty for him. I enjoyed seeing the look on his face as we stopped for our picnic and took in the vistas around us, and the farmlands below, stretching across to the bay on the horizon.*

And naturally he was drawn to the sea, so often we would head out in the opposite direction too, walking the river banks down to the estuary. That way we would eventually find ourselves on the seafront at Cottsea, of course. There was a bench by the shore there, where we used to sit and watch the changing cloud patterns in the sky, and follow the slow progress of the waves as they crept towards us over the mud flats. Paul was intrigued by our vast sand banks stretching out over the bay : he would comment on the tide's seemingly hopeless surges to cross them as it inched its way to the shoreline – a shoreline that it often didn't reach. He said it reminded him of the futile advances of the armies on the Western Front.

He liked to compare the breeze in our faces with the stiff winds that come off the North Sea onto the Belgian plain. The smell of mud and seaweed we are used to here was a far cry from the sharp salt tang of the air on the Belgian coast.

It was on that bench, as I listened to him compare our drab beach with the coast across the Channel, that I came to realise how deep was his attachment to Belgium. Of course it should have been no surprise to me, but it was a while before I could bring myself to acknowledge that he would have to return there. There was a chance that some of his family had survived the German invasion, and there was no other way to find out what had happened to them but to go back himself. By that time we had become very close and I already had dreams of us living together here, in England, once the war was over. I have to confess that my great fear was if he went back I would lose him. He promised me this would not happen, that I meant as much to him as he did to me, and that he wanted to spend his life with me wherever we might choose together. But in the first instance he would have to go back alone, since he would be travelling as a military returnee.'

I nodded. She sat up in her chair and folded her arms. She breathed in and exhaled.

'I wonder if I should go on...' she murmured.

'Mmm... mmm...' I said, and nodded vigorously. I couldn't tell if she knew that I had a fairly good idea where things were leading. 'Mmm,' I added, for what it was worth.

'Well, the war was at a peak of brutality. After the battle of the Somme, as you know, it was clear that the fighting would get worse before there was an end to the bloodshed. I took comfort from the fact that Paul would not be called on to fight, and he wrote to say he had been given a desk job which meant he was out of danger. He had also managed to make contact with his surviving family members, which boosted his morale. We wrote to each other such letters as circumstances permitted, though the post was infrequent and unreliable and in any case of course neither of us felt able to express our true feelings. I wrote often, never knowing how many letters actually got through and how long it would take for a reply to come. The time hung heavy,

despite my attempts to fill the hours with my volunteer work. While waiting for letters from Paul, I found myself writing a sort of extended letter – not one I ever intended to send, but which was a way of keeping him in mind, so to speak, until I could read and answer his next letter. Little by little this writing became a sort of lifeline, I suppose you might say, during those weeks and months of uncertainty and fear, when our existences were at a standstill like the troops in the trenches.'

As Hilda talked, I sat on the edge of my seat and tried to will my recalcitrant features into an expression of curiosity, expectancy, whatever instruction I could get them to respond to : all in vain. In the end I had to make do with raising my eyebrows. Fortunately Hilda got the message : do go on.

She shifted in her chair. The next turn of events called for a change of posture.

'I had no plan in view when I began writing. I just jotted down whatever came to mind. But I was naturally drawn to my recollections of our happy time together when Paul was here convalescing... So I found myself writing a diary after the event if you like, an autobiography of sorts. I described our walks, how I had introduced Paul to the countryside around here, our one trip to Westmoreland, his reactions to the places we visited. His meditations on the tide fighting to cross the bay...' She shook her head in disbelief as she said, 'I can't believe I wrote so much.'

I was suddenly tempted to ask what became of this document. I was glad I wasn't able to blurt out the question, because in the instant that the impulse occurred to me I had a pretty fair idea. Now I had another reason for keeping her talking. If I could induce her to go on for long enough she might well reveal all herself. And I wondered if Hughie knew about this – wherever he was, and whatever had become of him.

Hilda roused herself from thoughts her recollections stirred in her. Her tone was suddenly brisk: 'Months went by and the war dragged on, and all I could think of was when the fighting would stop and Paul and I could be reunited.'

26

She paused, drew breath, pursed her lips, and breathed out tensely : she was approaching a difficult admission.

'Then one day a letter arrived from the War Office. It said they believed that Thomas had been found in a sanatorium attached to number 24 General Hospital, part of an encampment set up near Étaples, in Northern France.' She spelled out the precise details emphatically : she had reason to remember them. 'It was an international medical installation, treating not just British casualties, but German prisoners of war and wounded troops from a number of other countries too. There were Portuguese, Greeks, I don't know what else...'

She sighed. 'This letter arrived in the summer of 1918. It seems that part of the site at Étaples was a military base and had been targeted in an air raid. The hospital premises nearby were what they called unintended casualties. Wards and operating theatres were destroyed, and there were hundreds of deaths, medical staff and patients. The survivors had to be evacuated in the ensuing chaos. And among them was Thomas.'

Her shoulders had drooped and her hands were clasped in her lap. Her eyes looked down : for a moment she was a picture of dejection. Then she explained softly that months earlier Thomas had been dragged from a crater on the battlefield, where he had lain unconscious for hours, with a severe head wound, unable to move, to give a signal or cry for help. His clothes had been all but stripped from him, presumably by the blast of the artillery shell. He had been rushed to a Clearing Station and then to a Field Hospital, where they managed to stabilise his condition but judged it too dangerous to attempt to get at the shrapnel fragment lodged in his skull.

Hilda was speaking in a low voice throughout all this and I had trouble hearing what she was saying.

It seems he had been found in territory that had changed hands several times during the previous twenty-four hours, so it was impossible to tell which side he had been on. His identification tags were missing, perhaps taken by someone who had intended to report him as dead and then was himself killed – unless they were carried off by a battlefield scavenger. This was never properly explained. He was transported to Étaples, and in the absence of information or through an administrative misunderstanding, he was allocated to a ward of foreign casualties, who tended to be relatively neglected. There he remained as an anonymous patient, unable to speak, virtually paralysed, incapable of explaining who he was – past being aware of who he was ; and as the hospital was daily deluged with numbers of dead and wounded, his case was either overlooked or classified as irremediable. Eventually he seems to have been left all but unnoticed in a minimally conscious state.

'I imagine that he became a fixture in a corner of the ward and people simply stopped seeing him,' Hilda concluded.

However, during the evacuation from the bombed-out hospital, the question arose of who this patient was and where he should be transported to. This must have been the first time for months that his case had attracted proper attention. Clinically he seemed beyond help and he was now an administrative problem.

'Then as he was being moved from the premises, a stretcher-bearer claimed to recognize him.' Hilda shook her head, as if she still could hardly believe the coincidence. *'The letter I received,'* she spelled out slowly, *'said that after further investigation the patient in question "answered the description" of Thomas Beaumont, though the patient himself was unable to confirm this. Can you believe it? Imagine the thoughts that went through my mind. Without the information I gathered later, I really didn't know what to think. All I was told was that the patient had been repatriated and I was invited to attend the convalescent holding unit in the Woodthorpe annexe to Nottingham General Hospital, to identify my... husband. Why Nottingham, I will never know.'*

She had pulled back a curtain and was looking out of the window as she spoke these last few words. She fell silent and continued watching the lumbering movement of the clouds reddened by the setting sun. Then she swung round to face me.

'I hardly need say that this came as a bolt from the blue. I had all but resigned myself to having lost Thomas... Don't misunderstand me,' she added

quickly. 'I didn't consider myself a free agent. I was still bound to his memory and still felt a tie of loyalty. But... well, as I've explained my circumstances had changed since the start of the war and a lot of water had flowed under the bridge since he had been reported missing...

So what was I to do? There could be no question really – I had no option but to respond to the "invitation" I had received from the War Office.'

I saw her lips tremble.

'But I was torn, naturally. And then to make matters worse, a letter arrived from Paul. Oh, it was a normal letter, just the kind of letter I had grown used to getting from him. Chatty, telling me his news. He had been transferred to Paris, and was working at the Foyer Franco-Belge, helping to provide for refugees. The story based on his wartime experiences was written up in draft, he was glad to report – though he had decided to wait till the war was over before sending it to his publisher. By all accounts there would be an armistice in a matter of weeks' time. Then we could plan for a reunion.

I couldn't think how to respond. Should I tell him we couldn't have a future together? It might be best to break the news to him right away rather than keep him living in hope.

Or should I say nothing – at least for the time being? Perhaps this rediscovered soldier might not be Thomas after all. If I was to tell Paul about him while I was still dazed from the shock, and then the invalid turned out to be someone else, it would upset Paul unnecessarily and perhaps sow seeds of doubt in his mind as to my feelings for him. The thought that my husband might reappear at any moment would blot out our prospects for a future together. So I decided not to tell him anything. I would go to Nottingham and see what – or who – I would find there.

But while I did that, Paul would be waiting for a reply to his letter. I hadn't the heart to sit down and write to him as if nothing had happened, pretending I was still living my usual routine. I couldn't bring myself to write lies. Then I had an idea : instead of a letter, I would simply send him my memoir of our time together here. That would keep him in good spirits, and would be a way of avoiding mentioning the problems I was trying to face up to. Now that he had a civilian address in Paris I could be sure the post would reach him without being intercepted by the censor ; and it would let him know I was thinking of him and remembering our happy times. I bundled the pages up in a large envelope and put them in the post.'

It was getting late, but Hilda showed no signs of fatigue. Evidently she had kept this story bottled up for so long that once it began to come out there was no stopping it. And of course I was eager to hear the rest.

'So...' she breathed out. 'I made arrangements to travel to Nottingham. I didn't know how to prepare myself for what I would find there. There would be dealings with administrators, I supposed ; I made sure to take my birth certificate, passport and identity papers with me, as the official letter had instructed me to do. And I dug out my marriage certificate. My hands trembled as I re-read it and recalled the day when I believed I was the happiest girl in the world. It had Thomas's signature on it. I wondered if he would still be as recognizable as his signature.

I didn't know what to expect. Would he be horribly mutilated, so that I couldn't bear to look at him? Would his handsome face be disfigured?'

There was a sharp intake of breath from both of us as we registered her words each in our different way.

'Oh! I'm sorry, Marion, that was thoughtless of me. I hope I haven't upset you ...'

I made a sound between a wail and a cough : It's all right, no offence taken. Do go on...

'On the train I tried to think of other things, but my mind was in turmoil. I had grown very fond of Paul, and had allowed myself to believe that with him I would be able to build a new life. I told myself that my marriage to Thomas had already proved a failure before he went off to war, and I was entitled to start again. And yet here I was, haunted by the memory of those first few weeks after I received the telegram announcing he had been reported missing. During our difficult days I had sometimes wished him out of my life, and now I was tormented by guilt and remorse, accusing myself of having driven him to his death... the lovely man who didn't deserve such a fate... and I had made a vow not to forget him, to make amends for what I had done...'

I stiffened to hide the pang of regret coursing through my own body.

Hilda took a moment to recover her composure.

'At our age we've learned to be sceptical about all that kind of emotion, those vows and promises that rarely stand the test of time. If we're lucky and have the strength to do so we can force ourselves to go through the motions... Perhaps that's the best we can hope for when our lives have not lived up to expectations.'

She looked me in the eyes and I saw hers were filled with tears. She dabbed at her cheeks.

'Sorry,' she said, a tremor in her voice. 'That's just play-acting too, I'm afraid.'

I tried a brusque shake of the head, to refute what she was saying. I felt the need to comfort her. The woman was wretched.

'I had no idea what to expect – or even what I really wanted. Every possibility seemed equally unbearable. But eventually it struck me that there was one simple – albeit brutal – solution to my dilemma.' She lowered her eyelids and gave me an oblique look, as if defying me to anticipate what she was about to say. Then she took a deep breath. 'I could disclaim Thomas ; I could decline to acknowledge whatever remnant of a human being I might find at the sanatorium.'

She had been right to imply I would be shocked. I tried to contain myself, unsure whether she really meant what she said

'After all, given that he was apparently so badly injured that he didn't know his own identity, he was unlikely to know who I was. He would have no expectations, so whatever I decided, it wouldn't affect him. And I still had a good deal of my life ahead of me, and the chance of a fresh start with Paul. I steeled myself with that thought, desperate as I was to salvage something from the impossible situation. So I arrived at the convalescent ward with that one idea in mind. I would make myself impervious to any other thought.'

She raised a rueful eyebrow.

'Slightly to my surprise, a team of VADs had been delegated to the unit. The sister in charge welcomed me with a warm and sisterly gesture : she had evidently been made aware that I had

served a term on the Western Front. And she had a lot of sympathy for my present plight, she said. It was a terrible thing to come home to recuperate and then be confronted with tragic news. I resisted the temptation to give in to her pity, determined to withstand any appeals to my emotions.

We went through the identity checks and then a Matron appeared and asked me if I felt ready to meet the invalid. I noticed she didn't mention him by name. I understood this was a concession to the peculiar circumstances, though from my own experience in the field I was sure that the nursing staff had given him a provisional one. I didn't allow myself to wonder what it might have been.

I followed the Matron along a series of corridors to the side-ward where... Thomas was to be found. I forced myself to adopt an impersonal manner, as if I was back in the field hospital. This was just another patient, just another wretched case that simply called for a clinical approach.

As the door to his room opened, I caught sight of a figure sitting motionless in a reclining chair. Of course, I thought, it couldn't possibly be him. Nothing about him resembled Thomas, that was for sure. And I maintained my bravado until I found myself in front of the slumped body. His head was lolling on his chest and I couldn't see his face.

The Matron spoke to him. "Here's someone to see you," she said, and touched his shoulder lightly. At first there was no response. But he noticed her feet and slowly raised his face to her. He seemed completely unaware of me. I was able to examine him in profile, and found myself marshalling evidence to confirm that he was a stranger to me. Cheek, nose, eyebrow, chin... the flesh had fallen from them and they were much more stark and angular in shape than my remembered image of Thomas. I was already beginning to shake my head.

And then I noticed his ear. External acoustic meatus : the term came back to me from anatomy lessons. And I couldn't help but recognize the shape of his lobe, the external helix, the pattern of the superior and inferior crus... it was Thomas after all.

I gave a sudden gasp and the figure turned his face to me, in a mechanical response.

I stood trembling before him. He raised a pair of blank eyes, the eyelids drooping, like those of a dejected animal.

He didn't make a sound and that's when I realised that behind that vacant stare there was nothing I would recognize, or that would recognize me...

That was my last chance to deny him.' She paused. 'But I couldn't take it.'

Hilda's face buckled as she relived that moment from forty years earlier. And a sound came rolling from my throat : I was sobbing despite myself.

We both pulled out our handkerchiefs and dried our eyes, then blew our noses. It struck me there was something slightly comical about our actions, as if they were coordinated.

When I had recovered my composure, I took out my notebook, wrote in it and tore out the page to show to Hilda.

'Your cousin in the nursing home – is he..?'

She closed her eyes and nodded. Then, brisk again : 'So I had to welcome him back and care for him. Which I did. Once I had decided, everything flowed from that. To begin with, I thought that with my nursing experience I would be able to take care of him myself. And I did so, for almost two years.

Thomas received a small pension and that helped us materially. But my parents were elderly and in poor health too, and eventually I had to acknowledge that I couldn't cope on my own. In the meantime, care homes were opening up to meet the needs of disabled veterans, and we found a place for him nearby. Over the years it has changed hands but it has always catered to his needs. As you have seen,' she said somewhat pointedly, though without malice.

'*As we were making arrangements for Thomas to come back to live with me, I got a letter from Paul in Paris. He had read my memoir of our time together and was full of praise for it. It was immensely affecting, he said, and it had made him relive the happy months we had shared. So much so that he had decided he must include it in his novel about his wartime experiences. "I have realized my book needs to be about what we both lived through," he wrote. He had already begun to translate my memoir into French and was in the process of inserting it as a chapter in the story. "And when I have finished, this novel will become merely the first chapter in the long, long novel I want to begin living with you as soon as the war is over and we can be together again."*

You can imagine how I felt on reading this. I was committed to bringing Thomas back home and being a loyal wife to him. It was impossible to continue a relationship with Paul ; it wouldn't be fair on him to try. Though I must admit I did consider leaving everything behind and joining him in Paris, where I was unknown and we had realistic prospects of living together. Thomas would be looked after in a nursing home and no one here would be any the wiser. But I couldn't bring myself to abandon him, and in any case my parents' health was deteriorating and I had a duty to stay with them too.

So I replied to Paul to explain my position. It was the most difficult letter I ever wrote to him. I asked him not to use my memoir in his novel, and told him we should stop writing to each other. Naturally he replied with attempts to dissuade me, promising he would find a way to live incognito nearby while pursuing his writing career under a nom de plume, and keep up our contacts without anyone else knowing. But I couldn't bear the thought of a furtive affair that would be haunted by secrecy and tainted by a second betrayal of Thomas. The die was cast – "les jeux sont faits", I wrote to him.'

She pursed her lips, furrowed her brow, said, 'So that was that,' and fell silent.

27

I tipped my head and squinted at her.

'Except,' she admitted sheepishly, 'that's not how the story ended.' She clasped her hands and pushed them into her lap. 'The armistice came, and people struggled to return to normal life, each in his own way. I did my best to adapt to the situation at home. For over a year I tried, but it wore me down ; so much so that I knew I was in danger of another nervous collapse. My Mother and Father were worried for my health as well as their own ; and in the end I turned to the nursing home for help with Thomas.'

I was waiting for a sequel, I confess : I looked at her aslant, with one eyebrow raised.

'Yes,' she said cautiously. 'I can see that you're wondering what happened next. The fact is, nothing happened for a while. I played the dutiful wife and daughter, taking care of my ailing parents and accompanying Thomas to the nursing home three times a week for daycare. That was quite enough to keep me occupied.

From time to time a picture postcard would arrive from Paul, sent from Antwerp where he was visiting relatives, or Milan or Barcelona where he was researching a magazine article or planning a new book, though he was still living in Paris. These souvenir postcards were always addressed to my parents and would contain renewed expressions of gratitude for the kindness they had shown him during the war. The message was brief, formal and would conclude with good wishes to me. These asides irritated and upset me with their covert pointers to what could have been. But of course I had to share in my parent's pleasure as they were reminded of the charming young man who had stayed with us for a while.

Then one day a parcel arrived containing a copy of Paul's novel, which it turned out had just been published in France. It was addressed as usual to my mother and father – who would never be able to read it, since they didn't understand French – and on the fly-leaf, in English, Paul had written a dedication to them. They were delighted by this new evidence that he still appreciated the hospitality we had shown him. The volume was given pride of place on the bookshelves. As soon as I could decently get my hands on it I took it away to read.

I remember how my hands shook as I opened the book and saw in print words I had first read in Paul's handwriting. My recollections of reading the original manuscripts were threaded like filigree between the formatted lines of printed characters. The book didn't teach me anything new and I didn't expect it to. In fact I was chiefly concerned to know whether or not it carried traces of my own writing. I was relieved to find that Paul had spared my feelings and omitted all reference to our story.'

She broke off and gave an impish grin.

'I say all ; but the truth is that where the story reaches Paul's admission to hospital, the text breaks off and three asterisks mark a blank before the narrative resumes with him working as a military adjutant. I admit that those asterisks meant the world to me – for what they concealed, and for what they signified. And the title he had found for the book : "À l'Abri de la Tempête" – "Sheltered from the Storm", fits very well with the situation of a narrator writing from his hospital bed ; but I knew it really referred to Paul and me during our period of seclusion.'

No doubt about it : this was what Hughie had been investigating. And the manuscript that Hughie discovered wasn't a translation from Paul Daubignac after all : it was a text written in English by Hilda Beaumont. If I could have spoken I might have mentioned him ; but mercifully that was out of the question. I reminded myself that Hilda was unaware of the connection between myself and the young Scotsman. For the time being she was intent on continuing her own story – one that Dr Storth himself probably had no knowledge of. Dr Storth would have to wait till later.

'My parents were extremely taken with the idea that Paul had included them in his literary career. My father was not a connoisseur of literature as such, but he certainly appreciated that a signed copy of a first edition was every bibliophile's dream.

One day, shortly after the book was delivered, my father suggested that we should invite Paul to come and visit us again by way of showing our appreciation for his gift – and for keeping us in his thoughts. "For old time's sake," he said. "Now the *war is over it would be nice to share some of the peace with him."*

To begin with I suspected he had sensed my fondness for Paul and was deliberately calling my bluff. At first I was horrified at his proposal : I didn't think I could cope with seeing Paul again, determined as I was to fulfil my commitment to Thomas. But no, my father was simply acting spontaneously from an attachment that had grown up during Paul's stay with us. "After all," he said, "Paul was like one of the family in the end... and who knows, another visit might give him an idea for a new book."

On the other hand I was relieved – grateful even – that Father was prepared to take the initiative and thereby spare me the responsibility for whatever came of it. He wrote a letter of invitation and sent it off.'

Hilda shrugged her shoulders and questioned me with a look that said : 'Well, what would you have done?' I tilted my head from side to side. If she expected me to take Thomas's part in her dilemma she was mistaken : I couldn't help sympathizing with her.

'Time passed and there was no news from Paris. Then one of Paul's postcards arrived, this time from Athens. Evidently he was travelling and he might or might not have made arrangements to have his mail forwarded. We had no choice but to wait. Father was mildly impatient, but I was going through agonies.

Eventually my father received a letter. Paul would be delighted to accept the invitation and proposed a visit the following month. Father consulted with Mother and me as a matter of course

; Mother was pleased and I struggled not to let my feelings show.

When the day arrived Father went to meet Paul at the station and brought him back by car. I stayed at home with Mother, a bundle of nerves. Watching the car draw up in the lane I was overwhelmed with panic. No good would come of this ; I didn't know how I would cope with having Paul in the house, sharing every day with him while bound by my loyalty to Thomas.

I needn't have worried. Mother and Father welcomed him with open arms and he took a genuine pleasure in seeing them again. I found I could share the general affection without feeling compromised. He became, as Father had said, like one of the family.

And Paul engaged with Thomas as if he was a brother. He had come to visit the family, he implied, and each of us meant something to him. The moment he saw Thomas propped up in his day-bed, he crossed the room towards him without hesitation and took his hand, murmuring a greeting. Of course Thomas was unable to acknowledge him : he raised his eyes but his face, like the rest of him, showed no signs of a sentient response. But there was no doubting the fellow-feeling in Paul's manner. For him Thomas was another damaged comrade among thousands of pitiful casualties from the trenches, and what they had in common overrode the rest.'

Her voice faltered and suddenly Hilda's eyes were brimming with tears again. She sniffed, but hadn't time for her handkerchief : she was anxious to go on speaking.

'Not for a single moment did I suspect him of taking satisfaction from Thomas's pathetic state.

He could have revelled in seeing a rival so... incapacitated, but all I could discern was profound compassion.' She glanced down sideways as if considering an unworthy thought. 'You might be tempted to imagine it was hypocrisy. In a lesser man, perhaps, but not Paul. I had my feelings on a very short rein and I was in no state to be taken in.'

She took out her handkerchief and blew her nose.

'In any case,' she went on, 'he made no attempt to suggest there was anything unusual between us. From the first days he did take on some of the burden that Thomas represented, in a gesture aimed at me. Eventually I let Paul drive me to the daycare unit where we left Thomas for the morning – and not till then were we able once more to spend time alone together.

Even on these occasions, however, we struggled to find words. I think each of us was on edge, frightened of saying the wrong thing, fearful of a response we didn't want to hear. We would exchange pleasantries : Paul said what a change it was to find himself in a landscape that had not been a perpetual battlefield for centuries ; and I tried to recall the names of local sites where skirmishes occurred during the English Civil War. But sometimes a painful, clenched silence would fall between us as we sat side by side in the car.

On the other hand it was only natural that we should walk out together with Thomas in his wheelchair. This was a novelty for me and Thomas, since it was something I hadn't felt able to do on my own ; the wheelchair was cumbersome and if Thomas should slump forward he was too heavy for me to lift back up. But with Paul we relaxed when we could share a picnic in the fresh air rather than sit with Thomas cooped up indoors.

It also struck me as a good idea for the three of us to be seen out together – it showed we had nothing to hide. Passers-by would nod sympathetically ; relatives caring for their injured veteran were a common sight in those days. Sometimes people would strike up a conversation. They would begin by addressing our invalid, and when they realised he could not respond they would turn to us and cast around for something to say, like whether he was glad to be home. Occasionally other groups with convalescents of their own would stop to compare notes : which action was he injured in ? Would he recover?

One day a fellow stroller, casually pausing to pass the time of day as we crossed on the path, asked if Thomas was a brother. I had taken Paul's arm as I stepped around a puddle, and our interlocutor took me for his wife. I replied 'Cousin' before I could think, and the man nodded, smiled, wished us good-day and went on his way.

I had felt Paul's arm tighten as the word escaped my lips. We walked on in silence, each wondering what the other was thinking. It occurred to me that we could pass Thomas off as a relative... and Paul could assume the role that in effect he had adopted since he returned.

I dismissed this passing thought as a moment of madness and we headed home for lunch.

A few days later, Paul and Father went out for a walk with Thomas. Father enjoyed Paul's company and I think, to tell the truth, that our visitor represented a welcome change from his handicapped son-in-law, whose inert, nerveless presence in the house weighed on him.

The three of them had been gone for almost an hour when the telephone rang. It was the hospital.

Father had been taken ill and was being given emergency treatment for a heart attack. I had just replaced the receiver when Paul arrived at the front door, with Thomas in the wheelchair. My father had been wheeling Thomas along, he explained, when he had collapsed. Fortunately another man out walking lived nearby and had taken father to hospital in his car.

When Mother and I arrived at the hospital, my father had already died.'

Hilda wrung her handkerchief in her hands. She was speaking of events from many years before but I could see that the shock of losing her father was still fresh. She stifled a sob.

'He was a man of few words, my father, but his instincts were always sure in the way he responded to me... I honestly don't think I have ever experienced a more reliable affection – love – from anyone. And I don't believe I shall ever mourn anyone more than I mourn him, still today.' Her voice trailed off and she had to pause as her words caught in her throat.

She coughed, swallowed hard and wrestled with her emotions to regain her composure.

'His death left a terrible void, and I found myself adrift without an anchor in a maelstrom of emotions. I had envisaged talking with him about my feelings for Paul. He could see what the burden of Thomas was doing to me and I'm sure he noticed that having Paul with us had lifted my spirits. His sympathy was reassuring to me even though he never put it into words. Now I had to deal with everything on my own.

For a while the situation felt unbearable. Mother was obviously distraught and her failing health left her without the strength to cope with her bereavement. When Paul, courteous as ever, suggested tactfully that he should cut short his visit and return to Paris so as not to intrude on our grief, – I felt the ground open up beneath my feet. I was terrified of what would happen with the three of us – Mother, Thomas and me – left alone. I begged him to stay, though he felt it might be improper to have a stranger lodging at a house in mourning. In the end he gave in to my pleas – and his presence proved a great comfort. In fact I was grateful for his help with the funeral arrangements, which I could never have managed alone.

We arranged to leave Thomas at the nursing home on the day of the funeral. He had no idea what was happening and for Mother and me he would have been another worry in the chapel and at the cemetery.' She looked at me apologetically, acknowledging what my feelings might be. She gave a sigh. *'To be blunt, heartless though it might seem towards poor Thomas, I didn't want to be distracted from my grief.'*

She paused again, no doubt sifting her memories of the sad day.

'At the funeral service and then at the committal, Paul stood alongside us, giving Mother a steadying hand whenever her frailty became apparent. He was a tower of strength, as the saying goes.'

Then, to my surprise, she brightened.

'What I remember distinctly is that no one in the congregation seemed to question Paul's presence on the front pew – none of our neighbours, none of the local worthies come to pay their respects, none of the very few distant relations and remote acquaintances who had been able to make the journey. We stood in line together to acknowledge condolences as the mourners left the church. Paul's

hand was shaken as much as mine and Mother's, and I had to conclude that it was the most natural thing in the world for him to be beside us. He was one of us. And,' she drew breath, then : 'that's what decided me as to our future. It was clear that many, in the distracted way of bystanders and members of the congregation, automatically assumed that Paul was my husband, and considered it natural for him to be grieving for his father-in-law. We made no attempt to dispel the misapprehension. I was determined that that was the role he would play from then on.'

She knitted her brow and a vertical crease appeared between her eyes. This was what her determination looked like, I reflected – and she would brook no opposition.

'When the will was read, I was the sole executor and my first priority was to do what was best for Mother. For her part, she said she could not bear to stay on in the home she had lived in with Father. She had a spinster niece who was happy to have her come and share her cottage. She moved in there six months after Father's death – and died herself barely six months after that. Which left Paul and me alone in the house – with Thomas. We had had lengthy discussions and Paul had made it clear he would be content if this state of affairs were to become permanent. However, when it came to the crunch I was immensely uncomfortable at the prospect of a tripartite domestic arrangement. Even if we persuaded all and sundry that Thomas was a distant cousin – that was the least of my problems – I could not live under the same roof together with these two men. It just wouldn't do.'

Here she blinked a few times, pressed her lips together, and braced herself for what she had to say next.

'So I paid a visit to the care home. I was on good terms with the owner and her manageress. They agreed to take in Thomas for residential care. A small legacy from Father would cover the costs for as long as necessary. And for a consideration they consented to a tacit change in his status and his personal history was, shall we say, informally edited. Over the years this alteration became a fait accompli as various managers and staff succeeded each other ; so nobody now has ever known any different. He is a veteran of World War I who never recovered from his head injury, was placed into care forty years ago and to whom his surviving relatives have remained deeply attached. The care home, for its part, is committed to protecting our privacy.'

She blinked and fell silent, evidently self-conscious. Having at last spelled out the full story she was wondering how I would react to her confession.

I had been hanging on her words for over an hour, listening intently as the pieces fell into place, some confirming my suspicions, others catching me off-guard, some actually taking my breath away. My mind was in a whirl, but I could have found nothing to say even if I had not lost the capacity to put my thoughts into words. I nodded repeatedly, rolling out a string of inarticulate murmurs, in an effort to show my appreciation for her candour.

So the old man into whose arms I had virtually fallen at Faircroft had indeed once been my beautiful Thomas, my poor young fiancé who had been mauled and mutilated by life and had finally been washed up as a derelict on the shore of the care home. I wondered how he had looked, at twenty-four years of age, and how his wound had scarred him before it was camouflaged by the ravages of old age. For forty years he had survived there while all around I and others got on with our lives, oblivious to his fate. I wondered : what if I had known and had offered to care for him myself – or at least become a regular visitor who could take him for walks? I could have done that ... for a few years at least, before I had my stroke. But Hilda would never have entrusted me with her secret when she had so many reasons to resent me.

And who was this Paul, the writer whom she had succeeded in passing off as her husband? I imagine time had blurred his story too, and slid it sideways : doubtless the local gossips had established that he was the husband who had first gone missing in action and then had been miraculously restored to his loyal wife... But he had acquired a strange manner of speaking as a result of what he had gone through on the battlefield. Some kind of speech impediment due to shell-shock...?

And where on earth did Hughie fit in here?

Meanwhile, my distracted silence, which she could tell was not only my inability to speak, was making Hilda restive. She coughed lightly to get my attention and said,

'So there you have it.'

I stared at her and she held my gaze. She took a breath, but before she could speak, there was a catch in her throat and her words seemed to freeze on her lips. She tried a second time and the words finally spilled out.

'Thomas is dying.'

28

I knew that Hilda had spilled the beans the day I saw her arrive at Faircroft with Mrs Horton.

I was looking through the window of the side room when I recognised the car coming up the drive. Thomas had been moved in there after Hilda and Doreen had conferred over what to do during his final days or hours. The home had no proper facilities for terminal care and the manageress had adopted the procedure of using a side ward, which also served as an isolation room for those inmates who had caught something contagious. Hilda had evidently come to an understanding with Doreen so that Thomas could pass away in seclusion, without there being any need to move him to a hospice.

The job I had been given was mainly just to help out, since the nursing home was already working to capacity. Sheila had left suddenly, apparently under a cloud, and I was brought in to ease the extra pressure on the staff at Faircroft by making myself useful with some of the day-to-day chores that didn't call for specialist skills. I was prepared to have a go : it made a change, and the rest of the staff, who were amiable enough, were glad of a

294

replacement pair of hands. Hilda had persuaded me that by lightening their load in this way I could acquire experience that would eventually help me qualify for a permanent position. In her opinion my work with the elderly in the guest house showed that I had a gift for dealing with geriatrics. She assured me that I could train on the job and that there was the prospect of a long-term career. In the event, she was not wrong about my aptitude for this kind of work ; I've been doing it now for longer than anything else I've tried. But as I said at the beginning, this isn't meant to be the story of my life.

Doreen had warned Mrs Beaumont that Thomas was showing signs of failing and she had reacted by telling Mrs Horton. To judge by what had passed between them when Mrs Beaumont told the full story to Mrs Horton, the two of them had agreed, quite spontaneously, that they should both be by his side when the time came for him to go.

They entered the building together, Hilda pushing Mrs Horton in the wheelchair. Mrs Horton nodded to me and held out her hand, which I squeezed gently. She didn't seem surprised to find me there ; I assumed Hilda had explained things to her. I felt awkward at not having told her myself – but Mrs Beaumont had insisted that if she got me the job I should – for the time being – not tell anyone where I had gone to. I had no doubt my name would be mud with Mrs Dugdale, but that couldn't be helped. And perhaps when the truth emerged she and the others would be sympathetic.

I stood aside as they headed off down the corridor towards the room where Thomas lay on what was to be his death-bed. Watching them from a distance, one hunched in a wheelchair and the other a stooping figure unsteady on her feet, it occurred to me that they might not be much longer for this world either. And yet by making their way here at this moment they were giving a new breath of life to their feelings for the same man. Watching figures like them shuffling by in the street, their footfalls ever lighter on the ground as their past receded from them, one might feel their pale existence had no other purpose than to peter out progressively until the inevitable end. But here they were asserting that what they had lived, what they had lived for, still counted for something. And as the door of Thomas's room opened to let them in, they advanced towards an encounter that would be as significant as any they had known in their younger days. It would complete the unfinished business of their lives.

After that there was nothing for me to witness, nothing for me to report. Their last moments together were private. I went about the modest tasks I had been entrusted with, occasionally glancing at the clock on the wall and calculating how long they had been in with Thomas and how much longer he might still have to live.

I say 'live', but for forty years or so he had existed as a mere vestige of what is called a living being. I could count my time with him only in minutes, not even hours, and nothing had passed between us even when I was helping with vital or intimate functions. He submitted in silence and without reaction to all the indignities that flesh is heir to. There were moments when I found myself wondering how he might have responded when he was a healthy young man. Struck down in his twenties, he had probably been denied the chance to properly familiarise himself with the intricate potential of his own body, let alone that of lovers or wife.

What passed between him and Hilda and Marion I cannot tell, but the sense of an impending bereavement touched everyone in the building. The staff would catch one another's eye as they went about their duties, and the looks they exchanged spoke of a shared sentiment of loss and a mutual fondness in the face of collective sorrow. They redoubled the tenderness and affection they brought to their treatment of the other patients whose days were numbered but who still had time to live. I noticed, too, that they reserved special signs of sympathy for me, young as I was, and unaccustomed to the departure of those I'd soon be growing attached to in this line of work.

*

As she had promised, Hilda gave me a lift home after our conversation, but dinner was over and everyone had returned to their rooms when I got back, so I didn't see Geraldine. I was apprehensive about meeting her again : she had clearly been hurt at having been asked to leave Quainton. I owed her an apology and an explanation : it had pained me to see her retreat into that haughty, prickly demeanour which hides her insecurities but tends to put people off her.

I weighed my words as I composed a message. My 'speech impediment' served me well in this instance, since it saved me from blurting out some excuse put into words on the spur of the moment and liable to come out wrong. Instead, I wrote a note – several notes in fact, revising and rewriting until I thought I had got the right formulation.

The next morning, as usual, Geraldine was not present at breakfast. This too made matters a bit easier for me, as I could simply put my message under her door rather than struggling to find a way to catch her attention – which might have been difficult if she had opted to snub me by way of retaliation for my betrayal.

This is what I had written:

'Dear Geraldine, Please excuse the way our evening was cut short. Hilda sends her apologies for what must have seemed a very rude end to our conversation. The fact is she had received some distressing news about an acquaintance we have in common, and she was anxious to share it with me since it was an urgent matter. It concerns a person who is dying and whom we both wish to visit before it is too late. I'm sure you will understand if in the heat of the moment she (and I) were less than courteous, torn as we were between the pleasure of your company and the painful call to assist an old friend's last moments.'

I rushed to get myself ready and was waiting in the porch of the guest house when Hilda drew up outside.

'Paul and I decided that he should not come along with us,' she said as we drove off together.

She didn't offer an explanation but I could well imagine what had prompted them to this conclusion. The long-standing version of the relations between the three of them was an accepted fiction but at a time like this it was best not to draw attention to it.

'I had a telephone call this morning,' Hilda said. 'His condition is stable but he doesn't have long. I trust we'll be in time...'

I nodded, and for a few minutes there was silence as Hilda drove faster than was usual for her. Soon we were out of the winding narrow lanes and on the long straight road that cuts across the landscape towards Neatby.

'There's something else I should let you know,' Hilda said.

I turned and stared at her, but she kept her eyes on the road.

'You may have been wondering what became of young Graham.'

I started. She shot me a sideways glance and returned her gaze to the road.

'The fact is I – more exactly the management at Faircroft – offered him a job and he took it.'

'Aah,' I managed to force out.

'A vacancy had arisen since Sheila was dismissed... I believe you may have met Sheila?' she asked.

It was a rhetorical question. I nodded.

'Yes,' she continued. 'It seems Sheila had become rather lax. A trifle over-zealous and... profligate when administering medications...'

She paused to let her words sink in. Then went on:

'And as for Graham, he had pieced together some of the details we had been keeping to ourselves ; and in the interests of confidentiality I proposed a change of job – it pays well and keeps him at this end of the parish.' She tipped her head towards me while continuing to watch the road. 'I think he has an aptitude for the work. He certainly seems happy doing it, and Doreen is very pleased with him.' She braked as we approached a corner. 'He's been staying with us until he finds new lodgings.'

I pursed my lips and gave a 'Hmm' that carried a sceptical note : And you can keep an eye on him.

'I can tell what you're thinking,' she said, alert to my tone. 'Let's just say the arrangement suits us all for the time being.'

I gave a murmur of approval. Whatever else might be the case, Graham would benefit from the new job.

And then it struck me : could she and Paul have come to a similar arrangement with Hughie? His arrival at Quainton Lodge would have presented a dramatic threat to their 'confidentiality'. Imagine their reaction when he told them about the manuscript that had led him there. What kind of scheme would get him out of the way while ensuring that their secret stayed safe? They surely weren't murderers, but they could hardly have kept him prisoner indefinitely...

I was distracted from these thoughts when we pulled up outside Faircroft. Hilda helped me out of the car and we were admitted through the entrance door with the stained-glass panes. I spotted Graham right away, standing in a corner looking slightly sheepish, poor boy ; he had been expecting us but didn't know how I would react to seeing him again. I gave an affectionate snort and held out both my hands, which he took in his as he said a soft Hello. No one said anything more. There was a hushed air on the corridors: everyone was aware that death was about to visit.

Doreen led the way until we stopped in front of the door behind which Thomas lay. I heard Hilda take a deep breath and felt her hand on my shoulder. I reached up and touched her fingers with mine. Doreen opened the door and stepped aside to usher us in. She stood in the doorway and watched as we drew close to the bed. Hilda reassured her with a gesture and she withdrew, leaving us alone with the motionless figure that lay there.

I hadn't had a chance to examine his features so closely since... the days when we were fiancés. The mere thought of this word I couldn't speak provoked an ache in my throat. Hilda placed a comforting hand on my shoulder again as she wheeled me up close, and then she moved around to sit on a chair that had been placed on the other side of the bed. I raised my eyes to her across the body. She caught my look and the expression on her face froze. Distressed as I was in this moment, I was conscious that her anguish had accompanied her for decades.

Thomas's eyes were closed. Would I have a chance to see into them before he was lost for ever? His skin was already white, announcing the pallor of death, and his complexion was growing waxy. The creases and wrinkles in his face were stiffening and his features were beginning to settle into what would be their final lifeless mask.

I stared at this face. Hilda had recognized him by his earlobes, she said : but now these were the ears of an old man, larger than I remembered, and the lobes more pendulous. His cheeks had been lean when I knew him, the bones high ; there were signs that he had filled out in his maturity, and the cheeks had turned to jowls. He needed a shave : bristles stood out on his chin and his jawline was cross-hatched with stubble. I felt an impulse to ask if I might be allowed to shave him – but I could not know if he would have wanted that. I wondered too how Hilda would respond : did she view me as his first love, come rightfully to reclaim him after her attempt to make him hers? Did she have the feelings of a widow, after all that had transpired? I glanced at her. She was studying his face like me. Her expression was as inscrutable, in its way, as mine must have been.

I recalled how his tousled hair had remained unruly despite the best efforts of barbers to keep it cropped. Now only tufts remained above his ears and the back of his head. It was white, as were his eyebrows. It occurred to me that he had been unconscious or unaware throughout the process of his hair loss and its change in colour : no staring into the mirror each morning to note his advancing baldness and count the remaining dark hairs as they turned grey.

And then, all of a sudden, came a stab in the heart as I recognized a slight bump on the septum of his nose. I had looked up the word for it one day as we decided, laughingly, that this was his special distinguishing feature. Our past together rushed in and overwhelmed me as this relic of his young face, untouched by time, thrust through the layers of ageing and the sediments of history, and brought him back to me. I had to catch my breath and tried to hide my reaction from Hilda. I didn't want her to think I was taking possession of Thomas, enveloping him in my grief, on the strength of an adolescent reminiscence.

I took out my handkerchief and wiped my nose. Hilda watched me. She smiled. 'His breathing is so steady' she murmured. And it was : something in him was taking deep breaths, drawing the air down into his lungs, then exhaling it slowly, taking a long time over each respiration.

I raised my face to Hilda to confirm her words. There were marks of fatigue in her face ; visibly she had not slept. When she sensed my eyes on her, she gave a wan smile. This was it, she seemed to be saying ; the long years of leading a double life were coming to an end. As her smile faded I read signs of nervous exhaustion in her features. This last trial of her loyalty to Thomas was proving to be the most taxing. I clasped my hands together, attempting to acknowledge her feelings. Then I looked away, not wishing to intrude.

We both fell silent and the minutes passed. There was a clock on the wall but I had no desire to consult it. I sank into myself and ruminated over memories of a young Thomas. But this brought me to the hurt I had done him, and I flinched. Hilda must have noticed my brow furrowing, for she gave me a questioning look and mouthed 'Are you all right?' I nodded and let my eyelids fall briefly, to show I felt calm.

Thomas's breathing had become shallow and we noticed this together. After each respiration there was a pause before his chest rose again ; and we found ourselves waiting each time for that next intake of breath, wondering whether it would come.

I had an urge to place my hand on his arm, but forced myself to wait until Hilda made a move. She was staring intently at his face. Eventually her fingers rose and brushed his arm before coming to rest on his shoulder. I followed my instinct and touched his wrist. My fingers flexed slightly but there was no response.

Thomas seemed to labour over another deep breath. But was it him making the effort? I wondered. His continuing existence depended on a life force which was ebbing away. There was a long exhalation, and as we looked intently at his mouth, his eyelids flickered and sprang open. I was transfixed, shocked at the sudden lifeless stare. I suppose I had hoped he would notice me before he died, but that empty gaze told me I was nothing to him.

The next intake of breath did not come.

Hilda stifled a sob and I looked up at her ; we wept together as we stared down again at the poor features fixed in their final repose. His mouth was slightly open and I noticed a fine strand of saliva suspended between his lips.

29

Mrs Horton and Mrs Smith are the best of friends now.

At Mrs Horton's suggestion, Mrs Smith was invited to Thomas's funeral : she could push Mrs Horton in the wheelchair while Mrs Beaumont and Paul occupied the front row. The service was a perfunctory affair, by design ; but Mrs Smith took the opportunity to stand out. She came dressed in a superb fur coat and hat, and cut a statuesque figure, all poise and solemnity throughout. She graced the funeral, one might say ; and poor Thomas, though he had never known her, would have had reason to be grateful for the touch of glamour she added to the proceedings in the windswept cemetery.

The wake too was a small gathering, since those who had known – really known – the deceased were few in number. Doreen attended to represent Faircroft. Mrs Smith was also there, of course, taking to her role as Mrs Horton's carer with evident pleasure. For all her distinguished manner, she showed herself full of affection for her silent companion in the wheelchair. She had set aside her cigarette holder and from time to time she would lean down and murmur to the old lady, who nodded warmly in response. The two of them were clearly comfortable in each other's company. While the other guests at first seemed awkward when approached to make conversation with the invalid who couldn't speak, the couple put everyone at ease through the display of their new-found affinity. They communicated easily through gestures, and Mrs Smith was apparently developing an ability to understand and translate some, at least, of the incomprehensible sounds that Mrs Horton occasionally uttered.

When the guests had gone and we were left alone, silence filled the room : complicated feelings hung in the air and Mrs Horton was not the only one struggling to express them. Hilda had spent the wake accepting condolences with a pale smile and soft words, and in the stillness that followed the departure of the guests, emotion drained from her face. My first impulse was to excuse myself and retreat to my room ; but as I moved to leave, Hilda stopped me in my tracks with a gesture of her hand. Like it or not I was a part of the story now, and would be a part of the sequel.

Still no one had spoken. Hilda looked around the room and her face creased in a brusque spasm of grief. Paul, standing unobtrusively in a corner, made to step forward but again she raised a hand.

'Dear Paul,' she said, and heaved a deep breath to stifle a sob. 'My constant comforter and loyal companion through all these years. Now here we are, alone together.'

She could no longer control the sobs which racked her whole body. She strained to speak as she gasped and shuddered. For a fleeting instant I thought she might be having a seizure and I glanced at Mrs Horton who could be harbouring the same thought.

Words began to tumble from Hilda's mouth, interrupted by more sobs, and we listeners struggled to grasp what she meant.

'Guilty… life… again…'

She looked at Mrs Horton, tears filling her eyes and glistening on her cheeks.

'So... sorry,' she gasped.

Mrs Horton seemed to understand. Perhaps she was the only one among us who really appreciated what Hilda meant. But she had no words to reply with. Tears of her own had to suffice.

All I could gather was that Hilda was tormented by guilt at the prospect of resuming her life with Paul. They were about to close the chapter that contained Thomas's life, and continue leaving only a memory of how they had contrived to endure while he continued to exist. Their life together could only be provisional as long as he was in the world, and with his disappearance they might spend the closing years of their lives in a different way. But they were old, frail, and it was a challenge they themselves might not survive to accomplish.

Paul understood this. They had talked about it over the years, stifling their impatience while Thomas clung on to life. But tactful and discreet as ever, Paul looked on impassively now as Hilda struggled to regain her composure. He was not one to take advantage of this moment ; he would not seek to deny or erase what Thomas still meant to her. But once she was calm again, he stepped up to comfort her and murmured words of consolation.

Mrs Smith wheeled Mrs Horton closer to the couple and the two of them offered comfort and sympathy as best they could. It was not clear how much Mrs Smith understood the true nature of Hilda's bereavement, but somewhat to my surprise I realised, as I stood by and watched, that her instincts were attuned to the other woman's sorrow.

*

I was very pleased to see Graham again, and his presence at the funeral helped me too. He was perhaps the only one there who could appreciate everything that Thomas's death might mean to me. He caught my eye occasionally to show his concern, which I found very touching.

I had been missing Graham when he disappeared from the guest house ; but watching his manner at Faircroft, I could tell he was surprisingly at ease here. No need to humour passing customers with their unpredictable requirements, or pander to the idiosyncratic ways of long-term residents. Here he was called upon to give care ; and manifestly he had a vocation for it. He had found his métier, as Paul Daubignac would say.

It wasn't just fondness for Graham that decided me to move into Faircroft. For some time I had been aware that I could no longer look after myself as I would wish, and the staff in the guest house could not be expected to provide for my particular needs. I required personal care, and it was logical for me to turn to Doreen and her establishment. She was happy to take me in, and Graham saw to it that the transition went smoothly.

As a matter of fact I quickly found myself among old friends : for my acquaintance with Margaret and Janet has blossomed into a real friendship. Quite spontaneously we have got into the way of complementing each other's separate disabilities : I can see, Margaret's hearing is very acute, and Janet, partially sighted, can make out what I am gargling about when I have spotted something but can't put it into intelligible words. I listen to their conversations, which are always entertaining, and interject as best I can, confident that they will pause and make time to comprehend. We have found ways of doing crosswords together, and we enjoy listening to plays and concerts on the radio : I have learned to appreciate music I would have had little time for previously.

A curious bonus is that I have visitors. I had feared that Geraldine would take it badly when I defected to Faircroft, leaving her alone in the guest house. But on the contrary : from what she tells me when she comes to call, I infer that she is happy presiding over the day-room without having to compete for attention with my bizarre mannerisms. And away from that milieu we find that we get on well together. She walks me in the grounds and willingly attends to my burbling, which she understands better and better. We can laugh companionably at the follies of our younger days and are oblivious now to the friction our different outlooks might once have given rise to. And when Paul and Hilda come to call, they sometimes arrange for their visits to coincide with Geraldine's, which usually makes for a jolly outing and cream tea at a café by the seaside.

Paul and Hilda are clearly happy together. Amidst the spinsters and widows that life has created around me, their couple radiates loyalty and devotion and serves to remind us that sometimes life brings exceptional blessings.

Postface
by
Professor Hugh R Storth, MA, PhD
Officier des Palmes académiques

The inhabitants of Quainton Lodge had let it be known that Mrs Beaumont's husband, at first reported as 'missing in action', had eventually returned home injured from the war. The aftermath of shell-shock had left him with a speech defect, which meant that people could not easily understand what he said in reply to their questions. Gradually the awful patience with which we address the incapacitated had worn thin, and so had people's curiosity regarding his wartime experience and his current life at the Lodge. Over the years the number of people to whom his presence in the area might matter diminished, and eventually the couple who went by the name of 'Mr and Mrs Beaumont' thought they were out of the wood. Their only continuing concern was the seriously incapacitated 'cousin' for whom they had assumed responsibility and whom they visited diligently at the care home.

Of course I was unaware of this when I began my research into the abandoned fragment I had established as a part of the novel *À l'Abri de la Tempête* by the then little known Franco-Belgian novelist Pierre Daubignac. I was simply an academic on the trail of a literary enigma, in the hope that it might afford me some publications, promotion and a reputation among scholars of French. As is the way of scholars, I was quite oblivious to the potential consequences of my zeal in the real world. After all, the Great War had been over for some forty-odd years and my work was of little more than antiquarian interest. Be that as it may I can remember, with an intensity that only literary researchers will appreciate, the thrill I experienced when I came across this curious manuscript in the library of the *seizième arrondissement* in Paris. It had been archived along with relics and documents left behind by Belgian refugees ; it meant nothing to anyone except myself, who happened to have been studying the manuscript and first edition of *À l'Abri de la Tempête* in the Bibliothèque Nationale the previous summer.

So I deciphered this manuscript and it brought me to Cottsea, and from thence to Quainton Lodge where I met a charming couple. Charming... but when I told them what had brought me to their home they became at first defensive and then distinctly hostile. With my arrival on the scene came the prospect of a sensational disclosure to a generation who knew nothing of the past, suspected nothing in the present, and who merely thought of the couple as eminently respectable people who kept themselves to themselves. The neighbours would be scandalized by a historic revelation that the wife of a disabled hero, a woman who had once passed herself off as a war-widow, had actually been cohabiting for some forty years with a foreigner who had moved into the marital home and taken the place of her spouse. The scandal-sheets would have a field day : the monstrous *News of the World* would drag them through the mud for the delectation of its nine million prurient readers.

Naturally I did what I could to reassure them. Delighted to discover that Daubignac had not died after all, I flattered him by insisting that his novel was a significant contribution to the literary history of the Great

War. I explained to Mrs Beaumont that the translation of her memoir, which I proposed to include in my critical edition of *À l'Abri de la Tempête*, would mean nothing to its French-language readers beyond confirming the close links between Belgian soldiers and British civilians in the war years. And of the few British people interested in reading French, the coded versions of the place names in her manuscript would more than adequately camouflage the real localities – and people. In any case, I argued, the novel was a work of fiction and as such it could disclaim any connection to the real world.

I could tell that M. Daubignac was touched by my interest, and in spite of himself saw some advantages in having his reputation revived at an age when most writers have sunk into oblivion, eclipsed by successive generations of young literary Turks. He had after all published little under his own name since moving to Britain. Writing under a *nom de plume* he had built up a small readership in France, but their numbers were dwindling with the passing years.

However Mrs Beaumont was terrified at the prospect of unwanted notoriety and was adamantly opposed to my taking my research any further. She had never intended for her memoir to be published and had specifically told Paul so. Could the manuscript be retrieved from the library where it had been conserved? she asked. Paul explained that it had become a part of the *patrimoine* and could not be withdrawn except perhaps via a special request from the author – who would have to have their identity confirmed... It would be best not to go down that path.

Finally, M. Daubignac invited me to stay with them for a few days while we discussed the possibility of finding an amicable way forward. I could tell that he was reluctant to abandon all prospects for a publication along the lines I had outlined to him ; but Mrs Beaumont's peace of mind was his prime concern. He suggested I might like to examine the archive of his work at Quainton Lodge ; he could show me other manuscripts and drafts that did not present the same difficulties regarding erudite publications. Above all, I soon became aware, neither he nor Mrs Beaumont would let me out of their sight for the time being, for fear that I let my scholarly fervour run away with me and prompt unwelcome indiscretions.

I didn't mind my confinement ; for a *rat de bibliothèque* such as myself, the prospect of being sequestered among shelves of books and manuscripts held no fears. Quite the reverse, in fact : this diversion actually opened my eyes to other aspects of Daubignac's writing – aspects to which my own career would subsequently owe much. Thanks to my analyses of these documents, Daubignac's work has been progressively rehabilitated and now figures among major contributions to French literature of the interwar years. And as a leading specialist on the author, I have achieved a modest scholarly standing in the field.

None of this seemed particularly likely at the time of which I write. In fact the first imperative was that I should lie low lest my presence in Quainton Lodge attract unwanted attention. Meanwhile, to throw others off the scent it was agreed – insisted on, by Daubignac and Mrs Beaumont – that I write an apology to Mrs Dugdale explaining my failure to return to the guest house. M. Daubignac would personally put this letter in the post and that would set their minds at rest. I volunteered a Scottish postage stamp, to support the spurious claim I made in my letter that I had been recalled on university business ; and M. Daubignac would contribute the balance of my outstanding rent. That served to settle things with Mrs Dugdale. But I felt I owed a moral debt to poor Mrs

Horton whom I had befriended ; it pained me to think of the old lady, abruptly abandoned without a word. So I indulged in a minor subterfuge : I decided to slip covertly into the envelope a second missive addressed to her. Naturally I couldn't tell her the truth directly, but it occurred to me that I might send a hint in the form of cryptic clues of the type we had amused ourselves with when doing crosswords together. It would serve as an entertaining souvenir of our friendship. I found a form of words that implied I had been detained elsewhere, intended to allay any anxiety she might feel about my disappearance ; and then I returned to my studies, closeted among the archives under the eaves of Quainton Lodge.

I was not to know that Mrs Horton would enlist Graham Rawcliffe's help and try to find me, or that her attempts to track me down would unearth a story that extended well beyond my investigations. Her first appearance at Quainton Lodge, accompanied by her young accomplice, set alarm bells ringing in the household. To begin with, Mrs Beaumont was mildly interested in echoes of her schooldays ; but Paul quickly alerted her to the risks involved in reviving the past. Their worries were all the greater in that they could not know what had motivated Mrs Horton's initial visit. They were unaware of her connection to me. As soon as I learned what I had inadvertently set in train, my first thought was to keep that connection secret. If our acquaintance was to come to light, my own underhand action would be exposed, and the chances were it would compromise the prospects for my research.

As I pondered my predicament, Paul and Hilda became anxious to avoid being unmasked by this old lady's unwitting curiosity. When news came from the care home that she had paid them a visit and caused an incident, they were increasingly uneasy. My presence in the house was an added source of concern, and I could tell that they were constantly on edge having me around, however discreet and self-effacing I tried to be. It was clear that compared with what I was working on, Mrs Horton's prying was liable to implicate them in a major disgrace on their doorstep.

In the end, I took it upon myself to propose a course of action. I suggested, quite simply, that I might leave, which would release them from my uncomfortable and perhaps embarrassing presence in the house. Naturally Hilda reverted to her initial reaction of panic concerning the potential of my research to cover them in shame. I explained the detail of my plan to Paul. I would take sabbatical leave from the university and would go off to France to pursue my archive research on his other works. There I would be at a safe distance and present no threat to them. Hilda was immediately suspicious. What was to prevent me revealing all, once I was free to do so? I looked at Paul and set out what I had in mind. As the author of all the works I was proposing to study, I reminded him, he had the right to prohibit publication of any material he wished to keep away from public view. And I would be bound to adhere to whatever he decided. I would like to continue my research, I said, on the grounds that his work was important and merited better understanding ; but I would publish nothing without his permission. Paul's reaction was immediately favourable. He pointed out to Hilda that what I said was indeed the case and meant that they would be protected from any attempt to divulge material that might compromise them. I could see that Hilda was still hesitant. I went further. I said I was prepared to sign, in good faith, a solemn and binding statement to the effect that I would do nothing to put into the public domain any material that they wished to keep confidential.

At this, Paul fell silent. He was turning things over in his mind. Then he asked me to leave the room so that he and Hilda might talk in private.

After half an hour of anxious speculation on my part, he called me back into the parlour. He invited me to sit down and then explained that as the years advanced and they were growing increasingly elderly, the time had come when he and Hilda must give thought to what would happen when they passed away. Hilda had already drawn up a will in her name, but he had had to make separate arrangements, for reasons he preferred not to go into. And he had decided, with Hilda's agreement, that with regard to his literary estate, I should be named his executor. I had shown a remarkable appreciation and understanding of his work, he said, and he was convinced he could trust in my integrity and commitment as to the care of its posterity.

Naturally I jumped at the chance but took pains not to let my eagerness show. It would have been unseemly to rejoice at the prospects that Daubignac's demise would open up for me. Nevertheless, he proceeded to draw up a document that I was happy to sign along with him.

Since that memorable evening, I have continued to study M. Daubignac's life and work, having written and published an authorised biography as well as numerous in-depth studies of his literary texts – with the sole exception of *À l'Abri de la Tempête*, which I have been keeping in reserve for obvious reasons – and I can safely say that I am by now a recognised authority.

With the sad death of Mrs Beaumont in 1971, M. Beaumont-Daubignac, whose health was also failing by then, confirmed the responsibility that he had entrusted to me some ten years earlier, and I renewed my undertaking to abide by the terms we had agreed on. There would be no critical edition of *À l'Abri de la Tempête* until ten years after his death. It is true that I had already prepared an authoritative text and variants, as well as an extensive introduction explaining the unusual history and genesis of the novel, but this has remained under seals until such time as its publication may be authorised.

Meanwhile, Mrs Horton, who moved from the guest house into a nearby care home where it transpires that Graham Rawcliffe is currently the manager, has recently also passed away at the age of eighty-three. Mr Rawcliffe made enquiries as to my whereabouts and discovered without too much difficulty that I currently hold the Chair in French and Francophone Studies at the University of Brantigen in Denmark, where I have pursued my academic career for the past decade. When he notified me of Mrs Horton's death, Mr Rawcliffe also revealed that they together had compiled a record of her life which impinges on my own research, bringing to light certain facets of her biography of which I had remained unaware. The completion of this little volume placed me in a curious position, since I am still legally bound by the undertaking I made not to publish any documents pertaining to the novel for which Daubignac is best known. However Mr Rawcliffe is not subject to the same constraints, and my authority as executor of the Daubignac estate does not extend to non-literary publications of the kind he has brought to my attention. In the circumstances, therefore, I am honoured to have been able to enlighten its readers as to a dimension of this story which will be more fully revealed when my critical edition of *À l'Abri de la Tempête*, extensively revised in the light of Mrs Horton's role in its gestation, can finally be published.

Brantigen, September 1974

About the author

David Walker is an internationally recognized specialist on the literature and culture of France. He is the author of numerous critical works, including *Outrage and Insight : Modern French Writers and the 'fait divers'* and *Consumer Chronicles : Cultures of Consumption in Modern French Literature*. He writes in both French and English, and is well-known in France and beyond as a leading expert on the writings of Albert Camus and André Gide. He has published three previous novels, *Migrating Voids*, *An Uncertain Shore*, and *Storms in the Midi*.

Printed in Great Britain
by Amazon